Plenty More Fish

Only dead fish go with the flow.

To Melanie,

Enjoy the read!.

Dawn Martin.

Dawn Martin

ISBN: 978-1-7384354-0-1

Typesetting by Let's Get Booked.

www.letsgetbooked.com

Abandoned

Chloe's life seemed to change overnight. One minute she was a normal hard-working mum of four, complete with dog, house, husband, and mortgage, and the next, her world was turned upside-down. She wasn't sure how or why it had happened but suddenly and without warning, she appeared to have joined a long queue of single parent families that not so very long ago she would have frowned upon. She wasn't a snob, at least she didn't think she was, but being married carried a certain status, and the prospect of ticking the separated or divorced boxes on forms filled her with dread. She didn't need pity, and she certainly didn't want people thinking she couldn't keep hold of her husband; she was after all, a proud woman who had carved a successful career out for herself, and her work colleagues thought highly of her. Failure was never an option, so she was going to put it right - she had to put it right - because as a nurse it was her job to make things better.

Her marriage to Pete hadn't been perfect, but then

nobody had a perfect marriage did they? So she hadn't been unduly concerned when he didn't return home from work on Friday night. Pete came from a large family that he adored, but she had very little to do with them, and she frequently told him his sisters were far too possessive for her liking, not to mention ridiculously overprotective of him. He was a grown man for God's sake, and therefore quite capable of fighting his own battles, and it was about time they let him stand on his own two feet. As an only child with a boarding school education, Chloe learned to be independent at an early age and was fiercely proud of her resourcefulness and ability to juggle family life with a nursing career. She achieved her goals in life on her own and resented being told what to do. She certainly didn't need telling how to look after her own husband by a bunch of interfering busybodies, so as far as she was concerned it was easier to keep out of their way.

By eight o clock the dinner had gone cold, and she was angry, yet at the same time, she felt slightly apprehensive. 'Why couldn't he just phone and say he was going to be late?' she mumbled to herself crossly. She checked her phone for messages, but there were none, and that irritated her even more because he knew she would be worried by now, and at the very least he could have sent a text to warn her he was going to be late. She rang his mobile, but it was switched off, so as a last resort, she decided to ring round his family to see if any of them knew of his whereabouts. Having never been close to Pete's family, she dialled the numbers from the little black book next to the phone with a familiar feeling of unease that caused her stomach to lurch uncontrollably. Annoyingly there was no reply from his brother Ian, who she could at best tolerate, and the number that belonged to his youngest sister Ruth, went straight to answerphone. She didn't bother to leave a message because she knew Ruth could talk for hours on the phone, and chances were by the time she picked up the message Pete would be safely back home again. Reluctantly she dialled the number of his eldest sister Anne, who seemed unsurprised by her call. Chloe knew Anne would be home because apart from her obsession with craft fayres, her life was pretty dull. They had only met a few times over the years at the dreaded family Christmas parties which Anne insisted on organizing. She always rented out a church hall somewhere and decorated it with handmade items from the craft fayres that Chloe despised. Parties forced Chloe out of her comfort zone, and after tolerating them for the first few years of their marriage, she started making excuses not to attend, forcing Pete to go alone. He never argued about it, but she knew he was disappointed, especially as the kids never went with him either.

Being the eldest, Anne assumed the role as the head of the family, but Chloe thought she was a patronising snob, who just liked to be in control. They had no common ground, although Pete always insisted they were very similar, and Chloe thought Anne's hoity-toity attitude was pathetic considering she lived in a modest two up two down terrace in a remote rural village somewhere and had, to the best of her knowledge, been a frigid spinster for the best part of her life. When she answered the phone, her tone was polite but cold, and Chloe felt sure she was smiling when she explained that Pete was staying with her and would not be coming back, except to collect his belongings. She tried to reason with her, but Anne refused to offer any further explanation.

Chloe couldn't deny that she and Pete had argued a bit lately, but nothing serious enough to justify him leaving her. She was frustrated, and the perpetual flutters in her stomach were beginning to make her feel queasy. She liked to be in control, and the usual coping strategies that she used in emergency situations appeared to have deserted her. Her panic quickly turned to anger. How dare Pete do this to her and the children without a single word of explanation? She grabbed her keys and prepared to drive over to Anne's house to confront him, before realising that it wasn't an option because she had no idea where Anne lived. Slowly, it began to dawn on her that after twelve years of marriage she should probably know where her husband's family lived. She made up excuses in her head about being too busy with her job, and bringing up the kids, but deep down she knew she had been too preoccupied with her own needs to recognise his. Her own childhood had been lonely, and she craved love and affection. She had longed for a little brother or a sister, but one never came along, and she never felt wanted by either of her parents. Deep down she knew she was jealous of her husband's relationship with his family, and now it seemed her deep-seated insecurities may have pushed him away for good.

The weekend came and went, and Pete still hadn't been in touch. The children were starting to ask questions and were no longer of an age where they could be fobbed off easily. She had always believed in being honest with them, but she wasn't in the mood for answering any awkward questions, so she decided it wouldn't hurt to be a little economical with the truth. Chances were, they would never need to know the real reason for his absence anyway because he would be back, she was sure of it. She told them he was staying with their Auntie Anne because she was having a few personal problems and she needed him around for some brotherly support. The children, two girls and two boys were engrossed in some trashy reality television programme and barely batted an eyelid at her explanation which was a huge relief because it meant she didn't have to explain to them who Auntie Anne was, and, perhaps more importantly, why they had never met her.

Chloe had a dilemma on her hands, but problem solving was her speciality, and she prided herself on her belief that no problem was insurmountable. She was confident that she and Pete would work things out eventually, but in the meantime, she was going to need a contingency plan of some kind. She had no idea how she was going to balance home and work without some sort of financial support from him, but as his wife and the mother of his children, he would be expected to pay maintenance so they would manage just about. It wouldn't come to that, she was sure of it, that was the worst-case scenario, and they hadn't had a chance to talk things through yet. Her brain was buzzing with unanswered questions, and she couldn't just dismiss them. How would she pay the bills and meet the monthly mortgage payments? Where was the nearest foodbank? Oh my God was that a real possibility? Food banks, bailiffs, repossession even! She took a deep breath to steady her breathing. She was clearly overthinking the whole situation and now wasn't the time to have a panic attack. There was no point making a bad situation worse, especially one that was sure to be quickly resolved, and she quietly scolded herself for being such a drama queen. Nevertheless, as a precautionary measure, she phoned her employer and arranged two weeks emergency leave, and in that time, she convinced herself that Pete would return, and their lives would go back to normal again.

But Pete did not come back; he sent his brother Ian, to collect his belongings with a message saying that all future contact should be made via a solicitor. At the same time, he declared himself bankrupt to avoid paying maintenance for the children and dodge mortgage payments. He promised to make arrangements to see the children once he was settled, but he was cagey about giving any timescale and refused to be more specific about his plans.

Chloe felt very alone again for the second time in her life, but this time things were different because she had children of her own to consider, and she was desperate not to let them down in the same way her own parents had let her down.

An
Acrimonious Divorce

In the months that followed, Chloe experienced a barrage of mixed emotions. During the daytime she kept herself busy balancing work, while trying to retain an element of normality at home for the sake of the children, who appeared to have taken the news of the breakup in their stride. Evenings though were empty, and she felt encompassed in a fog of overwhelming loneliness which she found difficult to shake off. To make things worse, rumours were spreading that Pete's financial problems were escalating. His once thriving building business had fallen victim to the recession, and rumour had it that he intended to claim his share of their home and its contents at the earliest opportunity. As Pete still had a key to their family home, Chloe decided to change the locks to protect what little she had left until the court issued a financial order. Her solicitor had warned her it was illegal, so she wasn't all that surprised when an authoritative letter from Pete's solicitor arrived in the post a few days later. She read the letter out loud because it seemed more real that way. It seemed that Pete wanted a divorce on the grounds that the marriage had irretrievably broken down because of her unreasonable behaviour, but later she would learn the real reason for Pete's hasty divorce request.

It came as a surprise to Pete that new divorce laws made mediation compulsory prior to a court hearing as a chance to resolve things amicably, but Chloe had already done her homework on this and arrived at the mediation meeting fully prepared to do battle with him. She hadn't seen Pete since the day he left, and she was afraid she might cry. Her head kept telling her to stay strong, but her emotions were all over the place, and the only thing that stopped her fleeing from the room were thoughts of her children. As it happened, she didn't have to worry about breaking down and showing her vulnerability because Pete didn't bother turning up. He clearly had no conscience because he also failed to show up on two further occasions when the meeting was rescheduled, so eventually the mediation was abolished, and the case went straight to court.

On a chilly November morning, Pete and Chloe arrived separately at court. Fiercely independent, Chloe turned up alone just in time to catch a glimpse of Pete scurrying off to hide behind one of his sisters who she immediately recognised as Anne. Chloe chuckled at his pathetic, cowardly behaviour before questioning how her judgement of this man could have been so wrong. Maybe she hadn't been wrong at all, maybe they had both just changed, especially since the children came along, but never-the-less they were still both adults and they were supposed to be responsible parents; she had been certain that Pete would always put their children first. Disappointingly, it seemed he wanted something different now, but she was not privy to that information which only served to increase her frustration more. She had so many unanswered questions, and by the looks of it they were destined to remain that way, because he was too much of a coward to face her. She assumed it was the guilt he was hiding away from. He'd fled to his man cave to do whatever it is men do in those places, but eventually he would have to come out, and the truth would soon follow.

In front of the judge and without his sister to hold his hand, Pete suddenly found his voice and Chloe was shocked at the extent of his arrogance and greed. He clearly had ulterior motives which she was yet to uncover, but she would soon find out that Pete had news that was going to turn her world upside down again once more.

From the outset, Chloe realised it was unlikely there would be any poignant emotional reunion with Pete in the courtroom, and she thought she'd come to terms with that. She kept telling herself she didn't need him anymore, but she was shocked and completely unprepared for his selfish demands, and she listened helplessly as he pleaded poverty to the judge as a result of his failed business and subsequent bankruptcy. He asked for the family home to be sold so he could raise funds to pay off some personal debts. He made no mention of his children, and Chloe made up her mind there and then that they would all be better off without him. From what the judge told her, she had two choices, sell while she was still solvent - which was purely courtesy of her dwindling savings- or succumb to the bailiffs when the mortgage went into arrears, which would ultimately be unavoidable under the circumstances. It was a no brainer; she would sell, so she and the children could pick up the pieces and get on with their lives, and Pete could do whatever it was he wanted with his.

Chloe left the court with her head held high. The judge wasn't allowed to appear biased, but he commended Chloe after the proceedings for her remarkable composure under what he described as difficult circumstances. Her strong family principles concerning her children would, he said, hold her in good stead for the future, and she hoped his optimism was contagious because she wasn't feeling quite so confident. Chloe was about to start a new chapter in her life. She had no idea what that involved yet, but it didn't matter because she had already made up her mind that whatever it was, it was going to be better than the previous chapter. Pete's performance in court had confirmed without a shadow of doubt that she had been stuck on the same page of the same book for far too long, and it was time for her to move on with her life.

Moving On

Not long after the court hearing, the decree nisi arrived in the post followed by the decree absolute a few months later. The formal paperwork simply stated that her marriage to Pete was now legally dissolved, and she was free to re marry if she wished. Chloe reflected on the term 'dissolved.' Was her divorce comparable with taking an Alka- Seltzer tablet, capable of 'dissolving' the pain away? She thought the wording was inappropriate, but the legal eagles had obviously spent years at university devising fancy vocabulary to justify their extortionate fees.

The family home was now on the market and the estate agent was confident that there were enough interested parties for Chloe to secure a good price. With four children, two of them teenagers, she needed a good size three-bedroom house at the very least with a decent size garden for the dog. Chloe was looking forward to moving out. The house was laden with memories but was no longer a home. When she thought long and hard about it, she came to the conclusion that the so-called family home had been nothing more than a dysfunctional unit for years and she wondered why she hadn't spotted it earlier. There had been warning signs of course, but with their busy lives they had both chosen to ignore them, and their ignorance had led them down the road to divorce. Well-meaning friends and work colleagues attempted to humour her with comments like, 'you're better off without him' or annoying clichés like, 'there's plenty more fish in the sea.' Maybe there were plenty more fish in the sea, but as a forty- something newly divorced woman laden with an armful of heavy baggage, Chloe was convinced her only catch would be great white sharks or piranha fish with huge teeth capable of inflicting even bigger holes in her already dented ego.

The house sale completed in early March and Chloe moved her family to a delightful semi-detached turn of the century cottage with oodles of character on the outskirts of town. The cottage was in need of some minor renovation work which had made it affordable, but its rustic charm made it feel warm and homely. The children settled in quickly, and even her moody teenagers seemed to positively embrace their new surroundings. Chloe was cautiously optimistic that this home could offer her the new start she so desperately needed. As the days gradually merged into months, she thought less about Pete and more about her own future, and she finally felt able to move on. It had been years since she had dated anyone, and she had no idea how to go about meeting a man. Social networking sites were not her thing although her kids' lives seemed to revolve around them. It was a lovely bright sunny Sunday morning when Chloe's eldest daughter dropped the bombshell. Pete had sent her a Facebook friend request and she had accepted it because even though he had not given her a second thought since the divorce, she still wanted him to be a part of her life. When she opened up his profile page he was standing on Copacabana beach holding hands with a bronzed Brazilian floozy and a number of equally tanned looking kids who she assumed had to be the floozy's offspring. The woman was proudly holding out her left hand, and on her ring finger there was a large diamond rock. Pete was engaged, and it seemed this was his cowardly way of breaking the news to his own kids. Chloe stared at the page for some time before coming to the conclusion that he must be having some sort of midlife crisis, but then things all started to add up and his desire for a quickie divorce started to make sense. It wasn't long before her anger turned to hate, and hate soon turned to tears of despair, and before long she had turned into an inconsolable blubbering wreck. She was furious with herself for allowing him to hurt her again, but she was even more angry that he still had the power to do it. It suddenly dawned on her that he must have been having an affair during their marriage and was spending the money from the proceeds of their house sale on expensive foreign holidays with his bimbo. Chloe stared at the photograph and instantly hated this bronzed South American harlot with the skimpiest of bikinis and enormous silicone breasts. Impulsively she searched eBay and found a homemade voodoo doll which realistically she had no intention of buying because all things of an occult nature scared her. She briefly laughed at the thought of sticking a pin in it to puncture those obscene silicone balloons until they were all shrivelled and deflated. Pete had once told her that anything more than a handful was a waste, but she knew he was only trying to convince her that her saggy post- baby boobs weren't as bad as she made them out to be. He knew she had a complex about them, so one day he had surprised her with a Wonderbra, and she had never looked back, until now that was. She needed something to boost her confidence again, but she knew a pair of gigantic silicone breasts were not the answer. She and Pete were history, and his new-found passion for watermelons was none of her business.

Later that evening while she was surfing the net, checking her emails, and hunting out eBay bargains, an unexpected pop- up for an online dating site caught her attention. She was curious and impulsively clicked the link. Before long she had created a personal profile and uploaded what she considered to be a half decent photo of herself tastefully dressed (unlike the floozy posing shamelessly with her ex-husband on a public social networking site.) Mixed emotions flooded her troubled mind, but the anticipation turned somersaults in her stomach, and she treated herself to a celebratory glass of wine. This was progress. This was an attempt to move her life forward and have some fun and it could even be the start of an exciting new adventure. Life had taught her to have few expectations, because from her experience, expectations usually meant disappointment. She mulled over the words of her friends in her mind. If there really were 'plenty more fish' in the sea she had taken the first step and cast her net. Now all she had to do was reel them in.

Within twenty-four hours, thirty-six eligible men had viewed her profile and twelve of them had registered their interest by sending her a wink or a poke which Chloe thought was distasteful. It made her feel vulnerable, a bit like walking past a building site to the sound of taunts and wolf whistles from sweaty testosterone- filled labourers. Her email account flagged up five new messages from male admirers inviting her to take a look at their profiles. She was intrigued, but secretly wondered if these were the type of men that hit on every new female profile in the hope of notching up another score on their bedposts. She reflected on her newly acquired scepticism but reasoned that this was new territory for her, and far better to be safe than sorry. Her work colleagues had concerns of their own. Most seemed convinced she was going to fall prey to the local axe murderer, and co-workers young enough to be her daughter offered advice on safe meeting places and the importance of carrying a pepper spray or rape alarm in her bag at all times. She pretended to listen but refused to take their concerns seriously. She was a grown woman after all, and this was the first time she'd felt excited about anything in a long time, and absolutely no one was going to spoil it for her. She didn't yet know it, but the time would come when she would regret not taking their advice. She was far too excited to think about the dangers, and she secretly thought her colleagues were being a bit too overprotective, but the extent of her naivety would soon be revealed.

She opened the first email from a pleasant-sounding man called John. She reflected for a moment on the word pleasant. The dictionary definition defined it as pleasing and nice which she thought was likely to mean he could turn out to be incredibly boring. She always believed in going with her gut instinct, but this was her first date in years, and she wondered if she was being unfairly judgemental about him. She always prided herself on being a good judge of character and it usually took no more than thirty seconds for her to decide whether a person had potential or not. She defended this quickie evaluation of people as a trait learned from work, since the pressure of working in a busy doctors' surgery meant she often had to make life or death decisions following a short ten-minute consultation with a patient. She hoped she wouldn't have to make any life-or-death decisions if she were to date John, or any other man for that matter, and then she laughed at how ridiculous that sounded. She convinced herself that meeting John would be okay, after all he was just a small fish in a big pond, and she would have to start somewhere.

John

J ohn lived about twenty miles away from Chloe, far enough she thought if he did turn out to be a madman or a stalker. His profile picture depicted a fairly ordinary looking man, but Chloe thought he had kind eyes, and he said in his profile he was just over six foot tall. Height was important to Chloe because at 5'10" she was tall for a woman, and she liked to wear heels to show off her long slender legs. She would never date a man shorter than herself and was acutely aware that some people might think she was shallow, but she didn't care because she had stopped worrying about other people's opinions a long time ago.

Chloe arranged to meet John in a village pub approximately halfway between their two homes. The pub had a reputation for good food and live jazz music on some nights. Chloe reasoned that if the conversation dried up between them, the meal would justify the lack of dialogue, and the music would provide an outlet for her selective hearing if the evening became boring. She asked for advice from her two trendy daughters about what outfit she should wear for the occasion, and they spent a fun afternoon together going through her wardrobe and throwing out all the stuff she was hoarding from her hippie days. She had been reluctant to get rid of them because she associated them with happy carefree memories of her younger days, but by the end of it there was a large bag full of clothes ready to go off to the charity shop. She had no idea what a woman was supposed to wear on a first date these days, especially a blind date, but her daughters convinced her the hippie phase was long gone. She didn't want to give the wrong impression by wearing one of her signature, 'come and get me' short skirts which were, in all probability, a bit too short for a forty something mum of four, but on the other hand she didn't want to dress too formally either in case the poor man thought he was there for an interview. Pete had loved it when she wore short skirts and actively encouraged her to buy them, which is probably why she had ended up with so many of them. Whenever they went out, he would proudly showed her off to his friends and work colleagues but in hindsight she wondered now whether she'd been nothing more than a trophy wife to him. Well now he had the opportunity to show off his latest tart, the floozy with the huge artificial boobies and the bronzed skin that would age and shrivel long before her pale, slightly freckled skin would. Eventually, she settled for a pretty floral dress just above the knee with small kitten heels just in case John had exaggerated his true height. With a spring in her step Chloe gracefully climbed into her pride and joy; her gleaming black 1997 low mileage BMW convertible that she had lovingly cherished over the years and the same car she had fought Pete with the ferocity of a wild animal to keep as part of the divorce settlement. They had shared a mutual love of cars. Pete liked fast cars with big flashy wheels and go faster stripes while Chloe preferred the more standard vintage models, unspoilt by would- be boy racers. Nowadays the closest she got to car shows was a Sunday morning car boot sale on the common. If she hadn't been driving she would have been tempted to have a glass of wine before setting out to provide her with some much-needed Dutch courage, but she'd never needed alcohol to talk to a man before so she could see no reason why she would she need it now. For a brief moment, she almost doubted herself before laughing out loud at the absurdity of it all. Displaying all the outer confidence of a tigress stalking its prey, she set off to meet John at the pub.

They had arranged to meet in the pub car park. She secretly planned to arrive early and park away from the entrance on the basis that if she saw him first, she could make a swift exit if he failed to meet her expectations. She inwardly scolded herself for using the 'E' word again. No expectations meant no disappointment, but she was human after all, and she knew her theory was littered with flaws. She had safety nets in place. She had told a few close friends where she was going, and her girls were under strict instructions to keep their mobile phones switched on in case she needed to employ her, 'get out of jail quick' card. John hadn't given much away about himself, but he mentioned he would be driving a silver Ford. Chloe found a parking space with a good view of the entrance and waited. A few cars trickled in, with couples stepping out laughing hand in hand before making their way in to the pub, which by now was getting busy with music radiating from the open windows. Chloe reminisced sadly. Only a few years ago she and Pete would have been one such couple. She hoped John wasn't going to be late because lateness annoyed her intensely, and it was even worse when no explanation or apology was offered. She hated it when patients turned up late for their appointments and expected to be seen even though it meant she would run late for the rest of the day, and other people, who had arrived on time for their appointment would be kept waiting through no fault of their own. She mentally scolded herself for thinking about work when her knight in shining armour could arrive at any moment. An old silver Ford Fiesta drove cautiously into the car park and stopped, and Chloe instantly knew that her dreams would remain fantasies for the time being at least.

She watched as John stepped out of the car. He was plumper than she had expected, with a larger than average nose, and dressed rather too formally for a date wearing a grey suit complete with shirt, tie, and jacket. To her dismay, his trousers were too short and were flapping around his ankles, giving him the unfortunate appearance of an overgrown schoolboy. They looked like his work clothes and Chloe wondered whether he hadn't had enough time to change for their date. If he was there for an interview, he would have passed the dress code with flying colours. All he needed was a leather briefcase and he would have been well on his way to getting the job. From what she could see he also looked to be no more than an optimistic 5'9" and he was carrying a small bunch of flowers in his hand with a sticker which looked like a hasty purchase from the local petrol station. She wondered if now was a good time to phone her kids and declare a state of emergency that required her to leave immediately, but she knew that would be unfair. She would have one drink with him, and then politely make an excuse to leave. Reluctantly, she forced herself out of her car and slowly made her way over to where John was standing. On closer inspection he looked older than his forty-six years and Chloe suspected he had uploaded an old photograph of himself to improve his chances of securing a date. Chloe was the bait but something was telling her that this date was already doomed to fail.

Initial greetings between the two parties were awkward. John appeared nervous and dived in headfirst to kiss her on the cheeks, but she had instinctively pulled away and offered him her hand instead. He looked disappointed and Chloe felt the tiniest bit guilty, but she didn't welcome presumptuous gestures and felt it was important to set boundaries to avoid misleading him. Reluctantly, she walked into the pub with him inwardly nervous in case someone recognised her. This was an occasion when a burka would have come in handy, but she didn't even have a hood on her jacket. She made up her mind, one drink and one drink only, and then she would make her excuses to leave. She ordered a diet coke and John had a pint of bitter. She pretended not to be hungry because if they ate, she would have to stay longer. Attempts at small talk were strained, and after half an hour John had still only drunk about one inch from his glass of beer because he said if he drank it too quickly it would go to straight his head and make him silly. Chloe spluttered to stifle a laugh. Surely he meant sillier, after all one look at his schoolboy trousers said it all. When he made a trip to 'the little boy's room' as he so aptly called it, Chloe forced herself to take a few large gulps from his glass to make the contents disappear a bit quicker. On his return and to Chloe's utter dismay he was keener to resume conversation than he was to finish his ale and he appeared completely oblivious to her negative body language and one-syllable answers to his pointless questions. He went on speaking enthusiastically about himself for what seemed like hours. His 'engineering' job involved working on an assembly line putting printed circuit boards into car radios. Previously he had worked as a salesman selling fire extinguishers and proceeded to explain how to use each different fire extinguisher in the pub and the importance of keeping the fire exits clear. In a desperate attempt to change the conversation to something that might keep her awake and stifle her yawns, Chloe asked John about his previous relationships. She doubted he had ever actually had any so was flabbergasted by what he revealed next. John launched into a sorry tale from his past, and for a moment she thought he might actually cry. Following a road traffic collision ten years previously in which his fiancée was injured, John had only recently developed enough confidence to start driving again so she could excuse him for driving into the car park like he'd just passed his driving test. His fiancée, who was also his childhood sweetheart, had sustained a minor head injury which left her with amnesia. After the accident, she no longer recognised John and their engagement was terminated. John was devastated because he firmly believed he had lost his one and only opportunity of finding true love, and Chloe remained silent because she thought that was probably true. She didn't know whether to laugh or cry and inwardly scolded herself for her lack of empathy, and her unkind suspicion that this girl had deliberately developed selective amnesia in order to avoid making the biggest mistake of her life.

Unable to think of an appropriate response to John's revelations about his past, Chloe made her excuses and dashed off to find the ladies. Now was definitely the time to employ her emergency exit plan. She reached for her phone, but to her dismay there was no reception to make that much -needed rescue call to her kids. After standing on the toilet and hanging out the window waving the phone around like a crazy ninja for about ten minutes, she was forced to admit defeat. Her antics were attracting unwanted attention from a group of merry lads in the pub garden, and she didn't want them getting the wrong idea. On the plus side, she had been gone long enough to convince John that she had something seriously wrong with her stomach and really needed to go home, and as luck would have it, John showed nothing less than gentlemanly concern for her wellbeing.

After a quick goodbye involving an exchange of only the most basic of pleasantries, Chloe made a hasty retreat back to her car. She took a long deep breath. John had mentioned meeting again same time, same place next week, complete with her choice of 'pub grub' providing her tummy was ok. Chloe had been so relieved to escape she couldn't remember her exact response and was worried she may have unintentionally nodded her head in agreement, so once she was safely home with a much-needed cup of tea in her hand, she opened her emails and started writing a 'Dear John' message. She kept the message polite but to the point, emphasising how 'nice' it had been to meet him but due to the lack of shared interests there would be no further dates. It was cowardly but as she pressed the send button she sat back and breathed a huge sigh of relief before bursting out laughing. Her email flashed to say she had twelve new messages waiting to be read. She knew she should go to bed because she had work tomorrow but curiosity got the better of her. This online dating malarkey was actually quite addictive; or perhaps it was just the need to feel wanted by someone that was addictive? She knew she was in denial about the latter. She tried hard to convince herself she was a strong woman who didn't need a man in her life but deep down she knew that wasn't entirely true. She was kidding herself in to believing it was just a bit of fun, a way to fill those long empty winter evenings until she could find something better to do but it wasn't that simple. She wanted someone, of course she wanted someone, because everyone wants to feel loved and needed, but her fear of rejection was steering her in the wrong direction.

She opened the first email. A photo popped up and to her dismay there was a guy called Jim who looked like a clone of John and could easily pass for his twin brother. Jim and John had a certain ring to it, and she wondered whether it was just a coincidence or whether he might actually have a twin brother. She quickly pressed the delete button without reading his message and moved on. The next message was from a guy called Mike. He looked okay in the photo, but she knew photos could be deceptive so keeping that in mind she opened the mail to find out more. Mike lived about fifty miles away and worked shifts at a major international airport. Like Chloe, he was divorced with four kids, all boys, but seeing as she secretly thought boys were easier to get along with than girls she thought that might be a bonus. From his profile he seemed like a regular type of guy with no obvious 'red flag' features. She used the red flag system when triaging patients at work to quickly identify clinical symptoms which could indicate a serious underlying illness. Her system was helping her to develop a basic strategy to spot potential online dating psychopaths too, but as she would later discover, that strategy was flawed and would need revisiting over and over again.

Mike

C hloe and Mike exchanged only a couple of emails before deciding to meet up. Hiding behind realms of pointless dialogue wasn't to Chloe's liking, and Mike made it clear he wanted to meet up sooner rather than later. Chloe thought emails made it far too easy for a person to live in a fantasy world and pretend to be something or someone different, and she didn't want to give him the opportunity to pull the wool over her eyes. She admitted she was overcritical, and first impressions were important to her, and anyone who said looks don't matter had to be delusional, because of course looks mattered. She arranged to meet Mike at a different pub because she didn't want the landlord of the little village pub to think she was using his premises as a meeting place to hook up with the type of men who paid women for certain services. Luckily, Mike seemed happy to drive and meet her at a location of her choice, which was just as well because she had no intention of driving fifty miles to meet him on unfamiliar territory. She congratulated herself for following at least some of the safety rules that were clearly outlined on the first page of the dating website. He said he would be driving a silver BMW which Chloe assumed, given the nature of his work, might be a company vehicle.

Once again Chloe arrived early so she could park up with a good view of the entrance. She had enough time to let her thoughts drift back to Pete who was by now playing happy families with his new floozy and her kids. She couldn't imagine Pete taking on another man's kids any more than she could imagine herself taking on another woman's kids. Other people's children were of no interest to her, she had four of her own and didn't need to complicate things with more excess baggage than was necessary. A dog would be better than kids. She liked dogs and her thoughts turned to Norman, her scatty boxer dog waiting at home for her. Dogs didn't answer you back, although they did sometimes drool, and unlike Pete, they remained loyal companions until their dying day without seeking affection elsewhere, unless of course there was a tasty biscuit on offer.

Mike had four kids and Chloe had four kids which made a total of eight kids between them, and if Chloe and Mike got married and their kids all had four kids each that would mean thirty-two grandchildren. Bright headlights and the sound of a car jolted Chloe back into the present. She hadn't even met him yet so why was she worrying about grandchildren for God's sake? It was indeed a silver BMW that entered the carpark, driven by a white male who appeared to be scanning the area for someone or something. Her nerves started to kick in and she wondered whether she should duck down and hide, but it was too late because he'd already spotted her, and the next thing she knew he was parking up next to her. The floodlit carpark revealed a tall man with dark curly hair, wearing jeans and a white shirt. He smiled when she got out of her car and immediately held out his hand to introduce himself. He appeared confident, maybe too confident Chloe thought for a first meeting. He also had thin lips and his eyes were a bit too close together, physical traits her mother had warned her about because she said they were signs of a devious nature. Chloe stifled a giggle thinking about her mother. She had been married six times and was currently seeking her next victim. Chloe couldn't remember a time from her childhood when her mother had been truly happy. Every time she came home from boarding school, she seemed to have a new stepdad. She still cringed at the memory of returning to school after the long summer holidays with yet another new surname. The girls at school thought there was a new kid on the block when her name was called at registration and although it was embarrassing at first, they soon got used to the frequent name changes and stopped asking questions. After her dad left, her mother craved attention and married anyone who showed her the slightest bit of affection. It saddened Chloe to think her mother had never found true love and she didn't want to make the same mistakes. It was bad enough that she had inherited all of her mother's mad superstitions, including astrological compatibility. Not only did she now drive around roundabouts twice to spot the second magpie, but she also tried to avoid dating any guy born under the star signs Pisces, Taurus, Gemini, or Virgo. John was a Pisces and Mike was a Gemini, so if her mum's theory was correct, this date was also already doomed to fail. Chloe brushed all thoughts of her mother to one side. She was her own person now, and capable of making her own decisions in life. All this superstitious stuff was total nonsense, but she kept her fingers crossed behind her back just in case there was an element of truth to it.

As they walked into the pub Chloe was cautiously optimistic about the evening ahead. Mike wasn't bad looking, although he wasn't the type of guy she would usually go for. She wasn't used to white collar workers and generally preferred the more rugged type of guy, the sort who got his hands dirty for a living, but at least Mike had what sounded like an interesting job, so she hoped they would have something to talk about. He had been married and had kids so presumably he wasn't gay or transgender, or non-binary whatever that meant, but you could never be sure of course. She scolded herself for making assumptions again, she had learnt long ago in her job never to assume anything because assumptions were often very wrong and could easily backfire. An ex-wife and kids didn't mean he wasn't gay, it could just mean he had taken a bit longer than normal to come out of the closet and his wife wasn't happy to share her wardrobe with him. Chloe inwardly smiled at her overactive imagination. She was creating problems that didn't exist, and she had nothing to worry about.

Chloe took a quick look around the pub. There was no one she knew but she did spot the location of the fire extinguishers. As they were both driving, they ordered non-alcoholic drinks before settling into a cosy alcove for a chat. Chloe was tempted to order a small glass of white wine, but after seeing Mike order a lime and soda she changed her mind and settled for a diet coke instead with no ice. Fleetingly, she thought back to another of her discarded emails from the dating site. Gregory, a frightfully posh solicitor specialising in licensing laws, had messaged her asking if they could meet for afternoon tea. Much as Chloe loved tea, she drank enough of it at home and work to sink a battleship, afternoon tea was the sort of social event her mother might suggest. When she replied suggesting an alternative venue, he became defensive and responded with an essay- sized email lecturing her on the perils of drinking alcohol. It turned out he was a reformed alcoholic and now ran AA meetings in his spare time. It had made her feel like a naughty schoolgirl, so she had quickly pressed the delete button followed by the 'block this member' button just in case he felt the need to lecture her again on her rebellious behaviour.

Chloe found Mike to be an attentive listener, but he was reluctant to talk much about himself. He had a clever way of turning questions around that forced her to provide all the answers, and much as she enjoyed talking about herself it became a bit tedious after a while. Her job meant she was very much a people person; she was used to doing all the listening and her naturally inquisitive nature craved information. Just as she was beginning to think he had something to hide, Mike opened up a little more about himself, and she wondered if he had picked up on her frustrations. Mike said he worked as ground staff for one of the small airlines at a London airport. He said his job frequently brought him into contact with all sorts of famous people, but for some reason Gail Tilsley, a character from Coronation Street was the only one he spoke about. He spoke about her at length, and Chloe started to think he might actually be related to her. By the time he had finished, she felt certain she was probably a very nice woman because he told her so time and time again, but surely if he worked at a large international airport there must be other, slightly more interesting high-profile people he could find to talk about.?. He worked shifts, so he instructed her to always text him and not phone in future communications in case he was busy checking passengers in, and although she took this information on board, something didn't feel quite right.

He spoke about his ex-wife with venom in his voice. He had no contact with his boys aged between twelve and seventeen years, and the one time he bumped into them in the street the youngest boy had spat in his face. Chloe wondered what could have provoked feelings of such intense hatred from a young boy and it worried her. Her safety net, her list of 'red flag' warning signs, had launched and she needed to escape. In the past her gut feeling had never let her down, so it had to be right. What on earth was she thinking, of course it was right, she needed to run for the hills as fast as she could. Mike seemed to sense her tension. She had been so busy thinking up a plausible escape plan she hadn't realised she hadn't uttered a single word for a full five minutes. He attempted to put her at ease by smiling and offering her another drink, but all she could think of was axe murderers and serial killers. She had clearly been watching far too many crime documentaries on television and her imagination was running riot. She needed to regain control of the situation, and quickly, before he realised she was on to him. Mentally, she had him convicted without a trial. He was guilty of something, she was sure of it, and if she didn't get away soon, she could be his next victim. Under normal circumstances another drink would have been good. She needed alcohol to steady her nerves, but alcohol wasn't an option because she was driving, and she could already visualise Gregory's scornful look at the sheer mention of the 'A' word. Chloe took another quick look around the bar. There were still quite a few people around, but it was beginning to thin out and she was seeking safety in numbers. She asked him to order her another diet coke without ice and then made an excuse to visit the ladies so she could instigate her emergency escape plan. Relief flooded through her when her eldest daughter answered the phone on the second ring. Chloe had made a no questions asked pact with her daughter early on. This involved nothing more than her daughter calling her exactly ten minutes from now and asking her to come home because the dog, who suffered from bouts of colitis, was ill and needed urgent veterinary attention. She was aware how lame an excuse this was but there was an element of truth in it. Norman did suffer from colitis, but she kept 'rescue remedy' medications indoors for acute exacerbations. He had been close to crossing the rainbow bridge on more than one occasion and she didn't want to take any chances with his health. The first time he got ill was after devouring an entire easter egg which her youngest son had left under his bed. She had since had strong words with all four of them about leaving chocolate hanging around and to their credit, they hadn't done it again. Norman was an opportunist, and she couldn't help wondering if Mike might be one to, but she was certain he was after something more than just a chocolate bar. Norman was the only male she had left to rely on in her life, and he was very special to her. He was special to everyone he met, and she loved him, even if he did slobber.

As soon as the phone call was out of the way she went back to join Mike in the alcove. He cast her a questioning look and she smiled briefly to try to reassure him; she didn't want to answer any awkward questions at this stage of the plan. She wished now that she had picked a table in a more central position so other people could see them, (just in case Mike did in fact turn out to be a psychotic axe murderer), but to change now would be futile and might arouse Mike's suspicions. She managed another half-hearted smile and thanked him for the coke.

Chloe had to try and act normally, whatever normal was, in what she suspected might be the longest ten minutes of her life. She forced herself to make small talk with her date, at the same time as digging a ridiculous number of ice cubes out of her coke glass. Chloe hated ice, it set her teeth on edge, and she was annoyed that Mike hadn't remembered this. Mike apologised for forgetting about the ice and after ten minutes of pointless discussion about the benefits of using a specialist toothpaste, her phone finally rang. The screen displayed an unknown number and to Chloe's dismay she answered and listened to an automated message about PPI reclaim. Inwardly seething, she kept calm and apologised to Mike for the interruption. She willed her phone to ring and within minutes it did. After making all the right noises on the phone so Mike would sense the urgency of the situation she hung up and grabbed her bag explaining to him that the dog was ill, and she had to go home. He seemed annoyed, he had driven fifty miles after all, but he obviously wasn't a dog lover otherwise he would have understood. He offered to escort her to her car and as a large group of people were about to leave Chloe nodded. At least she wouldn't be alone in the car park with him.

Outside by the car, Chloe apologised for cutting the evening short but thanked him out of politeness for an interesting evening. She couldn't bring herself to say nice, because frankly it hadn't been nice and her thoughts about serial killers were likely to give her nightmares for weeks to come. The group of people who had left the pub at the same time, were now beginning to get into their vehicles and drive off, so Chloe took the opportunity to quickly jump in her car and do the same. She knew Mike needed to travel in the opposite direction to her so was somewhat surprised when he turned the same way out of the car park . Surely, he wasn't following her. She had given him her mobile number but not her address, another box ticked when following internet dating safety guidelines according to page one of the rules. She felt a surge of panic rising in her throat before putting her foot down hard on the accelerator, after all, a speeding ticket was better than getting murdered any day.

To her relief when she looked in the mirror, she could no longer see him. Perhaps he had realised his mistake and turned round, or maybe he needed to stop for fuel. She slowed back down to comply with the speed limit and tried to breathe normally again. She would be home soon. As she turned off the dual carriageway, she noticed a car about four hundred metres behind her signalling to turn off. It was dark outside with only a handful of streetlights, making it impossible to identify the model from that distance. She was tempted to put her foot down again, but she was entering a

30mph speed limit and at that time of night the cops were everywhere waiting for the pubs to throw out the drunks. She convinced herself she was just being paranoid. There were loads of cars on the road still and this was a slip road so she should expect other cars to be behind her. The closer she got to home the quieter the roads became, and the streetlights cast eerie shadows on the surrounding buildings. The wind gained momentum causing the trees to forcefully shake their branches and shed any remaining leaves. They were only trees but something about them seemed sinister tonight. They appeared hostile, the shaking branches were trying to tell her something- she was sure of it.

Not too far behind her, there was a man in his car, slamming his fist on the wheel as he drove. He was angry, very angry. His plans for the evening had just been ruined by a bloody dog and he wasn't ready to give up on it just yet.

Chloe hurriedly pulled into her driveway. She was eager to get out the car and into the house as quickly as possible. In her haste to get inside, she failed to notice the subtle dimming of a car's headlights nearby. She felt uneasy yet she had no idea why. Even though she was home, her gut feeling was telling her the evening wasn't yet over, and it unsettled her. She wasn't usually a nervous person and she scolded herself for being such a drama queen. She convinced herself it was because she was out of practice with the whole dating scene, and things would get easier if she could only relax a bit more around men. She suspected she might have misjudged the poor man but given that he wasn't really her type, she had no regrets. The evening was over, and Mike was history.

Mike was sitting in his car not too far away. He watched as Chloe switched the lights on. For him, the evening was only just beginning.

Chloe opened the fridge to grab the milk for a cup of tea but the remains of a half-drunk bottle of wine were calling out to her just begging to be poured into a glass. She convinced herself that wine used for medicinal purposes was perfectly acceptable, after all, she'd given herself a bit of a fright, and it would help her sleep. Obviously, the saintly Gregory would disagree, but she was an adult woman and had no need to justify her decisions to him or anyone else. As she sipped the cool wine her phone rang. It was Mike, just checking she had got home alright and asking if the dog was okay. Chloe spluttered an answer. She had completely forgotten that the dog, who was happily wagging his short stumpy tail next to her, was supposed to be ill. She thanked him for his concern and wished him a safe journey home because he must have been calling from his hands free and would surely be almost halfway home by now. Feeling relaxed for the first time that evening she made her way upstairs to get ready for bed.

Mike watched as the upstairs lights flickered on and then phoned her again. He might as well push his luck and see if there was any chance of a second date with her, so he offered to take her for a meal. He was keen to get to know her better and as far as he was concerned there was no reason why she wouldn't feel the same way. He was disappointed when she declined his offer mumbling something about long distance relationships being too complicated for her. If she felt that way, why had she agreed to meet him in the first instance? She was clearly nothing but a time waster and he didn't appreciate that. He was looking for a long-term relationship with all the benefits, including somewhere to live. He had been a little economical with the truth because he had been trying to impress her. He couldn't admit to her that he was back home living at the hotel of mum and dad rent- free because he was unable to hold down a job for more than two months. His wife had become sick of him because she had no choice but to take on the role of the main breadwinner in the family and now his parents were sick of him too. His sons wanted nothing more to do with him because he had let them down time and time again, and as a result, had become fiercely protective of their mother. They had no respect for him but deep down, he knew he didn't really deserve their respect. His mother had always told him that respect was earned. He had failed as a husband, son, father, brother, uncle, and employee, and in his gut he felt the sharp stab of shame, a searing ache that stayed with him, reminding him of his inadequacies..

He had been on the dating site for months now and had never got further than a first date. The frustration was beginning to take its toll, he was on the edge and close to a breakdown. He had told his parents he wouldn't be home tonight, and they had willingly given him some pocket money to enjoy his night out, as if placating a small child. He couldn't go back now with his tail tucked between his legs like a naughty dog. Talking of dogs, he had witnessed Norman eagerly greeting Chloe at the door on her return to the house.

The dog certainly hadn't looked ill, and it didn't take him long to realise he had been duped. His parents were under the impression he was making progress, and he couldn't face the humiliation of losing face in front of them yet again. He had to persevere, at least that's what his therapist had told him. Everyone deserves a second chance, now all he had to do was convince Chloe of that.

Chloe's phone rang for a third time and alarm bells were starting to ring. Her instincts had been right, it looked like she had picked herself up a stalker. She was tempted to ignore it because she wanted to go to bed, but something told her that if she did that he would continue to call, if not tonight then tomorrow, and she didn't want that. Surely, he must be almost home by now, so he didn't pose much of a threat, more of a nuisance. She answered in an assertive tone, fully expecting Mike to report his safe arrival home so she wouldn't worry, not that she was in any way worried. Instead, he announced that his car had broken down about a mile away from the pub. He hadn't wanted to bother her, but it was getting late, and he hadn't been able to fix it and he wondered if she might come out and rescue him? Chloe was flabbergasted. She had no intention of getting trapped in yet another unpredictable situation with him so she politely declined, and suggested he might like to try calling a breakdown service instead, then hung up the phone.

Mike was furious. How dare she just hang up on him like that after luring him fifty miles from home? In her emails she had sounded keen to meet up and he wasn't the sort of guy to waste an opportunity. Most girls wanted to know more about you before meeting up and that made it difficult for him to hide behind the imaginary lifestyle he had created for himself. This make-believe world had become real to him because he had written about it so often. He had lived in a four-bed detached house in the London suburbs, the fact that it was no longer his house was irrelevant wasn't it? The house he had once shared with his ex-wife and kids had been repossessed when they couldn't meet the mortgage payments on her income alone.

His job at the airport had been terminated after his probationary period – a detail that he also omitted from his imaginary profile. He had spent most of his two months there off sick with a doctor's note which just said, 'Workplace Stress.' He had managed two weeks there though, and in that time had met Gail Tilsley from Coronation Street which had put him into a state of permanent euphoria. She had taken an interest in him which was unusual because, in his experience, most passengers were unnecessarily rude to him. A doctor's note had saved the day and he'd gone sick with only statutory sick pay to support his family.

His brother Luke was a successful entrepreneur and had built his own catering business up from scratch. He was two years younger than Mike but had always been the golden boy as far as his parents were concerned, and Mike had never felt able to compete with him. He was jealous of Luke's success. Luke didn't need or want for anything. He had a beautiful wife and two daughters, but Mike had nothing to do with them anymore. At one stage Luke had offered him a menial job within his company. Mike believed the job offer had been more out of brotherly duty than actual need, so he declined to save his brother from further embarrassment.

His thoughts wandered back to Chloe. He had misinterpreted her motives and his 'good time girl' had turned into a goodnight girl. She clearly wasn't interested in him, but he had a long night ahead of him stuck in the car and he needed to do something for entertainment. If he wasn't going to be sleeping in a comfy bed tonight, then she wasn't either. He enjoyed playing games, his ex-wife constantly accused him of playing mind games with her, but that was her problem for not having a sense of humour. He hoped Chloe had a sense of humour. He hadn't really spent enough time with her to find out, but if she could make up fictitious stories on the spur of the moment about the dog being ill, then he assumed she must have a sense of humour. She obviously found it funny that she had duped him so easily, but he hadn't quite bought her storyline which is why he had followed her home. Now the joke was on her. He picked up his phone and rang Chloe's number again. One ring then straight to answerphone. He left a message, then another, and soon he had left about thirty something messages before he presumably filled up her message box and wasn't able to leave any more.

Chloe was lying in bed listening to each and every message alert. She picked up her phone, thirty-two missed calls from Mike's number and twenty-nine unread messages so far, and as the phone continued to ring, she was getting angry. She was tired and needed some sleep because she had a long day ahead of her at work tomorrow. How dare this moron intrude on her life in such a personal way.

To the best of her knowledge Mike was stuck on the A3 somewhere so he didn't pose an immediate threat to her safety, but she decided to err on the side of caution by ringing the non-emergency police number to report nuisance calls. The police advised her to keep her phone on so they could monitor the calls overnight. She drifted in and out of a restless sleep before waking abruptly at 4am to find her eldest daughter standing by the bed.

"Can't you hear that commotion outside?" she demanded angrily.

Chloe rubbed her sleepy eyes and listened. Someone was calling her name through the letterbox, and she recognised his voice immediately.

"Chloe please let me in, I'm cold and I need you to warm me up."

She grabbed her phone, which now registered thirty-five unread messages and three hundred and thirty-nine missed calls. She must have been comatose not to have heard all that, so she made a mental note to herself not to drink wine so close to bedtime in future. Her instincts had been right, and this creep had followed her home after all. Suddenly she felt very afraid and vulnerable and without further ado dialled 999. The police only took about five minutes to arrive but to Chloe it seemed more like a lifetime, knowing that Mike was still lurking around outside . A police car and police van turned up simultaneously with flashing lights and sirens wailing loud enough to wake up the entire neighbourhood; curtains were starting to twitch and bedroom windows began to flood with light. Chloe cringed with embarrassment knowing full well she would be the talk of the neighbourhood for years to come. It seemed her poor judgement concerning men had followed her like a poltergeist from her old life to her new one, wreaking havoc, and now her neighbours were involved in the entire fiasco too. She knew it was probably her own fault, but it was a lot easier to blame someone else and that someone else was Pete. Damn Pete for leaving her! It was his fault that her life was in such a mess, and although she knew that wasn't entirely true, the more she said it the more believable it became.

Chloe watched from the window as a burly male police officer handcuffed Mike and led him to the waiting van. She could hear his verbal protests as they secured the doors, but there was too much background noise to hear his exact words. Chloe imagined his vocabulary was probably ripe with expletives. The doorbell rang and two uniformed officers asked if they might step in. Chloe had a fondness for a man in uniform and now, standing in front of her, there were two of them. A bit like buses she thought; you spend ages waiting for one, then two arrive together. She blushed with shame after catching a reflection of herself in the mirror, standing in her onesie and granny style fluffy slippers. It could be worse; she might have been wearing one of her silk negligees or baby doll nighties which left little to the imagination. Pete had bought them for her because, like the short skirts, they made her look incredibly sexy and emphasised her long lean legs and ample bust, but he wasn't the one who'd had to sleep in them all night was he? She'd hated them because they made her sweat and crumpled up awkwardly every time she turned over in bed and so, when he left, she was glad to get rid of them, and they had ended up in a charity bag with the rest of the junk she had collected over the years. Her onesie looked more like an oversized Babygro with poppers in the most inconvenient places, especially when she needed the toilet in a hurry, but right now it felt safe and comfy and that was all that mattered. She reeled her wandering mind back in and reminded herself that the coppers weren't there to vie for her affections, and if Pete had been with her instead of snuggled up with his Brazilian bimbo somewhere, they wouldn't be here at all. She smiled warmly at them and opened the door to let them in.

The taller officer introduced himself as detective sergeant Philip Russell and his partner as police constable James Owen. On closer inspection she thought that James looked about fifteen but that was probably because she was fast approaching middle age. She thought the same about the fresh-faced junior doctors that came into the surgery and realised she was most definitely getting old. Philip was closer to her age, an attractive man with piercing blue eyes and a generous mop of dark curly hair with just a hint of grey. Norman settled comfortably at his feet and Philip stroked him kindly. Chloe went by the motto, if your dog didn't like someone then she probably shouldn't like them either. She firmly believed that dogs had highly- tuned instincts that made them a good judge of character and wondered if she should get Norman to vet future male suitors on her behalf. Philip had obviously passed the dog test with flying colours, but she wondered if he would regret it later on when he got up to find his pristine black uniform trousers covered in white dog hair. She also noticed he was wearing a wedding ring on his left hand and for a brief moment, she felt disappointed. It seemed the good guys around her age were always taken, and knowing her luck she would probably have to wade through a sea of psychopaths like Mike before finding someone like Phil. She knew nothing about him, yet she was already affectionately calling him 'Phil' and not Phillip. Phil had a nice ring to it she thought and Norman obviously agreed.

Chloe made a mental note to check her dating emails once Phil had left to see if there were any policemen among them. A policeman would make her feel safe because it was their public duty to make people feel safe, much the same as hers was to do no harm. By this time, it was almost 5am and Phil offered to come back at a more reasonable hour if Chloe wanted to catch up on some sleep. Chloe declined, she couldn't go back to sleep now if she wanted to, and she had to be at work in a few hours anyway. Adrenaline was pumping through her veins, reminding her of the start line on school sports day. Her naturally competitive nature spawned from her mum's insistence that there were no prizes for second place; try telling that to an Olympic silver medal winner! Phil confirmed that they had monitored over three hundred incoming calls to Chloe's number, which in itself constituted harassment. He asked if he could listen to the answer phone messages so she handed him her phone. She hadn't bothered to listen to them which Phil said didn't matter, although the content would be needed as evidence if the case went to court. Chloe hadn't even considered court. She assumed Mike would just get a rap on the knuckles with a police caution. There she was making assumptions again. How many times had she told herself not to make assumptions for God's sake?

Phil seemed to sense her anxiety and reassured her that she would not necessarily have to attend court, it would all depend on Mike's plea and whether the Crime Prosecution Service thought there was enough evidence to charge him with harassment.

Chloe didn't want to attend court. She never wanted to clap eyes on that lunatic again. The very thought of him sent a chill through her body and instinctively she hugged a cushion from the sofa as a source of comfort. Phil noticed her unease and suggested a nice cup of tea to warm them all up before they got started on the statement and Chloe finally felt able to relax. James was ready to start writing and sat confidently with his pen poised and note pad on his lap, while Phil prepared to ask the questions. The statement took about an hour in total to complete and Chloe was asked to sign it at the bottom to say it was all true. The officers said Mike would probably be held at the police station for most of the day so his car would have to remain outside. She wasn't entirely comfortable with the car being there, but she consoled herself with the fact that she was going to work so she wouldn't have to look at it all day and be reminded of her close brush with a potential killer. She hoped they would lock him up and throw away the key and then laughed at the ridiculousness of it all because that was exactly the sort of thing her mother would say while watching the news. Oh God, she was turning into her mother, and much as she loved her, that would never do.

Phil and James stood up ready to leave and Phil said he would be in touch again later that day. Chloe stifled a giggle at the sight of Phil's discreet attempts to rid his trousers of copious amounts of dog hair but to no avail. By the time the coppers had finally left the house it was almost 7am and Chloe cringed as she watched the futile attempts of the curious neighbours trying to remain inconspicuous behind their net curtains. She felt tempted to wave at them but thought better of it because she had already drawn enough attention to herself for one day. She convinced herself that work would be a good source of diversion therapy, but she couldn't have been more wrong. She was tired, irritable and couldn't concentrate on anything for more than a few seconds at a time. Well-meaning colleagues expressed concern and brought in copious cups of tea, but this only added to her already grouchy mood. She couldn't bring herself to tell them about the events of last night because the majority of them had already turned into substitute mothers, and if they knew the full, gory story, they would probably have her under house arrest for the foreseeable future.

The front desk rang, it was detective sergeant Philip Russell asking to speak to Chloe. The receptionist looked at her questioningly and Chloe feared it wouldn't be long before she was forced to spill the beans, whether she liked it or not. Phil, as she liked to call him, was phoning to give her an update. Mike had pleaded guilty, and the CPS had charged him. By all accounts, he had driven the custody officers crazy by howling like a wounded animal in his cell and feigning claustrophobia, forcing them to move him to a larger one. For a brief moment, Chloe actually felt pity for him but that quickly passed. He had got what he deserved and hopefully he would think twice before harassing a woman again. Phil said they would shortly be bringing him back to his car and someone would follow him in a police vehicle to the county line. His court hearing was set for the following week and because he had pleaded guilty, Chloe was not required to attend. She breathed a sigh of relief and raced back to her room avoiding making eye contact with the reception staff. They would want to know what was going on because they cared about her, but they were also too nosey for their own good sometimes and she didn't have the time or energy to explain.

Her shift was almost finished but she couldn't face doing anything more, so she packed up and went home half an hour early mumbling excuses to the already highly suspicious reception staff. The kids would be in from school shortly and she didn't want them to be home alone while the police escorted mad Mike away from outside her home under the watchful eyes of the entire neighbourhood. When she arrived home, Mike's car was still outside with no sign of the boys in blue. She hurried inside to avoid questions by the no-doubt, well-meaning but nevertheless inquisitive neighbours, who were gathered together gossiping in a nearby front garden. The kids were sprawled out on the sofa eating snacks and watching television and Norman was sat drooling at their feet waiting for his usual supply of the leftovers. The kids were resilient, they had been through a lot of changes since Pete deserted them and had come to terms with being part of the broken family culture which appeared to be the norm these days, and had emerged relatively unscathed, it seemed. Friends with happily married parents were few and far between, so in their words the situation was 'pretty cool.' Chloe didn't share their opinion and there was a time when she would have done anything to turn back the clock and restore the family unit. She missed companionship, she missed physical affection, and she missed emotional stimulation. Damnit, she missed Pete, even though she didn't want to. Pete was all she had ever known. He was her first true love, and he was the father of her children. From the first time they met she knew he was the man she was going to marry and even though it was a bit of a cliché, it really had been love at first sight for both of them.

Pete was a gentle man with a placid nature. He had been in the same job with the same company for the past thirty years and he had no desire to do anything else which Chloe had found frustrating because she was sure he could do better. Chloe, on the other hand, was an ambitious workaholic. She was highly competitive, and her goal was to work her way up the career ladder to make her family proud. Her strong work ethic and high standards earned the respect of both patients and colleagues and her no-nonsense approach to problem solving had given her a formidable reputation. She and Pete were chalk and cheese, but Chloe believed their marriage worked well on the basis that opposites attract and she knew she could always rely on him to support her. Unfortunately, they had both ignored the warning signs which highlighted their marriage was failing and her desire to change Pete into someone he didn't want to be had cost their family dearly. Over time, she had become an expert at putting on a brave front and people relied heavily on her to be their advocate. She was proud of her reputation, but underneath her harsh exterior she was a pussy cat who was too afraid to let her guard down and allow people to see just how vulnerable and fragile she really was. It was easier to keep up the pretence to avoid getting hurt again although silently she was weeping inside.

A familiar looking car pulled up outside wearing the distinct Battenberg costume combination of yellow and blue check. No blue lights this time, but Chloe felt certain curtains would be twitching so she decided not to look. She didn't want to see him again anyway, him of course being Mad Mike but she caught a glimpse of him out the corner of her eye climbing into the driver's seat of his car. He had a downcast look about him like a scolded schoolboy, and he was staring at the ground, presumably to avoid meeting the gaze of the increasingly curious neighbours. Phil rang the doorbell just to explain that Mike had been warned to make no attempt to contact her in any shape or form. If he did, he would be arrested immediately. Chloe was given a crime number and details of victim support. She didn't think she was the type of woman likely to need victim support but there was no need for Phil to know that. It wouldn't hurt to let her guard down and play the part of the defenceless woman now and again, for a short while at least. It suddenly dawned on her that she didn't have to pretend anymore because she was a victim, and she was surprised to feel tears pricking at the back of her eyes. Without warning, she suddenly felt very fragile and exposed. Phil must have sensed the emotion within her and placed a reassuring hand on her shoulder to comfort her as best he could, and before long she couldn't stop herself and allowed the tears to flow. Chloe nodded her appreciation before closing the door and then sobbed her heart out. Norman was at her side within minutes trying to wash away her tears with his smooth slobbery tongue. He hated to see his human unhappy and lately she had been unhappy quite a lot. He was a dog, but he had taken on the role of man of the house. He was the protector, the comforter and more often than not the clown, but he was a loyal companion to. If only he could talk Chloe thought, perhaps then her world wouldn't feel so empty. Norman barked as if he understood, and Chloe embraced him with a reassuring hug; he responded enthusiastically by rolling on to his back with his feet in the air begging for a belly rub.

Chloe's next task was to contact the dating site to inform them they had a stalker on their books. She was sure there were plenty more on there that she hadn't yet met and hoped not to meet, but for now she had a single crime number that had the power to protect other women from Mad Mike. His profile was removed with immediate effect and the dating site thanked her for her vigilance and quick-thinking email. That done, Chloe looked at her remaining unread messages. She was tempted not to read them and delete her entire profile, but curiosity got the better of her once more and she didn't want to miss out in case there was a tall dark handsome police officer like Phil waiting for her somewhere.

The first few messages were disappointing to say the least, 'hey babe do you fancy hooking up sometime,' and 'hello sexy legs,' were not age- appropriate first introductions, although secretly Chloe was pleased someone had complimented her on her legs. Coincidentally, the third message was from a police officer but not your bog-standard PC Plod. This was from a detective chief superintendent called Alan whose job sounded awfully important because he was responsible for coordinating an entire team of detectives investigating serious crime like murder. Chloe thought it sounded exciting, unlike her own comparatively mundane job explaining the nature of viral illness to worried mums and dads still living in a nanny state triggered by overprotective grandparents. The parents always wanted antibiotics' just in case' it went to little Johnny's chest, and she was fed up spouting the same spiel every day. She felt like a tape recorder that was constantly running but which no one ever heard. All little Johnny usually needed was a few doses of kid's paracetamol and a tissue to wipe the never-ending stream of snot from his nose instead of making her feel sick by licking it off his top lip with his tongue while she was examining him. Chloe gagged just thinking about it, she hated snot and phlegm especially when it was presented to her in a tissue so she could see the colour. She didn't need to see the bloody colour for God's sake because snot was green, and she wished parents would use a bit of common sense before rushing their kids to the doctors at the first sign of a common cold. Google definitely had a lot to answer for. Colds were instantly pneumonia, all rashes were obviously meningitis, and it made her wonder what it was about children that made usually sensible parents lose all sense of logic. She was becoming increasingly certain she would have made a better police officer than a nurse, but it was too late now. She had applied to join the police force when she was just eighteen, despite protests from her safety conscious mother who was certain she would get murdered in the line of duty. Unbeknown to her mother, she had a higher chance of getting murdered now judging by current events. She had passed every level of the entry requirements bar one and was let down by her less than perfect eyesight. Her mother was of course euphoric, but Chloe remained disappointed to this day, especially as the rules had since been relaxed in the name of diversity. It seemed the more diverse you were, the better your chances of were of getting in, and she briefly wished she had been born a visually impaired dwarf.

Chloe decided to send Alan a quick message acknowledging his email and promised she would be in touch again later on. Later on didn't necessarily mean later today, she didn't really know what it meant but she knew she wasn't ready to do it right now. As she made her way up the stairs to take a shower, she started humming along to an old Broadway classic that was a favourite of her mother's, 'I'm gonna wash that man right out of my hair and send him on his way.' Mike was history and she had learnt from that mistake or at least she thought she had. At work the following day, she spent most of her time trying to dodge the inevitable questions from concerned colleagues and although she tried to brush it off as a minor misdemeanour, they went on and on at her until she was forced to relive the entire humiliating experience all over again. She fully expected lots of, 'I told you so's,' from them but she was pleasantly surprised by their sympathetic comments and the concerned expressions on their faces and although she knew they would have a good gossip about her behind her back, she didn't mind. Phil phoned with the date, time, and venue of Mad Mike's court hearing and quickly briefed her on Mike's fantasy make-believe world and his emotionally destructive relationship with his parents. She imagined him standing in the dock with that hang-dog look about him and his worried mother would be sitting in the gallery ready to make excuses for him. It was pathetic really but at least she would know to keep a tighter rein on her 'boy' in the future.

The court date came and went, and Chloe didn't hear from Phil until a few days afterwards. She wasn't all that surprised to hear that Mike had broken down and behaved like a blubbering wreck in court, but the judge had shown no mercy and issued him with a caution and a restraining order. If he violated this order the judge told him in no uncertain terms that he would be arrested and face a jail sentence which would probably be served in a secure psychiatric unit where they could treat his multiple mental health problems. Chloe was happy as it seemed justice had been done, and Mike now had a criminal record to add to his list of achievements. It would make it more difficult for him to secure gainful employment of any kind for at least five years, but as far as Chloe was concerned that was irrelevant because he was clearly far too much of a liability to be of benefit to any employer. If Chloe had been the judge, she would have added a minimum of six months community service to his sentence to get him in practice for the big wide world of work. She smiled as she tried to imagine him standing at the roadside in a bright orange high visibility jacket picking up litter from the gutter. Trash picking up trash she mumbled while congratulating herself on dodging another bullet. She heard nothing more from Mike but a few weeks after the court hearing, she did receive a personal email allegedly from his ex-wife which she ignored because she was convinced it had been written by Mike under the pseudonym of Tracey. It was just the kind of self-centred, self-pitying email that only Mike could have written. There was no remorse, only contempt for the ordeal she, Chloe, had bestowed upon him. According to 'Tracey,' he wasn't a bad man he was just misunderstood. It was a pathetic attempt to convince her that she had misinterpreted the situation, but it was futile, and with full knowledge of the consequences, Chloe forwarded it to the inbox of detective sergeant Philip Russell. Mike was dangerous, deranged, and delusional and he needed help; the only way he was going to get the help he needed was from behind bars. It was time to end this chapter of her life and move on to the next, because she had once read somewhere that one bad chapter didn't mean the whole book was bad.

Chloe opened her mailbox to respond to Alan's message but there was another message waiting to be read from a guy called Mel who she had already developed a type of crazy schoolgirl- type crush on. She refused to meet him because his status was 'separated,' which as far as she was concerned meant married, but they had exchanged a few emails and there was something about him which made her feel happy. She had given him her mobile number and although they hadn't yet spoken to each other something was telling her they would do soon. If nothing else she thought they could be friends and support each other, but deep down she knew it would be difficult to maintain a platonic relationship with a guy she fancied, and she was already one hundred percent certain she fancied Mel. She briefly read Mel's cheeky message which brought a much-needed smile to her face, but she decided to respond another time because she had logged in with the sole purpose of replying to Alan.

Chloe decided to be sensible and not dive in headfirst again. She would find out more about Alan before agreeing to meet him to avoid any nasty surprises. Her enthusiasm to meet Mike quickly had landed her in hot water and she didn't want a repeat of that fiasco. She needed to stay safe and although she was keen to ask some probing questions, she didn't want to appear too intrusive. She assumed that in his line of work he would be the one asking all the questions and she was concerned he might struggle with adapting to the role of the interviewee. As a police officer he would surely respect and understand her safety net, but in the end she talked herself out of asking too many questions because his job meant he would surely already possess a high standard of professional integrity and moral values. She was more concerned about whether her job as a humble nurse would meet his standards-surely an important detective like him would be seeking the company of a high-flying professional business woman who read papers like The Telegraph or Financial Times?

She had already made the mistake of trying to change Pete with disastrous consequences so she would lay her cards on the table, and he could take it or leave it simple as that, and if he chose not to meet her it would be his loss, not hers. She knew from experience that most guys loved nurses so there was every chance she would be able to fulfil all his fantasies, and at the same time be capable of holding down and following an intelligent conversation. She was happy with her plan and replied with a level of confidence that would show Alan she was more than just a pretty face.

Alan

Chloe quietly congratulated herself on her new, more cautious approach to internet dating. She and Alan exchanged several emails and they spoke at length on the phone. He spoke very eloquently, and they had more common ground than she had originally anticipated. His star sign was Aries, the same as her own, which according to her horoscope compatibility book made them a good match.

Alan's ex-wife, a barrister, had left him and set up home with another woman five years previously. According to Alan they had drifted apart after he gained promotion at work. His job involved working long hours with extensive travel, meaning he was away from home for weeks at a time. His ex-wife had become friendly with a woman from work and had begun socialising with her. The two women eventually bought a Volkswagen camper van between them as a renovation project, and the next thing Alan knew, they were going to music festivals together and enjoying weekends away. Alan was initially pleased his wife had found a 'friend' because he felt guilty about the amount of time he was away from home, but one evening out of the blue she told him she had something to tell him and blurted out that she wanted a divorce because she was a lesbian and her partner wanted to marry her. Alan struggled to use the word lesbian. His wife running off with another woman had made him feel inferior as a man, his role within the force commanded respect from colleagues. He didn't want to become a laughingstock or the subject of workplace gossip, so he was looking for a good woman to accompany him at social events. He felt that it would never do for his work colleagues to discover the truth. His private life was none of their business, but as far as they knew his marriage was dissolved affably on the grounds of irretrievable breakdown. After the divorce, Alan remained in the family home and his ex-wife moved in with her partner. They had shared custody of their two boys, aged nine and fourteen years, but as the boys attended boarding school they were only home during holiday times. Alan tried to protect his boys by urging them not to discuss their mother's sexual orientation at school. He was afraid for them in case they endured prejudice or bullying from their peers. He wasn't sure if they were embarrassed about it, but he most certainly was because having a lesbian ex-wife did not fit comfortably with his professional standing, and he did not want his work colleagues to think he wasn't man enough to satisfy a woman.

Chloe understood boarding school life. She had personal experience of boarding school education and knew how horrible other kids could be especially if you didn't fit in with a particular crowd or you were a bit different. Boarding school had made Chloe grow up quickly. She had acquired the resilience needed to stand on her own two feet and developed life skills that would enable her to cope in the big wide world at a later date. At school she pushed boundaries to their limits and challenged staff with her defiant and rebellious nature. Much to her mother's disgust, she had come close to expulsion on a number of occasions. She recalled the time when her arch enemy, the new girl from some foreign land whose daddy was a diplomat, made a derogatory comment about her after lights out one night. Chloe had done nothing to provoke such a disparaging remark and was lying in bed inwardly fuming and plotting her revenge which ultimately was to pull her out of bed by her hair and dump her unceremoniously in the centre of the room. Unfortunately, the house mistress came in to investigate the commotion just in time to witness the blubbering bully lying on the floor having perfected the role of the innocent victim. To the amusement of the other girls, the house mistress had shrieked at Chloe like an old fish wife which made the pompous little upstart smirk. It was clear she had provoked Chloe deliberately just to get attention and boost her own popularity knowing full well Chloe had a short fuse and would take the bait. Chloe she knew she would be punished for her behaviour and she didn't care so long as they didn't suspend her, because that would mean going home and she hated being at home nearly as much as she hated being at school.

Home was supposed to be a sanctuary, a place where she should feel loved and cherished, but her home was none of those things. As an only child, Chloe was also a lonely child. Her mum loved her in her own unique way, but her priority in life was men and booze. At the time of the 'dragging by the hair' incident, her mum's latest beau had been a sugar daddy

about thirty years her senior who had generously stumped up
the money to pay for Chloe's schooling. He told her mum he
wanted nothing but the best for Chloe, and of course she
believed him, but deep down Chloe knew that all he really
wanted was her out the way so they could live the child free
life they both craved. Her mum was completely blinkered
when it came to this man and could only ever see him through
rose tinted glasses, often to Chloe's detriment. He had money,
lots of it, but he came with a price and that price was getting
rid of Chloe; she had sensed yet another change of surname
in the not-too-distant future and dreaded it because his name
was Pratt. Pratt by name and Pratt by nature she thought, and
she knew she would never live it down at school, and worse
still it would give the stuck-up foreign brat something else to
taunt her about. As luck would have it, she wasn't suspended
but the head teacher gave her the laborious task of clearing
stones from a wooded area nearby to make way for the new
school tennis courts. It was only for two hours which she said
would give her time to reflect on her actions and provide an
outlet for her unresolved anger issues. Chloe didn't think she
had anger issues, but the irritating woman responsible for
pastoral care at the school disagreed. She was one of those
annoying women who nodded her head constantly like one
of those dogs that people put on the rear parcel shelf of their
car. She made all the right noises without passing judgement
which Chloe found tedious. She decided that the pastoral care
lady couldn't be all that bright, because she had sat without
flinching, and grinned like a Cheshire cat while Chloe had
hurled insults at her. Thinking back on it now, Chloe felt
ashamed because this poor woman was a nun who had

devoted her life to God and generously gave her time to the school to counsel the girls free of charge. The school didn't know what to do with Chloe, so she was forced into endless counselling sessions with the nun, who unbeknown to Chloe, enjoyed the challenge. This deeply insecure young, energetic, and high-spirited girl had reminded the nun very much of her younger self before she took her vows and devoted her life to God. Whenever she was with Chloe, she sang the song famously sung by the nuns in the film The sound of Music in her head - 'How do you solve a problem like Maria?'- because it had a better ring to it than, 'How do you solve a problem like Chloe?' In time, Chloe would turn out okay, she was sure of it, but she didn't think she was ever likely to become a nun.

Chloe had actually enjoyed her time- out, tossing stones into nearby bushes and tormenting spiders by destroying their intricate webs. She was in fact terrified of spiders, but this way she could get her own back on them for crawling under her bed covers without having to get too close to them. Had the house mistress not been mentally unhinged, then Chloe's punishment may just have been served quietly and without further incident but, as her fingers turned blue from the growing cold, Chloe had stopped work to put her hands in her pockets and warm them through. As she rested, she had glanced up at an upstairs window where, to her unease, she realised she was being watched (or rather glared at) by the house mistress. As their eyes met, the mistress began screeching in her fish wifey voice that, 'shirking on the job' warranted a further hour's stone clearing, meaning that Chloe would miss supper.

The house mistress wasn't authorised to issue

punishment to the girls, let alone additional punishment, but she just couldn't help herself when it came to Chloe, because she despised her. Chloe couldn't help wondering how such an evil woman had ever secured a job in a school, working with vulnerable home- sick young girls, some as young as five years of age. With a defiant look, Chloe had met her gaze, discarded the remaining stones, and made her way back into the main school building to phone her mum. Her mum may not always have been there for her, but right now she was all she had, and she knew she couldn't fight this despicable woman alone. Chloe's mum knew she was no angel, having inherited her own feisty personality and only abiding by regulations that she believed to be fair. Both loathed injustice and Chloe's mum had been incensed by what her daughter was telling her, but before she could finish her call, the door to the telephone kiosk had been flung open, and the spiteful house mistress grabbed the phone from Chloe's hand, slamming the receiver down hard. Fortunately for Chloe, the handset had failed to connect with the phone on the wall, and the loud slap and the vile obscenities that spilled from the house mistress's mouth were audibly witnessed by Chloe's shocked mum who was still listening from the other end of the phone.

Following the phone incident, the malicious house mistress disappeared. The vicious handprint on Chloe's arm served as evidence of physical assault and the last memory she had was watching her attacker being escorted from the premises by a squad of police officers. Chloe knew that nowadays such behaviour would be classified as child abuse, and emergency safeguarding procedures would have been launched by a whole host of multidisciplinary teams. Thirty years ago, it simply wasn't recognised the way it was now, and such events were easily dismissed and swept under the carpet to avoid any negative publicity. Life at school became unusually quiet following the eviction of the house mistress. Teachers seemed cautious, and even her arch enemy learned to hold her hostile tongue, which Chloe suspected had been excruciatingly painful for her. Chloe suspected that this current state of calm wouldn't last because stability had never been a permanent fixture in her life, so she decided to make the most of things while she could. She had longed to reach the magical age of sixteen so she could leave school forever, but now, as a much older, but not necessarily wiser, forty-five-year-old she wished she could turn the clock back, maybe not as far back as her school days, but certainly back about twenty years so she could meet Pete again for the first time and start afresh.

Chloe was surprised when Alan invited her over to his home to have a meal with him and his boys. She thought it seemed a bit early to be meeting the children when she hadn't even met their dad yet, but she dismissed her concerns by telling herself that the children would serve as a good safety net. She wasn't confident driving on unfamiliar roads, and as she made her way towards Alan's hometown, she started to doubt her judgement. His house was in a semi-rural location on the outskirts of town. Big sprawling houses with manicured lawns adorned the landscape and Chloe suspected local estate agents did very well from the sale of houses in this area. She hoped Alan was normal, as opposed to showy and pretentious like the properties in the area, although she wasn't entirely sure what normal was anymore.

As expected, Alan's home complimented the smart neighbourhood well. A long driveway led to a large double - fronted detached house with a solid oak front door and brass knocker. All the lights in the house were on and soft music was emanating from one of the open windows. Her nerves were starting to get the better of her and she struggled to control the nausea caused by the butterflies performing untimely gymnastics in her stomach. She wasn't sure she was being so sensible now, standing all alone on the doorstep of a man she was about to meet for the first time, and whose boys bizarrely came as part of the first date package. Tentatively she knocked on the door with one hand while attempting to pull down her skirt with the other. She regretted wearing it now because it was a bit on the short side, but it had been one of Pete's favourites, even though he would only allow her to wear it when she was out with him because he said it drew too much male attention to her legs. He'd been very proud of her legs but he didn't want her 'sharing them with every Tom, Dick, and Harry out there,' and as his wife she had respected his wishes. She had worn it tonight because she could, and because she was no longer answerable to Pete, but now, looking down at herself, she wondered if she was asking for trouble. She enjoyed dressing to tease but that didn't mean she was easy. He could look but he couldn't touch and those were her rules, and if he didn't like it that was tough. If he was a decent man he would be prepared to wait because, according to her mother all good things came to those that wait, and she convinced herself he wouldn't try it on with her with his boys there anyway.

Alan answered the door and smiled warmly; she blushed

awkwardly hoping it wasn't just the sight of her legs that lit up his smile. He was a tall, well-built man with rugged features that yielded an air of arrogance which Chloe guessed came with the job. He greeted her with a fleeting, continental, Parisian-style kiss on the cheek before introducing her to his two boys, Ben and Jake, who politely offered their hand to greet her more formally. She couldn't help but wonder if meeting new women was a regular occurrence for these two boys. She certainly hoped not because that would make their home nothing short of a brothel, and young boys needed to grow up with a healthy respect for women. She was offered a seat in the lounge while Alan returned to the kitchen to check on the dinner. The house was clean but undeniably lacked a woman's touch. It was a house that had probably been loved by a family once, but that love felt lost somehow in the absence of any family photos and traditional souvenirs from a previous life. Chloe felt sad for the boys because photos were precious memories and she wondered if Alan had deliberately removed them to erase that part of their lives. She was surmising of course, but she knew from experience that divorce was an evil word, capable of destroying an entire family; the thought suddenly made her feel nauseated. She was hungry, but she hoped Alan didn't pile too much food on her plate just in case she was sick.

Alan called to her from the kitchen. He was cooking steak with chunky homemade chips and all the trimmings and the boys were helping out, which Chloe thought was kind of them. He was asking how she liked her steak cooked and somewhat apologetically she blurted out, 'Well done please,' which unbeknownst to her, caused Alan to frown. He spent a lot of time in France and was used to eating his meat rare in top French restaurants. Asking for well cooked meat was considered to be bad manners in France, so Chloe was going to need some lessons in French etiquette if she planned on sticking around.

During the meal, Chloe sensed his disapproval but she hated rare meat and would push it away even if it showed the slightest hint of pink. If she cut it and blood ran out, she thought she would probably faint. Sadly, there was no dog to discreetly feed it to under the table if it was undercooked, so she waited anxiously for her meal and hoped for the best. As luck would have it, Alan's eldest boy Ben seemed to share her aversion to undercooked meat so she had a partner in crime. Ben often disappointed his dad with his choices which frequently provoked outbursts of verbal condemnation, even in public. Jake, on the other hand, was happy to experiment with different foods, but as the youngest boy he was always eager to please. Alan was used to getting his own way, and rarely listened long enough to hear both sides of a story. Ben protected his younger brother as much as he could from Alan's forceful nature, but there had been times when his anger had got the better of him and the boys had borne the brunt of his emotional cruelty. Ben looked at Chloe and pitied her, but it wasn't his place to tell her about his father. He hoped for her sake that she would leave at the end of the evening and never come back. He and his brother had been in this position many times before because Alan frequently used them as bait, using the opportunity to play the role of the doting father when he wanted to impress a pretty lady; it never ended well.

Alan was motivated by money and material possessions and was confident they could buy him anything, including love. Ben hoped Chloe would spot the red flag warning signs early on before Alan had the opportunity to manipulate her and reel her in with his undeniable charm. Chloe was in mortal danger and if she didn't wise up soon, he knew it wouldn't end well for her. Alan had tried to control their mother and turn her into someone she didn't want to be. When that failed, he'd become angry, and when he was angry, he was dangerous. For an easy life, they did their best to please him but nothing was ever good enough for Alan. Ben winced inwardly as he remembered the 'scene' he'd created in an exclusive Parisian restaurant when he was only ten, by refusing point blank to eat the frogs legs and oysters his dad had insisted on ordering for him. The only food he'd agreed to eat were the French fries, but Alan wouldn't allow him to eat them unless he ate the frog legs and there was no ketchup either – Ben had been physically ill, but his father had characteristically refused to back down. Such was Alan's need to control, he'd never truly forgiven Ben for such an outrageous faux pas.

They all sat down to eat together, and Chloe thought how well-mannered the two boys were. A combination of good parenting and a boarding school education had clearly influenced these boys and blessed them with high moral standards. She briefly thought back to her own boarding school education and reflected on her rebellious nature, and wondered why she hadn't turned out like them.. Alan opened a bottle of wine and Chloe placed her hand over her glass to politely refuse. She hoped he wasn't of the opinion that she was going to stay the night because if he was, he could think again. She planned to drive home after the meal, and drinking and driving was out of the question, and even more so when in the company of a high-ranking police officer.

Chloe asked for a soft drink instead and Ben saw his dad raise his eyebrows before getting up to find the lemonade. Alan was annoyed. He hadn't gone to this much effort for nothing and he was frustrated because he hadn't had a good shag in months. When she had turned up wearing such a short skirt he assumed she would be up for it, so this was an unexpected setback. As he poured her a glass of lemonade, she smiled softly at him and he noticed how pretty she was. He was going to have to work harder if he wanted to keep her; she met all the criteria and was definitely attractive enough to be seen out with him at work social events. Having an attractive woman on his arm would elevate his status and increase his popularity with the big bosses. He had already worked his way up the ladder, but he had his eye on a Chief Constable position which was pending due to the imminent retirement of the current post holder. If he was successful, he would have to move counties but that wouldn't hold him back. When his wife had left, the house became nothing but four walls, it was no longer a family home and although he hadn't told the boys, he would be glad to leave. The boys had lived there since the day they were born and were best friends with the neighbour's son, but they were happy at school and only came home for the holidays so as far as Alan was concerned the move wouldn't affect them.

The steak was edible although if she'd been in a restaurant Chloe would have asked politely if they wouldn't mind giving it a few more minutes under the grill . She washed down her dinner with the lemonade and couldn't help noticing that Alan had drunk his way through three quarters of the bottle of wine already. The boys only spoke when they were spoken to, which Chloe thought was slightly unusual given their ages, but then she remembered how strict mealtimes at boarding school could be so she interpreted their silence as force of habit as opposed to fear of their father. She wasn't to know that the boys were under strict instructions to keep quiet to give Alan time to work his charm, although it wasn't quite going to plan and the boys knew it.

After dinner, they were usually dismissed and told to go and amuse themselves so Alan could go upstairs for some 'adult play time' as he liked to call it. He'd deliver a knowing wink at the appropriate moment which Ben thought was vulgar. They had a fair idea what he was up to when he disappeared into the bedroom, because their mother had already sat them down and talked to them about the importance of meaningful love in a physical relationship. Ben already knew about the birds and the bees stuff, but their mum also taught them about the importance of showing respect to a woman; Ben wondered if his dad had missed out on that particular lesson because he always behaved as if women were just sex objects. As a mum, Alan's ex was desperate to protect her boys, but as a barrister she knew shared custody would prevail unless she could prove in court that Alan was an unfit father. When she left him, she didn't have enough ammunition to fight for sole custody, but she was waiting for her moment and she knew it wouldn't be long before Alan slipped up and displayed his true colours, she just hoped it wouldn't be at the expense of her two precious boys.

As expected, the boys were released from the dinner table but Alan had decided not to push his luck just yet, sensing that Chloe was likely to resist any attempts at seduction. Instead, he spent time humouring her by feigning an interest in her work and family and her bloody dog, which frankly bored him to tears. As far as Alan was concerned, nurses were failed, would- be doctors, but Chloe seemed to have worked her way up to a senior level and he commended her for that. He liked strong women, he found them sexy and exciting and there was nothing like a challenge to turn him on. He made up his mind to enjoy the chase, she was good on the eye and therefore worth the investment. He was planning a long weekend away with the boys in France and it would be nice to have Chloe around for company. It was time to turn on the charm so, with his most convincing smile, he invited Chloe to join them on an all-expenses paid holiday. He had more money than he knew what to do with and, as Chloe had mentioned in an email that she hadn't had a holiday for some time, it would be his treat. Chloe was flattered by his offer, but her sensible head was telling her she needed more time to think about it, and besides, she would have to check with work and organise her own kids.

Alan was arrogant enough to think that she would say yes eventually, he just needed to dangle the carrot a little closer; she'd be eating out of his hand in no time. He went on to elaborate in more detail, just to keep her focused; it wouldn't do for her to lose interest now. He planned to take the ferry from Dover to Calais, then drive to a quaint French seaside resort where they could stay overnight and eat out in a traditional French restaurant that he knew well. On day two, they'd be driving to Belgium to stay in the city of Bruges, a fairy tale medieval metropolis with dreamy canals steeped in history. He relished the idea of impressing her with his fluent French, a talent which unfortunately his boys did not share. Much to Alan's disgust the boys still showed no desire to learn a foreign language, despite learning French for years at school and having extra tuition; their grasp of the French language remained basic at best. He was becoming increasingly frustrated by their inability to learn, and insisted they persevere - what better way was there to improve than holidaying in French speaking countries?

Chloe had to admit it did all sound tempting, but she and Alan would have to get to know each other better first. She had a reputation for being impulsive, but in view of what had happened with Mike, to leave the country with a man she had only just met would be downright foolish, even by her standards. However, her resolve soon waivered, and two cups of tea later, she had fallen for his charms and agreed in principle to the weekend away providing she could make satisfactory arrangements at home. Alan was secretly congratulating himself on his powers of persuasion, but then he'd had plenty of practice due to the nature of his work. He would stop at nothing to catch his man and had a natural ability to intimidate colleagues and criminals alike. He wasn't popular at work, but that didn't matter to him because he didn't go to work to make friends and he enjoyed the power and authority that came with his status. Alan always had a victim and was usually spoilt for choice with the new recruits. He was quick to identify the vulnerable rookies and pursued them tirelessly like a predator hunting its prey. He made it clear that policing wasn't the boy scouts and if they were going to work in CID and join the big boys, they had to 'man up' because there was no room for error. His formidable reputation spilled over into his personal life where his standards remained high. His inability to accept criticism of any kind, coupled with unrealistic expectations, left family and friends exasperated and eventually friends disappeared off the radar. Most of his former friends had been people he'd met via his ex-wife and he wasn't surprised when they took her side after the divorce. There were a few that hung around for a while because they didn't want to appear biased, but in time they too had disappeared, and he was left alone to dwell on the life he had lost.

Chloe and Alan's relationship had progressed without incident and there were now only four weeks left until their planned weekend away; Alan made an extra effort to keep Chloe sweet for their trip. He'd been the perfect gentleman at all times and had spent his time wining and dining her and indulging her love of Indian cuisine. She was by now happy for him to hold her hand, and they had progressed from the continental kiss on the cheek to a slightly more intimate kiss on the lips. In an ideal world, he would have preferred things to move a bit faster and he hoped he wasn't spending money on a weekend away just to admire the scenery. He planned to see a lot more of Chloe and he had taken the liberty of booking a superior double room complete with Jacuzzi bath to make sure he got his money's worth. Chloe was looking forward to their short break. Alan requested that she pack some nice dresses as they would be dining out each night. He was hoping she would also pack some erotic lingerie because unlike Hugh Grant, Bridget Jones style big knickers didn't do it for him. He was a little worried because he hadn't been entirely honest with her and she was expecting her own room, but he was confident she would relax after seeing the exclusive suite he had managed to book, complete with a host of luxurious extras. If she made a fuss, he would apologise profusely and blame the hotel for the error. But he didn't anticipate any resistance because after all it hadn't cost her a single penny.

Chloe was excited when they set off towards Dover in Alan's unmarked police car. She was fascinated by all the technology inside the car which seemed to have as many buttons as an aircraft simulator. Alan enjoyed showing her how the flashing LED lights that sat either side of the front number plate worked, and they giggled like naughty teenagers as worried drivers instantly slowed down to comply with the speed limit. He loved the power this car gave him and today he loved it a little bit more because Chloe finally seemed to be warming to him. They sailed from Dover to Calais and then drove for just over two hours, with Ben in charge of map reading before reaching a tranquil coastal resort. Alan became unnecessarily agitated with Ben on a number of occasions during the journey because he had the map upside down and even accused him of deliberately trying to sabotage their trip, which Chloe thought was a bit extreme. Ben loathed map reading almost as much as he loathed French food. He suffered from motion sickness in the car and the constant waves of nausea were making it difficult for him to concentrate. Chloe felt sorry for him and thought about offering to help, but she couldn't pronounce the names of the places and the writing was far too small for her to see anyway.

The hotel was modern and overlooked the sea. It was well- equipped with state-of-the-art facilities including spa packages and a large indoor heated pool. The boys made straight for the pool while Alan tentatively prepared to show Chloe the room he had booked for them. The room was on the top floor with spectacular sea views and a balcony. Chandeliers decorated the ceiling and a rather grand looking queen size bed stood proud in the centre of the room. Chloe was instantly captivated by the grandeur and lavish furnishings and for a fleeting moment she was hypnotised by it all. She looked at the bed before looking over to where Alan was standing smirking mischievously on the balcony, and she instantly knew that this had been his plan all along. He was being very presumptuous but, just because there was a double bed didn't mean she had to sleep in it. She glanced around her and spotted a chaise longue tucked away in the corner; it looked hard and uncomfortable, and she suspected Alan would insist she was the one who slept on it if she made a fuss. Suddenly he didn't seem quite so gentlemanly anymore, and alarm bells were starting to ring in her head. She decided to say nothing because the sun was shining and the view from the balcony was glorious, and it seemed a pity to spoil the moment; they would discuss it later after they'd eaten. She checked her purse and was relieved to see her credit card tucked safely away which she kept for emergencies such as vet bills. At least now, if push came to shove, she could book another room for herself, although she hoped that wouldn't be necessary as the hotel looked pricey. Alan would understand, she was sure of it; at least she hoped she was sure, because police officers had to have integrity in order to do their job properly. There would be plenty of opportunities further down the line for them to develop a physical relationship if things went well between them; Chloe was in no rush for that and as a woman it was her prerogative to say no.

Alan watched as she gazed around the room and he knew what she was thinking, but he was confident that a good meal and a few glasses of wine would lift her inhibitions. Secretly he admired her tenacity. He liked a challenge, but most women had been too afraid to confront him. He knew she was different to the other women he had met because she was not driven by money or material possessions, meaning he was going to have to work extra hard to make the evening pleasurable. She didn't yet know it of course, but she was his top choice on the dessert menu, and he intended to savour every moment of it. His years of experience in the police force had served him well, and he knew he could be very convincing when he had to be. He had come this far and wasn't going to change his plans now.

Chloe showered and changed into an elegant dress suitable for dining out in the exquisite French restaurant Alan had told her about. He'd been chivalrous enough to let her have the room to herself whilst she got ready and she felt slightly reassured. She'd chosen the dress carefully to avoid any misconceptions and felt comfortable with the demure image staring back at her in the mirror. She applied a small amount of makeup and wore her shoulder length hair in a feminine half up, half down braid. Alan nodded his approval although secretly, he was slightly disappointed the dress didn't display a bit more flesh. Chloe was apprehensive about going to the restaurant. All she knew about French food was what she'd read in books about bloody meat, frogs' legs and slimy shellfish. She had the perfect excuse to avoid the shellfish because it brought her out in hives and an itchy raised bumpy rash would not compliment her dress. There was no way she was going to eat frogs' legs either because frogs lived in ponds and they might have made contact with the shellfish, which would increase the likelihood of an allergic reaction if eaten. She knew that this theory was ridiculous because shellfish clearly didn't live in ponds, but she had read somewhere that some Amphibia are salt tolerant and are able to survive in seawater; she couldn't possibly take the risk. Anyway, it was her excuse and she was sticking to it, however implausible it seemed. She hoped there would be a vegetarian option to choose from because she liked vegetables, but she was to be out of luck. The menu was written in French with a poor English translation in brackets, and the only food she recognised was cheese and biscuits which was in the dessert section. Alan offered to surprise her and choose her menu for her, but Chloe refused, insisting instead that he translate each and every item into English for her. Alan was frustrated by this, and Chloe watched helplessly as he spoke to their waitress in fluent French. She had no idea what they were talking about but, after a few minutes the waitress left so she presumed Alan had asked her to give them a bit more time to choose. She took a frantic look round the restaurant to see what other people were eating in case something took her fancy, but it all looked pretty revolting to her, and the prices were ridiculously steep too. She consoled herself that at least she wasn't paying to eat this muck, and she hoped the hotel might have a normal snack menu she could look at later. If worse came to worse she would raid the mini bar fridge stacked with goodies in their hotel room, and Alan could foot the bill. One way or another justice would prevail, and it would serve Alan right for being so damned arrogant.

Eventually Alan managed to convince her that she was right to assume that boeuf was indeed beef, and she would simply be served steak with a popular well-known French delicacy called Foie gras and frites which she recognised as chips. The waitress's English did at least stretch to 'rare, medium and well-done' and Chloe ignored the disapproving frown she received as she ordered the well-done option.. At least she would have the cheese and biscuits to look forward to for dessert; she only hoped that Alan didn't insist she finish every last morsel of her main course if she didn't like it. Alan smirked; he was of course testing her, and as expected she'd already failed the gullibility test, and he had little doubt that she would fail the taste test miserably too.

Alan knew that as a general rule, Foie gras was an acquired taste enjoyed by the French and often merely tolerated by experienced consumers of French cuisine and it was now quite clear that Chloe was a complete novice when it came to foreign food. It had been cruel of him to deceive her like that, almost certain that she was probably going to hate it,, but she had embarrassed him by keeping them all waiting so she would only have herself to blame if she didn't like it. Alan ordered mussels for himself and his youngest son Jake, but for once, Ben got away with ordering a kid's meal which Chloe was soon to wish had been an option for her too.

The mussels were served in a container that looked like a bucket, and Chloe couldn't help thinking it might easily double up as a vomit bowl if necessary. Her meat looked medium rare – which would normally have been a big enough problem - but her attention was drawn to the offensive smell radiating from what looked like a gooey mass of thick brown sludge on top of it. It smelled like a decaying corpse, not that she knew what a decaying corpse actually smelled like, but she knew Alan would be familiar with the smell given the nature of his work and her stomach lurched uncontrollably. Alan's grin was sinister as he explained that Foie gras was in fact a luxury food made from the liver of a goose or duck that had been specially fattened to provide the luxurious delicacy. Chloe could feel the blood draining from her face as he spoke. As hard as she tried, she simply couldn't lose the image of some poor innocent duck quacking away happily on the river before being cruelly captured, force fed until its liver exploded and finally slaughtered purely for the gratification of French cannibals. In that moment, she made an instant decision to become a vegetarian, and, as she glanced at her food again her insides lurched painfully, and she made an excuse to leave the table, hurrying to the ladies toilets where she puked until her stomach was empty.

Chloe returned to the table a while later looking quite green, and Alan couldn't help feeling a tiny bit guilty for playing such a nasty trick on her. As her watched her push her food awkwardly around her plate, she made a half-hearted attempt to eat one of the uncontaminated fries, and he hoped he hadn't completely blown his chances. It was an expensive meal but he was panicking in case it could cost him more than he was prepared to lose; and he was thinking about something other than money here. He was going to have to make up for it somehow so he offered to eat her meat for her as wasted food was impolite in France and as a frequent visitor to this restaurant he was highly regarded by the restaurateur. Ben was cross with his dad. He knew he was playing games with Chloe, but he knew better than to intervene, and now the rancid smell coming from the leftover gooey gunge on her plate had reached his nostrils too and was putting him right off his chips. Alan was sure that Chloe was probably still hungry and asked the waitress to bring her a large portion of cheese and biscuits. He spoke using his best French as he couldn't miss an opportunity to show off, but he needed Chloe to know that he wasn't really a monster, and he hoped she could forgive him and maybe even see the funny side of things.

When they left the restaurant Alan suggested a gentle stroll along the beach - with the boys trailing reluctantly behind. Chloe looked like she could do with some fresh air; he was beginning to regret his prank with the food because she looked fit for nothing apart from sleep, and the wine was already starting to make him feel amorous. The cool night breeze forced Chloe to pull her jacket tightly around her body and as she did so, she felt her phone vibrating in her pocket. She was too cold to answer it now so it would have to wait until she got back to the hotel; if whoever it was wanted to get hold of her badly enough they would leave a message. She told Alan she was cold and wanted to go back to the hotel to warm up. She hoped he wouldn't misinterpret her meaning;

after the way he'd behaved in the restaurant, he was going to be disappointed if he wanted his cockles warming tonight, or any night for that matter. She had guessed his intention the minute she'd seen the big bed but she had plans of her own - If he was cold he could always ask for an extra blanket.

When they got back to the hotel, the boys said a brief goodnight before going up to their own room. Alan wanted a night cap at the bar. Chloe thought he'd had more than enough to drink already, and her stomach certainly wasn't up to consuming another drink. She convinced him to enjoy his nightcap without her and she made sure to let him know how tired she was; with a bit of luck the alcohol would make him drowsy and he wouldn't attempt to pester her when he got back.

Back at the room Chloe took some pillows from the bed and a spare blanket from the wardrobe, making up a temporary place for sleep on the chaise longue – if that didn't send her message loud and clear, she didn't know what would. She pulled on her PJs and climbed into bed. Her PJs were her sanctuary and she wasn't ready to forgo that comfort zone for anyone. As she plugged her phone charger in, she remembered the missed call. She had one message waiting and it was from Mel. He had never phoned her before, and she was angry with herself for being out of the country and missing his call. She had no idea why, but just thinking about him brought a smile to her face. In one way, she was glad they hadn't yet met because that spared her from potential disappointment. She had tried hard not to build expectations, but it was difficult because her belief in him was heartfelt, and she felt certain he would never do anything to hurt her. His message was brief because he said he could tell from the ringtone she was out of the country but he hoped she was having a good time. His voice was incredibly soft and hypnotic, and for a short moment she was mesmerised by it. They hadn't met but she wished Mel were with her now because there was something about him that made her feel safe, and although she knew she was being ridiculous she wondered if she might already be in love with him. She cursed herself for being stuck in France with bloody Alan, but then she reminded herself of the reasons why she hadn't met Mel. He was technically separated, at least that's what he'd told her, but to Chloe that meant he was a married man, and she thought that would only serve to complicate matters. She put the phone down and let out a loud sigh. She was exhausted and even though she tried to sleep, her mind was still too busy evaluating the events of the day. She had been in bed for over an hour, and there was still no sign of Alan. She'd rather he didn't come back, especially if he was still drinking; he'd had already had a skin full at the restaurant and a top up could make him unpredictable. She was beginning to regret her decision not to book another room after Alan told her he was going to the bar. She figured if she was asleep when he came back, he would leave her alone – especially as she'd made him a spare bed - but now she wasn't so sure. Having grown up with an Auntie in the pub trade, Chloe had often witnessed volatile behaviour from regulars having 'one for the road' and she now felt very vulnerable. Suddenly, she heard footsteps outside the door, followed by the sound of a key fumbling awkwardly in the lock. She dived quickly under the covers and hugged the duvet tight to her body praying that if she pretended to be asleep, he would leave her alone and she would only have one night left with him.

Alan stumbled carelessly into the room tripping over Chloe's case and muttering obscenities. He smelled strongly of alcohol and Chloe felt uneasy. He noticed she was sleeping but he didn't care anymore because he'd had a few too many brandies to physically function properly now, and he'd had a pretty good time in the bar fumbling a busty French brunette who apparently couldn't get enough of him. He wasn't sure if it was him or his money she was after as she'd cost him a fortune in wine and spirits, but he'd had fun and that's what he was here for. He took another look at the sleeping Chloe. Her silky hair spilled on to the pillow and he thought how beautiful she was. He couldn't be bothered to undress because, by the looks of it there was nothing to get undressed for, so he slumped on top of the bed and passed out; he hadn't noticed the temporary bed on the chaise longue. Chloe stayed still and breathed a gentle sigh of relief before closing her eyes, but she was too afraid to sleep.

Still tired and starved of sleep, it had been a long night for Chloe and she was relieved when the sun finally peeped through the window. Alan was starting to stir, and the room reeked like a brewery. He was a sight for sore eyes slumped on the bed, fully clothed, his obscene breath invading her nostrils. He opened his eyes and uttered a few incomprehensible sounds before attempting to sit up. His eyes were heavy, but he forced them open and saw Chloe standing on the balcony in her winceyette PJs which reminded him of the pyjamas his mother had made him wear when he was a boy. They certainly weren't what he'd been expecting but then again, Chloe wasn't entirely what he was expecting either. He was used to getting what he wanted, and women were usually more than happy to give it to him. He couldn't remember much about last night but as he was still fully dressed, he assumed nothing had happened and those PJs of hers didn't exactly ooze sex appeal either. Chloe attempted a smile and a cheery good morning before heading to the shower. She emerged twenty minutes later as fresh as a daisy, casually dressed in Jeans and a light jumper. It was an improvement on the nightwear but not what Alan had in mind ,especially as he had been good enough to invite her on this all- expenses paid trip, the very least she could do was make an effort to dress nicely for him.

After a quick wash and brush up he would soon be ready for a hearty breakfast and then they would be on their way to Bruges. He was looking forward to Bruges, but first he needed some aspirin for his head. The boys were already downstairs waiting patiently for breakfast. Ben could see Alan was hungover and he looked anxiously to Chloe for reassurance. She attempted to reassure him with a warm smile, but he wasn't easily fooled, he had been in this situation many times before with other pretty ladies, and it worried him. Chloe hoped Alan would eat a big breakfast; he needed food inside him to soak up the alcohol before driving again today. Fortunately, he was happy to oblige. He ate one of everything from the buffet and went up for second helpings while Chloe settled for a bowl of cereal and a pot of tea. She didn't have much of an appetite and the dry crunchy cereal stuck in her throat when she swallowed. She didn't usually bother with breakfast at home, but her rumbling belly was reminding her she was hungry, and she felt forced to oblige, if only to shut it up. She wasn't sure if her poor appetite was down to nerves, or whether it was the sight of Alan shovelling down food like a pig. Just one more day and night and she would be back home in her own comfy bed. It should have been reassuring but instead it filled her with dread. She made up her mind there and then to pay for a room of her own when they got to the hotel in Bruges, but Alan didn't need to know about that yet.

Chloe waited with the boys in the hotel foyer while Alan paid the bill. Ben was feeling troubled but said nothing. He had been at the wrong end of his dad's foul temper before, and he needed to stay strong to protect his younger brother who was petrified of his father. Ben liked Chloe and wished he was man enough to protect her to because he knew how brutal Alan could be. He was counting the days until his sixteenth birthday. His mum had told him he wouldn't have to see Alan again if he didn't want to after that, but there was no way he'd let his baby brother go it alone. It would be like throwing him into the lion's den and bolting the door behind him, giving Alan the perfect opportunity to take out all his frustrations on the terrified boy. Ben knew alcohol was the trigger to trouble, but whenever he tried to say anything Alan became defensive and completely overreacted, so it was safer to stay quiet. In recent months, he'd had a string of girlfriends but none of them had stuck around for very long. Naturally it was never his fault, and he was always full of lame excuses which the boys didn't buy. They had witnessed firsthand the emotional blackmail and the physical and psychological abuse their mother had endured, but like all cowards, he was always deeply apologetic, and she would always forgive him until the day she decided enough was enough and left him to live with another woman. Thankfully, boarding school and the contact time they had with their mum was enough to get them through - for now.

As Alan was loading the suitcases into the car Chloe caught a whiff of his breath which still reeked of alcohol, and she knew that neither she nor the boys should get into the car with him. She wanted to grab her bags and run, but there was nowhere to go, so with a feeling of impending doom she climbed into the passenger seat and fastened her seat belt. Alan said nothing during the two-hour drive to Bruges, instead he put on a classical music cd and turned the volume up loud to drown out the brotherly banter of the boys sitting in the back. Chloe didn't mind classical music but there was something about this particular track that was melancholic and disturbing, and it frightened her. Alan didn't care much for the music either, but it was a good test of character. He fully expected Chloe to tell him to turn it down, but she remained silent which disappointed him - he was in the mood for a good argument so they could both enjoy making up later. She would soon learn that this trip was only free in monetary terms, and it was time for her to give something back whether she liked it or not. As far as Alan was concerned, she was nothing more than an educated prostitute and tonight he wanted a reward for his generosity.

When they arrived at the hotel there was a long queue of people waiting to book in, so Alan told Chloe and the boys to take a seat in the lounge. Chloe pretended she wanted to stay to keep him company which seemed to please him, but she was planning to book another room for herself. As it turned out, the couple standing in front of them managed to secure the last room which meant the hotel was fully booked and it seemed Chloe was destined to spend another night alone with him. As expected, Alan had booked another impressive room in a five-star hotel in the heart of Bruges overlooking the canal. Under normal circumstances, a room like this would offer an oasis of peace, relaxation, and tranquillity but to Chloe it felt more like a prison, and she knew she had to get out. In her most convincing voice, she feigned an interest in going out to explore the city because it would give her time to think; knowing there would be lots of people around meant safety in numbers.

Alan was delighted that Chloe wanted to go sightseeing because he knew the city well and it would give him another chance to show off his local knowledge. He hoped she might warm to him and give herself willingly later on, but her frosty demeanour told a different story. His headache had almost gone, and they stepped outside to a sobering cool breeze. As they made their way down the picturesque, cobbled lanes towards the main market square, Alan tried to take Chloe's hand but she quickly pulled away from him. He wasn't used to rejection but managed to hide his humiliation well, a trait he'd learned from his police academy days. Rookie cops who showed emotion didn't fare well in the force, and once he reached CID, he made it his priority to flush out the weaklings early on.

The market square was bustling with busy restaurants dwarfed by soaring towers, surrounded by historic churches and old whitewashed alms houses. It was picturesque like something out of a fairy tale, but Chloe barely noticed it. They found a restaurant that wasn't too busy and sat down to order food. She was relieved to see some familiar foods on the menu because she was hungry and, without seeking approval from Alan, she ordered omelette and chips and a pint of lager to wash it down. She didn't want to look at him, and in fact she didn't need to look at him to know he didn't support her menu choice, but she was having much more fun winding him up than she ever did trying to please him. To her dismay, Alan ordered a full bottle of red wine and didn't doubt that he would have no problem polishing off the entire bottle by himself; she felt very vulnerable once again. Ben gave her a sympathetic look, but dark thoughts filled his young mind once more.

After the meal they took a stroll around Bruges and Chloe was temporarily mesmerised by the city's charm. She wished she was there with someone else so she could enjoy its splendour especially as her travelling companion was becoming more loud and vulgar by the minute as a result of the wine. Alan was insistent they take a horse and carriage ride together and she reluctantly agreed but made sure she sat as far away from him as possible; she felt a pang of guilt as she ushered the boys into the space next to their father. Her mind was occupied with thoughts of running away but it was already beginning to get dark and she didn't have enough money to get her to an airport or back to the ferry. As it was, the ferry port in Belgium would have taken her to Hull, and Hull was further away from home than she was now. Calais was two hours away by car and the only airport she could think of in Belgium was Brussels and she had no idea where that was in relation to Bruges. She even thought about asking the reception staff at the hotel, but it would be difficult to talk to them without Alan becoming suspicious. Her last thought was to contact the police, but he hadn't committed a crime yet and they would think she was crazy. The word crazy echoed in her mind. Her gut was telling her she was in danger, but wandering the streets at night with little or no cash in an attempt to get back to England, wasn't exactly a safe alternative either. It was a question of balance, and she was struggling to determine who or what was the biggest threat to her safety.

By the time they got off the horse and carriage the main square was floodlit and the cathedral which stood proud among the smaller buildings was illuminated against the night sky. Alan suggested they made their way back to the hotel for a game of draughts and a night cap before bed and Chloe sighed. She tried hard to convince herself it would be okay, after all it was just one more night and she enjoyed playing draughts.

Back at the hotel Alan ordered coke for the boys and a large brandy for himself. Chloe settled for a small glass of Baileys. It was the only drink that seemed to improve with ice, and it would match the frosty atmosphere between her and Alan perfectly. The boys already had the draught board out and were ready to play. Alan insisted he and Ben play first so Chloe sat back to enjoy her glass of Baileys. Ben was an accomplished player since there was little else to do in the evenings at boarding school, and after only four or five diagonal moves, he had captured the majority of Alan's pieces and trapped him. Alan was furious and Chloe watched in horror as his face blushed crimson with rage as he threw the board off the table sending his glass crashing to the floor. Ben timidly picked up the board from the floor while Alan went to the bar to get another drink. He returned with another large brandy and insisted they play another game so he could win. Fuelled with alcohol, Alan prepared for the second game and Ben knew better than to win again. He deliberately made some stupid moves which gave Alan the opportunity to criticise his judgement before triumphantly declaring himself the winner. The score stood at one game each so Alan insisted on the best of three and returned to the bar for yet another refill while Ben despondently prepared the board for a third time. He had no choice; he would have to let his dad win again; Alan was a bad loser and Ben already feared for Chloe's safety.

Chloe had seen enough. She didn't think she could loathe this despicable man more than she did right now, but later that night she would find out she could. As he stood up to fetch another celebratory drink from the bar, she couldn't resist intervening and casually remarked she thought he'd had enough to drink for one night. She was totally unprepared for the backlash. The torrent of verbal abuse that spilled from his mouth shocked her, but it didn't shock Ben. She grabbed her bag and ran from the room. As she passed reception, she stopped to ask just in case there were any empty rooms available but there were none. The receptionist looked at her questioningly, but Chloe took off up the staircase without offering an explanation. Loud voices further down the corridor startled her. It seemed Alan and the boys were not far behind her, and she had nowhere to hide. She ran to the bedroom as fast as she could before locking herself in the bathroom where she planned to stay all night if necessary.

A few minutes later Alan came crashing into the bedroom and started pounding his fists on the bathroom door. Chloe was terrified. Within seconds he was standing in front of her, totally enraged; she knew for certain that her light frame was no match for his physical strength. She hadn't spotted the child friendly bathroom lock which had allowed him easy entry, but he was so angry she knew he would probably have kicked the door down anyway. She didn't know whether to start screaming loudly or make a futile attempt to pacify him. In the end she did neither because she was rooted to the spot with fear, and when she tried to speak her voice was nothing more than a pathetic little squeak. His face was crimson with anger and beads of sweat dripped unattractively from his forehead. As he spat derogatory words at her, his eyes filled with hatred and Chloe feared for her life. This was the sort of thing that only happened in fictional crime thrillers, it wasn't meant to happen in real life, and it certainly wasn't meant to happen to her. He was a police officer, so he was supposed to be the good guy not the perpetrator. She hoped he would come to his senses soon, and then she could make a run for it, but Alan seemed to read her mind and smirked knowing all the exits were blocked. Her fear was starting to arouse him and the bulge in his trousers indicated he was almost ready. She hadn't made it easy for him, unlike some of the other girls who were happy to drop their knickers on command, but that's what made her so interesting to him, and much as he enjoyed the thrill of the chase she had played hard to get for long enough; the time had come for him to claim the reward for all of his unreciprocated generosity.

By now Chloe knew without doubt that his intentions weren't honourable and she didn't know whether to fight him off or get it over and done with. She had always been a bit of a rebel so to surrender without a fight wasn't her style. Suddenly and without warning he grabbed her forcefully by the arm and threw her violently onto the bed. The sickly stench of alcohol and stale aftershave was nauseating and impulsively she kicked out hard with her feet striking a heavy blow to his forehead which briefly stunned him. For a split second he stopped to stare at her before letting out a piercing maniacal laugh which made him sound like a deranged hyena. If she wanted to play rough, he was more than happy to oblige but if she knew what was good for her, she'd keep quiet until he had finished. As she continued to struggle, his urge to forcibly take her increased. Viciously he pulled hard at her hair forcing her neck to bend back painfully and, seeing her stillness, seized the opportunity to force himself upon her while using both his hands to maintain a firm grip on her wrists and hair. She cried out and pleaded for him to stop but her cries fell on deaf ears; there was nobody around to save her. The commotion was heard in the adjoining room where the boys were attempting to sleep. Thankfully, Jake seemed to sleep through all the commotion, but as Ben listened sadly to Chloe's painful sobs, he placed his hands over his ears in a vain attempt to blot out her cries. He wished he could save her, but he knew he couldn't.

Eventually she succumbed to exhaustion. Her wrists were bruised, and her throat felt dry and sore from crying. She remained motionless and silent while he repeatedly violated her to satisfy his sadistic desires. She had no idea how long it lasted or how long she lay there afterwards but it seemed like hours. Her entire body ached and the sticky gunge running down the inside of her thighs made her feel cheap and dirty. Alan was snoring loudly on the other side of the bed with his trousers wrapped haphazardly around his ankles and beside him on the floor lay a discarded adult sex toy. She felt sick just looking at it because it meant he really was a monster. He had done more than rape her, he had humiliated her and violated her in the most despicable way possible and he had it all planned; Why else would he have bought such a filthy device with him that had already been God knows where? She tiptoed her way across the room towards the bathroom afraid that any noise might wake him, before quietly closing the door and switching on the light. As she did so she caught a glimpse of herself in the mirror and was visibly shocked by the reflection of the woman staring back at her. She could easily have passed an audition for the starring role in a horror film with her swollen red eyes and the dark tell-tale bruising on her wrists and neck revealed the true extent of the assault. Her thighs and clothing were stained with dried blood and without thinking, she ran a shower and scrubbed her body until her skin was sore. She felt dirty but no amount of soap could cleanse her of the filth, and she scrubbed over and over again until she heard Alan stir from his sleep in the room next door. She dressed hurriedly, fully expecting him to stagger into the bathroom so he could help himself to her tired and battered body for a second time, but to her relief she heard the bedroom door shut followed by the sound of footsteps going down the stairs. She waited a few minutes, frozen to the spot before cautiously opening the door to make sure the coast was clear. She glanced at the clock and was astonished to find it was already eight o clock.

Alan made his way downstairs to meet the boys for an early breakfast as they needed to be at the ferry port by midday at the latest. Ben wasn't surprised when Chloe failed to join them for breakfast; he hoped she was okay although deep down he knew that she wasn't. After hearing her cries, he had quietly phoned his mum in the early hours of the morning begging her to come and get them and despite her inner turmoil, she managed to calm him down by promising to wait at the house for them to return; she knew they would probably be safer that way, arousing Alan's suspicions could cause him to bolt and take them with him. It was to be their secret, and Ben promised not to tell his younger brother just in case he accidentally blabbed to Alan; somehow, Jake had managed to sleep right through it all, and for that Ben was grateful. Ben's call had deeply disturbed her, but this was the moment she had been waiting for and she would be there tomorrow to hold them tight and take them home; if she had her way, Alan would never see his boys again.

For months, Alan's ex-wife had been keeping a portfolio of evidence against him based on some of the things the boys had been saying at the dinner table. After their divorce, she hoped the boys would be able to maintain a relationship with their father but recently they had become anxious prior to visits and the school had expressed concerns about their behaviour. She knew he was manipulative and controlling, and judging by what Ben had told her about Chloe, it seemed he might have met his match, although this time he had gone too far. She hoped Ben was overreacting and it wasn't as bad as he said it was, but more than anything, she hoped the poor woman was alright, because from what Ben had told her she'd seemed to have their best interests at heart, possibly to the detriment of her own.

Alan was in an exceptionally good mood at breakfast and chatted away happily to the boys making feeble excuses for Chloe's absence. Jake bought his excuse about Chloe not liking breakfast, but Ben knew different, and was counting the hours until they were back home safely with their mother. Alan knew he looked scruffy because with Chloe hogging the bathroom, he'd not had the opportunity to freshen up, but he had worked up a good appetite last night and needed a hearty breakfast now to replenish his energy. Alan wasn't sure what he was going to do about Chloe. He knew he had behaved erratically but she had provoked him by shaming him in front of his boys, so she deserved to be punished. He couldn't afford to let her blab; any negative publicity or allegations against him would be investigated and threaten his chance of promotion. He sent the boys back to their room to pack and said he would knock when they were ready to leave. He wasn't surprised to find Chloe sitting in the reception area with her bags already packed. She stared coldly at him and for a moment he wondered if she had called the police. She made no attempt to hide the big purple welts on her wrists and neck and the receptionist looked at them both inquisitively. Her sad demeanour told a disturbing story, but the receptionist had been unable to persuade her to talk, despite her suspicions. Chloe had simply asked if she could wait in the foyer until it was time to leave. It was the only place she felt safe, and she needed time to think. Ben was visibly shocked at the sight of Chloe sitting so alone and forlorn. It was confirmation that he hadn't imagined last night, and that something truly terrible had happened to her; he wished his mum was there to take care of them all and give him a hug. Alan hurried the boys past Chloe as quickly as he could and up the stairs to their room. If she wanted a lift home, she was going to have to pull herself together otherwise she could make her own way to the ferry port.

Chloe had come close to asking the kind receptionist to call the police, but she was afraid they might not believe her because stupidly she had washed away all the forensic evidence in the shower, and it would be her word against his. Her only focus now was to get home as quickly as she could. She'd thought about alternative routes back to England but money was tight, and she wanted to avoid using her credit card because she was still paying off the balance from when Pete had left her and the kids with nothing to live on. Her car was still parked at Alan's house, and she needed her car to get home, so she didn't think she had any choice but to get back into his car with him. At least he couldn't attack her with the boys there.

He returned to the foyer without the boys and asked to speak with her privately. She declined and loudly pointed out that she would not jeopardise her safety again by spending time alone with a dangerous sex fiend. The kindly receptionist looked up and Alan smiled at her, but she just glared back at him and he returned his attention back to Chloe. He was taken aback by her allegation and wanted an apology from her – as far as he was concerned, he'd only taken what was due to him. Chloe continued to look straight through him with an icy stare. He had withstood derogatory remarks from women before, but no one had ever dared refer to him as a sex fiend, so he laughed out loud and pretended to be offended by her ridiculous accusations. Who was going to take her word over that of a highly regarded senior police officer with years of unblemished service? She was nothing but a dumb blonde who'd just spent hours in the shower scrubbing away any evidence. He laughed. She certainly was a scrubber, and a deluded one at the that if she thought she could blacken his name. There was the little matter of some telltale bruising on her wrists and neck and he needed a quiet word just in case she was thinking of pressing charges; he could be very persuasive if the situation called for it.

The foyer was buzzing with tourists and the receptionist kept glancing over at Chloe and Alan. She didn't trust this sleazy Englishman whose attempt to chat her up in French on arrival at the hotel had led to a stern rebuff. She had met his type before and couldn't help wondering what a pretty lady like Chloe was doing with such a pretentious, arrogant pig. Alan flashed his most obliging smile in the direction of the receptionist before draping an unwelcome arm around Chloe's shoulder and hissing a sinister warning in her ear. She cringed at his touch but his message to her was perfectly clear. If she mentioned the word rape to anyone ,he would personally make sure the justice system annihilated her; he was smiling broadly as he spoke. She thought it was interesting that it was he who had first mentioned the word rape and not her, and even though she knew he had indeed raped her, up until the moment he said it, it hadn't seemed real. The mention of the word rape suddenly made everything feel real again, and she wondered if Alan might be right when he said it was all her fault. Her heart started to pound rapidly through her chest wall as she relived the ordeal over and over again in her head, and for a brief moment she thought she might faint. In the end she was so desperate to go home and forget about it all that she found herself promising Alan she would keep quiet providing he got her back to England safely, and Alan grinned triumphantly before giving her a patronising pat her on the back and telling her what a good girl she was. He was glad she had seen sense because otherwise he might have been forced to take more drastic measures to keep her quiet and then she would have been really sorry.

Alan flashed his credit card to pay the bill and the receptionist gave him a frosty glare. She suspected foul play, and she was concerned for the welfare of this unhappy woman and the two children. She had seen the concerned expression on Ben's face and being a mum of two boys herself she had enough experience to know when a child was anxious. She had thought about calling the police herself but if Chloe refused to talk to them, she might risk jeopardising their safety further. Reluctantly, she dismissed the idea and handed Alan back his card. He had clearly got his money's worth, but she feared his pretty lady friend had paid a very high price indeed.

Chloe climbed silently into the passenger seat of the car. She would have preferred to sit in the back with the boys but there wasn't enough room, and she couldn't help noticing they were unusually quiet. Ben was thinking about the phone call to his mum and how he couldn't wait to see her again because she would make him feel safe. He liked to think he was grown up sometimes, but he definitely wasn't grown up enough to handle this, and he knew he wasn't man enough yet to protect his baby brother from the evil sperm donor they were supposed to call their father. He knew Alan would be furious to find her waiting at the house for them, but at the same time he knew he was unlikely to challenge her because she was the one woman who was no longer afraid of him.

The two-hour journey back to Calais felt more like twenty-four hours to Chloe. The queue for the ferry was long and they sat for a tense hour, moving an inch at a time before finally reaching the ship. Alan was becoming irate. He wasn't used to queueing with the minions, he was more accustomed to travelling business class with use of a VIP lounge where he could relax with a drink. They boarded the ferry separately and Chloe made her way to one of the inside seating areas while Alan stayed on the outside deck with the boys. She was relieved to be rid of him, even if it was only for a few hours. She needed time to think, she closed her eyes briefly, but his vile threats still echoed through her ears, and she wondered if she would ever be able to move on from this. She knew she would never be able to forget, but in time she hoped she might be able to forgive him, because if she didn't, it would give him the power to destroy the rest of her life, and that would be tragic.

The journey from Calais to Dover was approximately one and a half hours. It was the shortest route to France from England and therefore the most popular. The ferry was crowded with holidaymakers returning to England with fractious overtired children with equally tired parents. It was hectic and noisy, but Chloe found solace amongst them. She wondered if Alan would bother to come and find her before the ferry docked at Dover when they would be asked to return to their vehicles. She didn't actually care whether he did or not; if he didn't, it would save her from another long car journey with him. The ferry accommodated foot passengers and if necessary, she would catch a train home. Part of her hoped he would fall overboard never to be seen again so she could spare other women from the same fate as her and free his boys from future exploitation. She was shocked to think she actually wanted him dead, but right now, a quick shove into the cold English Channel to freeze his testicles was what he deserved and the jury was still out on whether he would live or die.

As they approached Dover, the intercom instructed all passengers to return to their vehicles. Chloe glanced round but there was no sign of Alan or the boys, and she didn't know if what she was feeling was panic or relief. She had misgivings about travelling by train because at some stage she would still need to collect her car from his house. A tap on her shoulder made her jump and she quickly turned around to find Ben gesturing her to follow him towards the stair well and back to the car. He looked sad, and she instinctively offered him a reassuring motherly hug which he welcomed. Alan was already waiting in the car with his youngest boy, and he continued to look straight ahead without bothering to acknowledge her. They were on the final leg of their journey home, but it was going to be a long drive and Chloe was dreading it. Alan turned the radio on to fill the awkward silence between them and the music comforted her. She had never really understood the phrase 'deafening silence' before, it was one of those strange oxymoron things that English teachers loved talking about, but today it was finally starting to make sense. Alan was looking forward to getting home and dispensing with this liability of a woman at the earliest opportunity. She had served her purpose but frankly he'd had better, and as he touched the painful bruise on his forehead, he made a mental note to choose his women more wisely in the future.

There were few hold ups on the M25, so they made good time. As Alan turned into his driveway, he spotted a familiar red car, and a confused frown crossed his forehead. What on earth was she doing here? According to the custody agreement he had another two days with his boys, and he didn't appreciate any last-minute change of plan without prior consent. Chloe had no idea who this woman was until the boys greeted her with the same enthusiasm her dog gave her when she returned home from work. It didn't matter to Norman if she had only been gone an hour or two; he still behaved like a dog possessed, acting as if she'd left him for an entire month. The thought of Norman brought a temporary smile to her face, and she was eager to get home and see him again. She also knew now that this lady had to be the boys' mother and relief flooded through her because she knew she could walk away from Alan knowing they would be safe at least.

Alan's ex-wife was different to what Chloe had imagined. She was only about 5'2" in height with short bobbed blonde hair and she was dressed in a smart suit. She looked like she meant business, and when she calmly asked the boys to climb into the back of her car, Alan didn't object. She looked at Chloe, saw the bruises, and recognised the pain behind her half-hearted smile, and her heart reached out to her. She wished she could help her, she really did, but right now her priority had to be her boys who had witnessed God knows what trauma, courtesy of her ex-husband. She knew Alan inside and out and felt blessed that despite being emotionally battered by him, she had remained physically unscathed for most of their marriage. The boys waved at Chloe and she smiled gently at them before getting into her own car and driving away. For her, the nightmare was finally over but something about the presence of his ex-wife told her that Alan's ordeal had only just begun and she smiled properly for the first time in days.

Alan stood sheepishly by the front door unable to make eye contact with the only woman he had ever truly loved. He knew now that Ben had phoned her, and he felt ashamed. She was a powerful woman, and he knew she was no longer afraid of him, a fact which made her all the more desirable to him. He wanted to hate her, but he couldn't because deep down he admired her and although he didn't want to love her, he couldn't help himself. He hadn't been surprised when she left him, but he hadn't predicted his love rival would be another woman. It had destroyed his male ego and left him hell- bent on revenge and, like all bullies, he always found someone weak and vulnerable to pick on.

He stood and watched silently as Chloe drove away followed closely by his ex-wife and two sons, and this time he feared he had gone too far. He had already lost his wife, but now he risked losing his boys too and the thought of that was unbearable. He hoped Chloe would keep her end of the bargain and stay silent, because if she reported him there would be an investigation, and there was every chance he could lose his job. He had the gift of the gab, but he had badly misjudged Chloe and he couldn't be certain of winning this time, he hated her, but at the same time he admired her for her integrity and resilience. In many ways she was just like his ex-wife.

Time Out

When Chloe returned home Norman greeted her with his usual enthusiasm. The kids were stretched out on the sofa watching television and their mobile phones beeped continuously with notifications of incoming WhatsApp messages. They glanced up briefly and said a quick 'Hi mum,' before going back to what they were doing, and for once she was pleased they were too engrossed in their own activities to ask how her weekend was. She had deliberately covered her bruises with a neck scarf and a long-sleeved jumper so the kids wouldn't notice but she wasn't convinced they'd have noticed anyway. There were times when she thought she was invisible to them until they wanted something of course, when they all of a sudden became uncharacteristically helpful. She had been naive in thinking her ordeal was all over, and she was ill prepared for the terrifying flashbacks. Her brain was working overtime and there was no plug to switch it off. She made her way to the kitchen to make a cup of tea; her mum always made a cup of tea when there was a problem. Once upon a time she had believed that tea could solve anything, but today it could not heal her tormented soul.

She took the tea upstairs and prepared herself for a long hot soak in the bath. Her body ached all over, and she was sore and bruised from the vicious assault. It was her first opportunity to relax in two days and though her body craved sleep, her mind denied her the luxury. She was jittery and nervous and every time her eyelids closed, she had visions of Alan standing over her causing her to wake with a start. He had raped her repeatedly, but he'd told her it was her own fault for teasing him with her short skirts, and now she was beginning to believe it was true. She had said no to him over and over again and put up a good fight, and that should have been enough to stop him, but he had carried on regardless and ignored her pitiful pleas to stop. She was still searching for answers when it occurred to her that she could phone Phil; the kind policeman who had come to investigate her last dodgy date turned lunatic. She had liked Phil and she felt she could have trusted him, but Alan had warned her off telling a soul; he'd said that no one would believe her, and she was afraid in case that turned out to be true. He was right, it was all her fault, she shouldn't have worn such a short skirt. She should have put up more of a fight, kicked him harder even, but if she had, she feared he might have killed her.

The next morning, she woke feeling hungover. Her head was aching, and her eyelids felt heavy through lack of sleep. Her lady bits were still very sore and despite drinking pints of water, her bladder was burning; she felt like she was peeing out shards of broken glass. Chloe had hoped that her doctor would agree to treat her over the phone, but she'd insisted on seeing her in person because her stupid annual asthma review was overdue, and she wrongly assumed it would be convenient to quickly run through both problems at the same time. Chloe really couldn't be bothered with her bloody asthma check-up under the current circumstances, but it had been easier to go along with it than to argue. Maybe that's why Alan had raped her, she hadn't put up enough of a fight, so perhaps he was right, it was her fault after all. She looked in the mirror and saw a stranger staring back at her. The bruises around her neck looked darker now and she was sure she had aged by at least twenty years overnight. If she absolutely had to go to the surgery, she would have to camouflage those bruises with some clever makeup; she didn't want the doctor asking too many questions just in case she cried again. Her mother firmly believed tea bags cured all ailments including swollen eyes, and Chloe smiled at the fond memory of their poor dog stumbling around with a tea bag stuck to each eye when he'd caught acute conjunctivitis from her when she was a kid. At the time she thought her mum was a bit crazy, but now it was her turn to look daft because she had nothing to lose by giving it a go.

By the time she arrived at the doctors, she looked more human and was secretly pleased to have scrubbed up so well. She thought it was amazing what a bit of carefully applied makeup and a roll neck jumper could do, and she congratulated herself for her clever attempt at disguise.

The GP wasn't her usual doctor and when she introduced herself, she mentioned that she was new to the practice. Chloe thought she had a kind face with soft features which made her feel vulnerable, so she tried hard to avoid making too much eye contact with her just in case the tears that were welling up in the back of her eyes escaped and gave the game away. The doctor tested her urine sample and agreed she most probably had a urinary tract infection before asking to check her chest. When the doctor asked her to remove her jumper Chloe literally froze to the spot and the doctor stared at her inquisitively. She hadn't anticipated this request, and she had no idea what to do. The kindly doctor gestured again for her to remove her jumper, so Chloe did as she was asked and was eternally grateful when the doctor made no comment. Despite not saying anything at the time, the doctor had instantly spotted the telltale bruises around Chloe's neck and wrists, and she had enough experience to know they weren't accidental. They sat quietly together for a moment, and the doctor hoped her patient might open up of her own accord, but Chloe knew she couldn't speak without crying so she sat staring blankly at the floor until the doctor gently placed her hand on top of hers and asked softly if there was anything else she wanted to talk about. She shook her head, because doctors had better things to do than listen to sob stories from women like her who had been stupid enough to get themselves raped, but the tears rolling down her cheeks told an altogether different story. Once she started, she couldn't stop, and she felt a huge weight lift from her shoulders because she was no longer so isolated and alone. The doctor encouraged her to contact the police, but Alan's words kept echoing in her mind and she knew she wasn't strong enough to see it through, not yet anyway. The doctor wrote a prescription for antibiotics and recommended a full sexual health screen at the local clinic to rule out other infections.

Chloe instantly knew she was referring to infections like HIV and hepatitis C and she was angry for putting herself at risk, especially as she had the children and Norman to consider, and she knew Pete would be hopeless if anything were to happen to her.

Chloe had never been to a sexual health screening clinic before but she frequently sent her patients there so she knew where to go. It was a walk-in clinic where she could sit and wait and people- watch if she wanted to, although she decided it might be better to hide herself away in the corner just in case there was someone there who recognised her. She reported to the desk and the portly receptionist handed her a number without even bothering to look up at her face. Names evidently weren't used in this clinic in order to maintain confidentiality, and although she understood the reasons for it, she didn't feel comfortable being referred to as a number. She didn't know why, but it made her feel insignificant, and she hoped she wouldn't have to wait too long to be seen. She took a seat away from a group of rowdy teenagers and waited for her number to be called. She had been given the number twenty-three and the board was currently showing number fourteen, so she anticipated a longer wait than she'd hoped for. She hoped she wouldn't lose her nerve because waiting made her anxious, and she just wanted to get the ordeal over and done with as quickly as possible. After taking a quick look around the waiting area she quickly realised she was the oldest person there by a good twenty years. The noisy group of teenagers looked no older than about twelve or thirteen. At their age, Chloe was still playing with dolls but it seemed to her these children might have been playing a far more realistic version of Barbie and Ken.

It was over an hour before her number was called and she was sorely tempted to jump up and shout, 'House!' because there was enough gossip going on to imitate a bingo hall. The noisy teenagers stared at her as she walked past and then giggled. She knew what they were thinking; she had teenagers of her own, and they were appalled to think that someone her age was still having sex. In the consulting room she was forced to relive her ordeal all over again and answer questions of an extremely intimate and embarrassing nature. She knew he had definitely used the revolting sex toy at the same time as his filthy manhood, but she had tried so hard to blot everything out that she had no idea what he had actually stuck where. The doctor kept nodding sympathetically and she reminded Chloe of the annoying nun at school, but she reminded herself it was her own fault she was here, and it wasn't her place to criticise the doctor for doing a thorough job. She didn't want counselling and she didn't want to join a rape support group either, but the doctor insisted on giving her leaflets just in case she changed her mind at a later date. She had gone there with the sole purpose of finding out if she had a sexually transmitted disease or crotch crickets or something much worse, but she was told she would need a blood test to find out for sure. If the test was negative, it would need repeating in six weeks and Chloe nodded because she already knew that.

Chloe was glad to get out, although in theory, it had been no different to any other clinic offering a service to the public, but it had a certain stigma attached to it that made her feel ashamed and dirty. The only people it seemed popular with were the teenagers who appeared to be using it as a meeting place for networking. She could picture their Facebook status, 'Barbie is with Ken at the sexual health clinic waiting for chlamydia results,' and she smiled at the ludicrousness of it all. To her relief, the following day she found out her blood results were negative, but she would have to wait another six weeks before she could relax completely, and she knew that six weeks was going to feel like a lifetime. She wished she had the time and money to run off and hibernate somewhere sunny and warm but she would need to win the lottery to do that and seeing as she didn't do it, her chances of winning were a big fat zero. The doctor at the clinic told her in a scary headmistress type voice to abstain from sex or to use condoms until the results of the second blood test. Chloe was furious by her insensitive approach; she had just told her she had been raped for God's sake and this woman was already talking about bloody sex like she was part of a harem. She didn't think she would ever want to have sex again, but she hoped she might, because otherwise Alan would have destroyed another part of her of her life, and she didn't want to give him that amount of power.

Chloe managed to keep herself busy with work, but she had been right, it was the longest six weeks of her life. She felt like a kid waiting for Christmas as she crossed the days off the calendar, the only difference being this was no advent calendar and there were no tasty chocolate surprises hiding behind the doors. She hoped there would be no surprises when she attended the clinic again. She had suffered enough humiliation and she didn't need a sexually transmitted disease to add to her résumé of disasters. She had made an appointment this time, which avoided the need to sit with the Barbie and Ken brigade in the waiting room. She was seen quickly by a nurse who she developed an instant rapport with, unlike the doctor at her first visit who had treated her like a common prostitute. She knew the doctor hadn't meant to cause any offence, but she genuinely believed nurses were more patient- centred and approachable than doctors, and she hoped her own patients felt that way about her. It took three days before all the results were ready and to her relief everything was negative. She didn't hear from Alan again and she made herself promise to put him and the events from that weekend out of her head for good; but in the weeks that followed, a nagging guilt lingered at the back of her mind that she found difficult to ignore. She wished she had gone straight to the police, but if she went now it could look like an afterthought and she feared they probably wouldn't believe her anyway because that's what Alan had told her. She researched unreported crime on the net and was shocked to find that eighty percent of sexual assaults remained undisclosed. She was up there with the majority, too ashamed to speak out and too afraid to face the consequences and as a result, the likes of Alan were free to seek out new victims.

Alan was keeping himself out of the spotlight just in case she changed her mind and went to the police. He knew what women were like when they got talking to each other and there was every chance one of her stupid friends would try and persuade her to dob him in to the authorities. He was arrogant enough to believe she wouldn't, after all, none of her predecessors had, but at one stage he feared he might have gone too far with Chloe. It had been more than six weeks now and he'd heard nothing so he was quietly confident he'd got away with it, but it had been a close call, and he knew he would need to be more careful in future.

Chloe deliberately avoided logging in to the dating site and ignored the message alerts in her email account. She thought about deleting her profile, but that would mean logging in again and if she logged in, she feared she might be tempted to read the messages, and whilst she wasn't ready to start dating again, she hoped one day she would. Her life consisted of work, coming home, cooking dinner for the kids and going to bed, and she felt physically and mentally exhausted as well as frustrated by her lack of motivation to do anything else. On days off, she stayed in bed and had duvet days because getting up and dressed involved too much effort, and there was no one out there she wanted to impress anymore. She wasn't convinced she would ever try to dress to impress anyone ever again and made a mental note to go through her wardrobe when she was feeling better and chuck out any item of clothing that ended above the knee. Friends and colleagues were worried because she looked so pale and tired, and she was losing a ridiculous amount of weight too, but she couldn't eat, because she wasn't hungry, and whenever she did try to eat the food seemed to stick to the roof of her mouth causing her to gag uncontrollably. The rape had changed her and that made her resent him even more. She was no longer the outgoing, fun loving life and soul of the party Chloe, that everyone loved and knew, instead she was a quiet withdrawn loner who could no longer bear to look at herself in the mirror, and she hated this stranger who had replaced her. Going out was out of the question and most of her friends had stopped asking her to join them at social events. Worried close friends patiently persevered, but she shut them out, because if she let them in on her dirty, sordid, little secret, she was afraid they'd think the same as Alan and label her as a cheap and dirty tramp.

Unsurprisingly, things came to a head and it wasn't long before she had a meltdown at work; forcing her to take sick leave and face up to the situation. Her line manager was sympathetic but insisted she went straight back to see her GP. Back at the doctors she wept openly and reluctantly agreed to try some medication and attend specialist rape counselling like the doctor at the other clinic had suggested. She wasn't used to talking to people about her problems and felt sceptical about having therapy, so she was pleasantly surprised when after only a few weeks of counselling her problems became more manageable. Chloe didn't know if it was the drugs or the therapy that made her feel better but her belief that the 'happy pills,' as she liked to call them, were for losers, was well and truly scuppered, because without them she knew she would be in a very dark place by now. With her new- found optimism she felt confident enough to get her life back on track and problems that had once seemed insurmountable, were now more manageable courtesy of her counsellor, and her new- found coping strategies. She wondered why it had taken a complete stranger to make her understand that she wasn't wholly responsible for the breakdown of her marriage or for making bad life choices. Her marriage like many others had failed but that didn't mean she was incapable of having another meaningful relationship one day, and with that in mind, she made the decision to become socially active again and meet up with old friends and hopefully make some new ones along the way to. Her profile was still active on the dating site, but she hadn't read any messages for weeks. Statistically she knew there had to be a few good guys among them somewhere, but she was so afraid of finding another bad apple that she couldn't bring herself to look. She still hadn't told her kids the full story of that shocking weekend because there was no need for them to carry the burden of it too, but they knew how unhappy she had been of late, and they wanted to help. Jokingly they suggested she had a go at speed dating instead, because you could 'try before you buy,' as they so aptly put it, but being on the wrong side of forty she was apparently past it. According to the criteria, the maximum age was thirty-five and even though she knew she looked good for her age, she didn't feel confident enough to try and pull that off. Presumably, they thought after the age of thirty-five you were past it, a bit like the teenagers did at the sexual health clinic and she laughed. If she wanted to find herself a man, she was going to have to stop being such a coward and plunge back in, because her prince charming wasn't going to come knocking on her door anytime soon, and she had no intention of living like a nun at the grand old age of forty-five. Friends kept reminding her there were plenty more fish in the sea and she wondered if Mel might just be one of those fish.

Mel

Chloe was staring at the photo of him again. Mel had caught her eye early on while she had been scrolling aimlessly through dozens of photoshopped photos on the dating site and she hadn't been able to resist taking a second look at his. There was nothing pretentious about his picture, and she liked the fact he wasn't trying to look like some trendy male model in a catalogue. He wasn't what she would necessarily call good looking, but he wasn't bad looking either. There was something about him that attracted her , and she felt a strong emotional connection between them which she couldn't account for. There was no logic to it whatsoever, but that made him stand out from all the others even more. She wasn't sure if she still believed in love at first sight, but she had never experienced feelings like this before, not even with Pete, although she might have thought she did at the time; she wondered now if she had ever truly loved Pete in the way a wife was supposed to love her husband. In reality, they'd become more like siblings than husband and wife, but she had put that down to the pressures of work and bringing up a young family. Four kids in just over five years had kept them busy, and raising them had pretty much taken over their lives meaning they rarely spent quality time together as a couple. Over the years, she couldn't deny that they had drifted apart, but instead of working together, Pete had chosen to seek solace in the arms of another woman, and all that was left of their marriage now was a small band of gold which she continued to wear on the ring finger of her right hand. There was a time when she had thought about selling it, especially as money was tight, but selling it felt like allowing someone to buy her memories, and they were not for sale... not yet anyway. Under normal circumstances, Chloe prided herself on being balanced and rational, but here she was staring at a photo of a man she had never met, believing she might be in love for the very first time. She felt like a teenager with a crush on a pop idol, and she smiled as she vividly remembered her schoolgirl crush on the tartan teens from Edinburgh, more popularly known as The Bay City Rollers.

As she gazed affectionately at the photo of Mel, she remembered the message he had left on her answerphone while she was in France, and the comfort it had given her. For some reason he always made her smile when times were hard and lately times had been very hard indeed. There were several reasons why they hadn't met, but the main reason was her insecurity. Mel said he was separated from his wife but until very recently they had still been living together in the marital home for the sake of the children. Chloe had heard this line before, and it was usually because a bored married man was looking for a bit on the side, but Mel assured her that wasn't his style, and she desperately wanted to believe him. His eldest son Lewis was away at university, but the other two boys Jack and Joel were living at home and were due to sit important exams at school. According to Mel, the time simply hadn't been right to disrupt their lives. Although his concern for the welfare of his children was commendable, Chloe had preferred to keep her distance because she didn't want to play a role in someone else's bitter marriage break up, and she was afraid of getting hurt again. She wasn't afraid of physical pain- somehow she believed without doubt that Mel would not hurt her in that way - but she was afraid of the emotional heartache that could come from such a relationship. She felt certain that Mel was a man she could fall in love with; if she wasn't in love with already that was. Momentarily she thought back to Pete who hadn't given her or the kids a second thought since taking off to shack up with his Brazilian bimbo. His behaviour had angered and disappointed her, but even now the latter was the greater emotion; she had truly believed he had strong family values and fathers weren't supposed to just walk out on their children and leave them with nothing.

Mel had his own doubts. His marriage to Claire had been going down the pan for years but she had been his first love and he didn't want to let go without a fight. Unfortunately, Claire had more of an emotional connection with the vodka bottle than she did with him, and her drink problem had all but destroyed them. He loved her dearly and could never imagine loving anyone else, but Claire didn't love him anymore, she loved vodka and she loved the attention she got from other men when she was out drinking with her friends. He had only joined the dating site to make Claire jealous and it seemed to have worked. She didn't want him, but she didn't want anyone else to have him either and, in a strange way, it made him feel loved. Her drink problem had been escalating steadily, but now she had gone a step further and had started to bring men back to the house while he was at work. They had been sleeping separately for some time now, but allowing strangers into their marital bed and home was too much for him to bear. The atmosphere in the house was taking its toll on the children so reluctantly he had found himself a room to rent and moved out. After that he went off the rails for a bit and was out getting drunk and meeting different women every night. He wasn't looking for a long-term relationship with any of them, he was just looking for what he had lost. He missed conversation and companionship and most of all he missed being needed by someone. He certainly wasn't looking for love, and Chloe's appearance had confused him; there was definitely a connection between them, and she had helped to fill the empty void in his life. By now, they were chatting everyday either by phone or by text and he thought it was about time they took the next step. He reasoned he had nothing to lose by asking her out, and she had nothing to lose by accepting, so he was delighted when she finally said yes to a date with him.

They agreed to meet outside a tapas restaurant in a busy shopping centre. The plan was to keep it informal to see if they clicked. Mel felt sure he already knew the answer to that and it worried him; he wasn't sure he was ready to commit to another woman just yet, and he didn't want to let her down. She hadn't said as such, but reading between the lines he suspected she had already been let down badly and he didn't want to add to her grief. Chloe was equally anxious and fretted about what to wear, changing her outfit about a dozen times before settling on a pair of tight jeans and a top that accentuated her slender figure. Mel had said to dress informally so she concentrated on looking elegant and feminine without going over the top. She had butterflies in her stomach; the last time she remembered feeling like this was the day she took her first driving test and that had turned out to be a complete disaster, so she hoped history wasn't about to repeat itself. She arrived at the shopping centre with plenty of time to take a quick look around the shops. She rarely shopped for herself these days because money was tight, and the kids needs were her priority. Pete used to enjoy taking her shopping, indulging her taste in expensive clothes and designer labels. He had said it was because he liked her to look nice for him, but in hindsight, Chloe thought she had been nothing more than a status symbol who helped to boost his ego; although judging by what he was shacked up with now, he must have lowered his standards.

Chloe kept checking her watch. She didn't want to appear too keen by arriving early, but she didn't want to be late either. She decided to browse round a shop closer to the restaurant so she could keep an eye out for Mel, but eventually anticipation got the better of her and, worried she might miss him, she ended up standing outside the restaurant alone, trying hard not to draw too much attention to herself.

Mel had the same idea and had been watching her from a different shop. He had recognised her immediately from her profile picture and was glad to see he hadn't been catfished. She was everything he had imagined, and probably more, and he knew he could fall in love with her if only he wasn't still trapped in the past. He didn't want to keep her waiting because she looked nervous, so he strolled over with an air of confidence that did not reflect his inner turmoil. She saw him coming and smiled with relief; surprising herself by holding out her arms for a hug. She was usually more reserved than this, but for some reason she already felt like she had known him forever, and it seemed only natural to offer an embrace. To her delight he responded warmly, and seemed reluctant to let go of her. Mel momentarily closed his eyes and sighed silently so that she wouldn't hear. If only she knew how much he wished he could hold her this close for ever. He took her hand as they walked into the tapas bar, and she squeezed it reassuringly. She sensed he was nervous too, and she liked that in a man. Her body tingled at his touch, and she shuddered as the overwhelming chemistry between them ignited a flame that she thought had long burnt out.

They sat down to talk, and the conversation flowed easily much the same as it had on the phone. Mel was nervous and ended up talking about all the things he had planned to avoid talking about, including all the women he had been meeting to avenge Claire, and the women he planned to meet later in the week. He had been keeping his options open for months now, but he hadn't wanted to tell Chloe that because she wasn't an option, she was a choice, and he knew he didn't need to dig any deeper into the selection box to find a better one.

He had her full attention now, but Chloe had devised a cunning little plan of her own to call his bluff, which involved inventing an imaginary date for herself at the weekend. She also had options, and it wouldn't hurt him to think she wasn't afraid to cast her net a little wider if necessary. She watched his eyes to gauge his reaction, and underneath all his bravado she saw another lonely soul not much different to herself, desperate to find love again.

Mel was worried, his nerves had got the better of him and he'd got carried away, and now he risked losing her to some other guy she was planning to meet at the weekend. He had told her everything except the things he really wanted to say; he'd given the impression he was a womaniser which couldn't have been further from the truth. He had to find a way to backtrack and start again, but what if he was too late, and she already had him labelled as the Camberley Casanova? Chloe sensed his dilemma but decided it would be fun to let him squirm for a little bit longer, after all he had talked himself into this predicament, so he could jolly well try and talk himself back out of it again.

Chloe had never been to a tapas restaurant before but there were so many choices it seemed a wonderful way of trying out new foods. They ordered a selection of eight different dishes to share between them, and Chloe giggled when Mel started to playfully spoon feed her. It was the total opposite of the showy cordon bleu French restaurant with the polished silver cutlery that she'd endured with Alan, and she didn't think she could be any happier than she was right now. They were completely comfortable with each other and there was no need to pretend anymore, so she decided to put him out of his misery by admitting there was no weekend date, just in case he was planning on asking her out again. Mel's face flooded with relief; he knew he'd been rumbled, but for once he was glad.

The evening passed far too quickly for Chloe, and she felt more than a little disappointed when Mel failed to pick up on her hint about another date. The evening had been almost perfect, and she could see no reason why he wouldn't want to see her again. Mel had deliberately ignored her cue and changed the subject quickly. Mel wanted to see her again, of course he did, but he just couldn't bring himself to say the words out loud. Claire was always telling him he wouldn't recognise a good thing until it had gone. Mel suspected that deep down, Claire had been projecting her own fears onto him, although after one of her many drinking binges, he could be forgiven for feeling otherwise. Right now Claire was a liability, a millstone around his neck, but deep down he still loved her, and he thought she probably loved him too.

Chloe was unusually quiet as they walked back to her car. There were so many things she wanted to say to him, but she felt humiliated for having misread the signals, and she wanted to get back to her car as quickly as possible. She thought he liked her, and she thought she had finally found her rock. Unbeknown to Chloe, Mel needed a rock too, he was just terrified that Chloe might be too fragile to withstand the inevitable pressure that would come their way once Claire got wind of their relationship. He knew Claire had a jealous streak, and he knew she would never allow him to find happiness with another woman. He suspected she would go to any length to destroy his happiness in much the same way as she had destroyed her own. Her excessive drinking constituted a form of emotional suicide, and as much as he loved her, he couldn't allow her to drag him down to her level.

His one-night stands irritated her, but they weren't a threat, and she knew it. If she knew about Chloe she would ruin their relationship before it got started; he was tempted to take the gamble, he just hoped Chloe wouldn't get hurt in the process.

After a lovely evening together the awkward silence between them was both unexpected and uncomfortable, and he felt wholly responsible. She looked close to tears, and he knew he had to act now before it was too late. He had mistakenly led her to believe he wasn't interested in her and nothing could have been further from the truth. When they reached her car, he impulsively picked her up and swung her around holding her close enough to feel her heart beating against his chest. She felt so warm and vulnerable, and he loved the way she clasped her soft hands around his neck. After mentally preparing herself for the big rejection speech, Chloe was startled by his spontaneous gesture. She could feel her heart beating furiously, and as she rested her head on his shoulder she wondered if he was feeling as confused as she was.

Mel was confused. He didn't want to complicate matters by adding mud to the already cloudy waters but he hadn't anticipated falling in love. He wasn't even sure if it was love, but it felt like love, or maybe it was lust? He couldn't let it go, not until he knew for certain; not everyone was lucky enough to get a second chance at love. The thrill of meeting a new woman every night had worn off long ago, and quite frankly it had become boring since Claire no longer saw it as a threat. In the beginning it wound her up, but when he stopped getting a reaction from her, he knew his 'shag fests,' as she had aptly nicknamed them, had served their purpose.

Committing to Chloe was going to be a bit of a gamble because the timing wasn't right - he wasn't sure if there would ever be a right time - but he knew if he didn't take a risk and move out of his comfort zone, which frankly was no longer very comfortable, he would be stuck in the same rut for ever.

Chloe drove home with her heart still pounding frantically in her chest. She didn't want to get too ahead of herself at this early stage, but something was telling her he could be the one and that excited her. His change in mood bothered her, but she had a tendency to overthink everything, so she decided to relax a little and go with the flow. He had spoken very little about his wife Claire, but to be fair she hadn't spoken much about Pete either. The term 'separated' still plagued her mind. She and Pete were divorced, and Pete had well and truly moved on, but being separated was open to interpretation; many couples went through trial separations before making a final make or break decision. The niggling doubts raced through her mind, what if this was only a trial separation and what if he still loved his wife? She forced herself to ignore her fears; she didn't want them to spoil what had been a lovely evening, but her concerns were real, and she knew one day she might just have to face up to them.

Mel's rented room was close to the family home he had once shared with Claire and their three children. Despite being located on a busy main road it was still too quiet and he felt isolated and lonely. He was used to a busy household, where there were always people coming and going and he missed being around to provide a free taxi service for the kids. His room was sparsely decorated and there were few home comforts, but it served its purpose as a base and somewhere to sleep. Claire had a decent job working part time hours as a specialist nurse at a local doctors surgery, but over the past few months the effect of the booze had taken its toll on her, and she was becoming a liability at work. Getting up in the mornings after a night on the razzle was becoming more difficult, and when she did finally stumble out of bed, she replaced her usual bowl of cornflakes with a glass of vodka. The kids were at an age where they could take care of themselves, and she took unfair advantage of them by using them as unpaid carers on days when she'd had one too many. Her employers had been sympathetic up to a point, but eventually they were forced to give her a written warning and some time off to sort herself out. She tried alcoholics anonymous but gave up after only a few meetings because she was in denial. Mel had gone along to support her, but he could see she wasn't engaging with it and the organiser struggled to cope with her relentless mockery and disruptive behaviour. Eventually he'd had a quiet word with Mel and explained that until Claire reached rock bottom she would be unlikely to benefit from the AA meetings. Mel struggled with the notion of letting someone he loved reach rock bottom and did everything in his power to help her, but she resented him for it and retaliated by drinking even more, along with prostituting herself to any man that showed her attention. If that didn't constitute hitting rock bottom then Mel had no idea what did, the only thing he knew for certain was that he couldn't stick around and watch her abuse herself any longer. He was a good father to their boys and even Claire endorsed his strong paternal instinct. There wasn't room for them to stay with him in his current accommodation but when the finances got sorted, he planned to find somewhere more suitable. It was better than nothing though and it provided a temporary bolt hole for the kids if they became desperate. He understood how hard it was for teenagers to adjust to a marriage break up because his own parents had divorced when he was just thirteen and he was forced to play the game of piggy in the middle for years after. His kids had the stigma of an alcoholic mother to deal with as well and had already been ridiculed by their peers after Claire turned up intoxicated at the school and made them a laughing stock. Fortunately, Mel had turned up in time to make excuses for her but not before some nosey busybody called the social services in.

Claire's life was spiralling out of control and she didn't seem to care. Vodka was the only thing that got her through the day, but she was drinking more and more of it to get the desired effect, and it wasn't long before she was knocking back an entire bottle every day. It was an expensive habit that they couldn't afford as well as a health hazard, and despite protesting bitterly when he bought home a cheaper brand, she still managed to drain every last drop. Mel had taken her to the doctors because she wasn't sleeping well but the doctor refused to prescribe anything as he said the medication was addictive. When asked about her drinking habits, she had lied. The doctor hadn't been so easily fooled and, given that his room smelled like a distillery, he had bravely attempted to probe Claire a bit more. He wanted to take some blood tests and refer her to the alcohol intervention team, but this had enraged her, and she stormed off in a huff shouting that it would be his fault if she died because he wouldn't give her the medication she needed. Eventually out of sheer desperation she bought some off the internet, but the drugs came from China and took weeks to arrive, and when they finally did arrive Claire had been furious that she had to collect them from the post office and pay a hefty handling charge. By this time, her vodka intake had more than doubled and she blamed Mel for this. She was angry that he hadn't supported her when they went to see the doctor, and claimed she wouldn't have needed so much alcohol if the stupid doctor had given her the tablets she wanted at the time. She was angry with him because he insisted she was an alcoholic, but she wasn't an alcoholic, she could stop anytime she wanted to; the fact that she had no incentive to was his fault. When they got married, he had been lively, fun, and impulsive and his energy invigorated her, but now she was bored with him. He had served his purpose and given her three wonderful children, but even the sex which was once wild and adventurous was now mundane, and she always needed a couple of drinks to get her in the mood. She wanted the magic back, and she wanted to feel like a real woman again. She loved being a wife and mother, but she wanted to be noticed and vodka had got her noticed.

Chloe wanted to trust Mel but she couldn't shake off the lingering doubts that plagued her already troubled mind. It would have been so much easier if he had been divorced or at the very least applied for a divorce, but he was still married, and seemed to be in no hurry to start divorce proceedings. She couldn't compete with a woman who had carried his children and she didn't want to try; there would always be a bond between them. Her mum always told her 'blood is thicker than water' and she had learned to her cost how true

127

that was. In hindsight she should probably have learnt that lesson before she married Pete because he refused to give up his family for her, and it wasn't until he'd gone that she realised she should never have expected him to. She had tried to ostracise him from his family because deep down she knew she had been envious of the attention they took away from her. Eventually her jealousy had pushed him away, and she knew the same could happen with Mel if she didn't try to modify her behaviour.

They had been dating for several months now and Chloe knew she was in love with Mel, but she wasn't sure if he was in love with her, or whether he just liked the idea of being in love with her. Friends had tried to warn her that she was moving too fast, but the strong physical and emotional connection growing between them, meant she took no notice of her well-meaning friends. Chloe loved how content they were just being together, enjoying the simple things in life like going for long country walks with Norman and stopping off for a bit of pub grub before going back to Chloe's house for some wild afternoon sex. She couldn't remember the last time she had felt this happy and naively believed that nothing could ever come between them. There were tell-tale warning signs of course, but she chose to ignore them. His phone was constantly ringing, and he always walked away to take the call mumbling something about his business partner, and she'd had no reason to doubt him, until now that was. They had just enjoyed a lovely lunch in a pub garden and Mel had popped back to the bar for another round of drinks leaving his phone unattended on the table in front of her. The phone rang and went to voicemail, and when she glanced at the screen, she noticed the call was from Claire. A few seconds later a message popped up to remind him there was a voicemail waiting and for a brief moment she was tempted to listen to it but thought better of it. His phone was none of her business and although the call made her feel uneasy, she decided to forget about it. As she took a sip of her cool cider, a text message flashed up and it was also from Claire. There was still a long queue of people at the bar and with no sign of Mel returning, Chloe decided to take a quick look and was shocked to find his phone full of messages from Claire. She scrolled down through the numbers and found no incoming calls from his so-called business partner either. She quickly put the phone back down and waited for him to come back with their drinks. He returned from the bar with the usual cheeky grin on his face and, although she was desperate to say something, she didn't want him to know she didn't trust him. She returned his smile before casually mentioning his phone had rung and watched as his cheeks blushed before making some random comment about how warm the weather was again. He apologised but seemed nervous as he quickly grabbed his phone from the table. He mumbled something under his breath about another problem at work and looked briefly at Chloe for sympathy, without registering the blank expression on her face. He was gone for about ten minutes - although it seemed much longer - and Chloe wondered if he would finally tell her the truth. He seemed uncomfortable and gave a worried look when she asked sarcastically why his business partner could never cope for more than a few hours without him at the weekend.

Mel could tell from the tone of her voice that she knew

something, and he silently scolded himself for not taking his phone to the bar with him. This was the moment he had been dreading for months, but he owed it to her to come clean, even though the truth meant he might lose her. She sat staring at him patiently waiting for an answer with her arms folded tightly across her chest. She had the feeling she wasn't going to like what he had to say, but she had been let down so many times already, another dent to her ego would be barely noticeable. He hadn't rehearsed what to say because he hadn't planned on telling her just yet, but he knew it was time for him to come clean. As it turned out it was a relief to be able to finally tell Chloe about Claire, and he hoped she would be a good listener;, thankfully she didn't let him down.

He had always known that Claire would interfere if she found out about his relationship with Chloe, but at the same time, he knew he wouldn't be able to hide it from her for ever. It was just a matter of time before she found out; stupidly, he had thought he was doing the right thing by not telling Chloe. Claire had been behaving like an overgrown schoolgirl for weeks now and had perfected the art of staging imaginary sob stories and insisting he came round to do non-existent DIY jobs that apparently couldn't wait. On one of his fruitless visits to the house, she had stolen his phone from his jacket and found Chloe's number; she had been blackmailing him ever since.

Claire didn't want him for herself, at least she didn't think she did, but she wasn't ready to hand him over to anyone else just yet either; besides, she enjoyed pretending he was still in with a chance. She congratulated herself on having him exactly where she wanted him, and like a loyal dog he would do anything to please. Having Chloe's number was an unexpected bonus and it gave her the upper hand, Mel knew her well enough to know her threats were real. His interest in Chloe disturbed Claire because he had never shown this much interest in another woman before and she had mixed feelings about it. A quick phone call to remind her he was still a married man wouldn't go amiss, but that was too predictable, and besides, she had a much better idea.

Mel knew that it wouldn't be long before Chloe received a message from Claire and he was fast regretting not coming clean and telling Chloe to change her number sooner, not to mention explaining the volatile relationship between him and his estranged wife, but he'd been afraid he might lose her if he did. His foolish behaviour could cost him the woman he loved, and he wondered if she would ever be able to forgive his cowardice. She was still sitting with her arms folded across her chest staring right through him, and he wished she would say something. Chloe couldn't believe he could be so gullible, leaving his jacket unattended had been nothing short of stupidity; especially as he seemed to know what Claire was like. If worse came to worse, she would have to change her number which would be mildly inconvenient but it wasn't exactly the end of the world either. She was more miffed that he hadn't felt able to talk to her.

Mel sat looking sheepishly at Chloe trying to think of something sensible to say. She hadn't responded to the news as badly as he thought she would, and he wished now he'd had the guts to come clean about Claire a bit earlier. He'd had his head stuck in the sand like an ostrich and acted selfishly, because like most blokes he wanted the best of both worlds.

He had tried hard to keep her out of his marriage problems but falling in love with her hadn't been a part of the plan.

Chloe had come too far to turn back now, and she could see from the worried look on his face that he was expecting the worse which only served to intensify her love for him even more. She wanted to be angry, throw a tantrum even, but her love for this man was an inexplicable, fiercely passionate, extraordinary kind of love that she thought only existed in fairy tales, and just like a fairytale she wanted it to last for ever. Friends laughed at her and said it was lust, but she knew differently and one day she was going to prove them wrong. It should have been easier now things were out in the open, but Chloe struggled to relax knowing one day she was likely to get a call from Claire. Under the circumstances most people would have changed their telephone number as quickly as possible, and Mel was keen for her to do just that, but she wasn't most people, and she couldn't help being a little bit curious about Claire.

Mel's birthday was fast approaching, and Chloe had a surprise meal planned for the two of them at a local Italian restaurant. She loved everything Italian and had dreams of getting married one day at an exclusive resort somewhere on the stunning Amalfi coast with views stretching out towards the sparkling sun kissed Mediterranean Sea. She knew she was way ahead of herself, after all Mel was still married and it was complicated, but in her dreams anything was possible.

Claire was in no hurry to spoil things for them just yet. It was all a game to her, and the timing was meticulously planned. She guessed Chloe would have made plans for Mel's birthday, so it would be fun to add in some extra entertainment free of charge. This would be the first birthday in fifteen years that she and Mel hadn't spent together, and she felt sad. Birthdays had always been special for the two of them - something they celebrated together - but this year she would be celebrating his birthday alone, with the remains of a bottle of vodka.

Chloe instructed Mel to be at hers no later than seven thirty. He wasn't sure what she had planned but he assumed it was a meal because she had given him strict instructions not to eat anything. He left work early because Claire had sent him yet another text and he thought it would be easier to pop in quickly and pacify her just in case she had plans to spoil his evening. When he arrived at Claire's, she was already half-cut and was dressed provocatively in a low-cut clingy dress that emphasised her slender frame. She had a card in her hand which she carefully placed in his jacket pocket before placing her arms around his waist and planting a gentle kiss on his cheek. Mel was stunned, and despite the stench of alcohol, he couldn't help noticing how she still scrubbed up well and he thought she looked beautiful. A few years ago, he would have been proud to show her off as his wife but now she was nothing more than a manipulative alcoholic who he still loved but no longer liked. She whispered softly in his ear, 'happy birthday darling,' before releasing her arms from his waist and wishing him a lovely evening. Mel had been speechless, but managed to thank her for the card before leaving. He had a forty-five-minute drive to Chloe's house and he still had plenty of time. He breathed a sigh of relief, having worried that Claire was going to make today far more difficult for him, he was relieved to have got off so lightly. Meanwhile Claire was laughing loudly with a celebratory glass of vodka in her hand. She stared at the phone, the one she had just removed from his pocket and couldn't believe it had been so easy.

Mel hadn't noticed that his phone was missing but so far Claire's devious little plan had worked out perfectly, and now it was time to amuse herself. He stopped briefly in a lay by and reached for the card in his pocket. Claire had drawn a heart around his name on the front of the card and for a brief moment he was tempted not to open it, but curiosity got the better of him and he opened it anyway. On the front it simply said, 'To my husband on his birthday,' but on the inside Claire had written, 'I miss you' and for a split second her words tugged at his heartstrings. She had written the card in one of her more lucid moments when she had been sober, and at the time she had meant what she said. She did miss him sometimes because they had been together for so long, but she didn't know what she wanted from one day to the next. The vodka confused her and messed with her brain so it wasn't her fault she couldn't think rationally, but another drink usually solved that problem. She knew he'd be getting a lot more than just a card from Chloe for his birthday and she was jealous. She was still his wife, and as his wife she had more right to him than Chloe did, so she had no qualms about spoiling their evening, after all she had nothing else to do.

Chloe was putting the finishing touches to her makeup. She looked in the mirror and smiled at the pretty face looking back at her. She looked younger than her forty- five years and she had dressed to impress tonight because she was secretly hoping Mel might be about to pop the question. She knew she was being ridiculous, and she didn't even know if you could be married and engaged at the same time, but she couldn't think of any reason why not apart from it being a bit unethical. Mel hadn't mentioned marriage to her of course, but they had looked around jewellery shops together and she had mentioned light-heartedly on more than one occasion that she wouldn't say no to a ring. For his birthday she had bought him a blue designer shirt. Blue suited him as a colour and she hoped he'd be pleased with her choice. She had already picked her menu and decided on the spicy Italian meatballs that she loved, but her choice of dessert remained a secret although it was fair to say it would be a whole lot spicier.

Chloe was still daydreaming about dessert when her phone pinged, and the display showed a text message from Mel. She smiled knowing that he would be on his way by now but when she opened the message, she was confused by what it said. The first message said, 'Sorry I won't be coming over because I am still in love with my wife.' This was followed quickly by a second message which said, 'Please don't contact me again, I have decided to make a go of my marriage,' and then there was a final message which simply said, 'Goodbye Chloe it was fun while it lasted.' The words were cruel and totally out of character for Mel because she felt certain he would never deliberately hurt her. Instinctively she picked up her phone ready to have it out with him, but something stopped her, and she was glad it did, because within minutes Mel was outside reversing his van into her driveway. Chloe couldn't contain herself and rushed outside to greet him, impulsively flinging her arms around his neck, her head burrowed into the softness of his shirt as she breathed in his fragrant smell. Mel sensed her desperation, and he could see the anguish in her eyes; he had no idea why she looked so troubled. Perhaps he should have phoned to say he was on his way? He started to apologise but before he could finish his sentence she silenced him by planting a passionate kiss on his lips, and he felt overwhelmed by his love for her. He wondered what on earth he had done to deserve such a phenomenal welcome; her vulnerability made her incredibly sexy and he adored her all the more for it.

As he surfaced from their kiss Mel, caught his breath, his eyes searching Chloe's for an explanation. Chloe took a step back and pulled her phone from the handbag slung across her body. As she scrolled through Claire's messages, Mel instinctively patted his own pockets in search of his mobile. The colour drained from his face as reality dawned. How could he have been so stupid? He couldn't believe Claire would stoop so low, but then again, hadn't she warned him that she'd use her trump card if she had to? He should have known that she'd lured him to the house under false pretences. He should have guessed she was up to something by her earlier behaviour, but time and again, he talked himself in to believing there was still some good in the woman he had married. He was still so gullible when it came to Claire, and he hated himself for being so damned predictable.

Claire was livid, her plan had backfired. Mel would have arrived at Chloe's by now, but the call she had expected from a desperate and heartbroken Chloe had never come. She couldn't bear the thought of the two of them laughing at her pathetic attempt to sabotage their date. She had drunk enough vodka to prepare herself for Chloe's call, but the wretched woman must have seen through her and the long-awaited call never came. Claire was curious about Chloe. Her husband had never once looked at another woman in the years they'd been marriage, and she couldn't help wondering what was so special about her.

The food at the restaurant was delicious, but after a few mouthfuls Chloe just pushed it aimlessly around her plate. She didn't want to spoil what was left of her evening with Mel, especially on his birthday, but she was deeply troubled by Claire's behaviour and it unsettled her. She wasn't prepared to take on the role of the 'other woman,' but Claire was still his wife, and as much as she hated to admit it, that made her his mistress, and she feared Claire may continue to have the upper hand.

Mel had been waiting for Chloe to ask the inevitable question all evening, and he still didn't know what he was going to say. He had no idea why he had gone round to see Claire when he could easily have made an excuse not to, but at the time it seemed like the right thing to do because they always spent birthdays together. He tried to convince himself it was just force of habit that had taken him there, but he could still picture how very beautiful she had looked and despite the booze, the years had been good to her.

He thought back fondly to the first time they met. He had been out for a few drinks with his mates when she walked into the bar with some girlfriends. She was a real head turner, and her presence literally lit up the room. As far as he had been concerned, she was the only girl in the room, and he'd made his mind up there and then that she was the girl he was going to marry. Claire was well aware of the effect she had on men, and she relished the attention. She attracted men like a magnet; other girls stood no chance when she was around. She could have any man she wanted but she liked a challenge, and it was the thrill of the chase that excited her more than the catch. Once she had caught them, she became easily bored and unless they had something exceptional to offer, she discarded them like a dirty rag. The minute she walked into the bar she had spotted Mel grinning at her like a schoolboy who had just found a new toy to play with. He was a bit ordinary looking and not her usual type, but he had a quirky lopsided smile and a mop of scruffy curly hair that yielded an innocent charm. He oozed potential and she thought he might grow on her, but after a couple of minutes he turned away to talk to a group of girls standing nearby and she wasn't used to making the first move. Mel had been trying hard to look busy but he couldn't resist watching Claire out the corner of his eye. She had a bit of a reputation when it came to men, and he wanted to be more than just another one of her conquests. He played hard to get for a while before conveniently bumping into her at the bar where he bought her a drink and the rest was history. They'd had a whirlwind romance and six months later Claire had suggested it was time he made an honest woman out of her. Within days she had a ring on her finger and before much longer, they were married with a mortgage and three young boys to care for. To the outside world they seemed like the perfect family, but Claire soon became restless and turned to alcohol to relieve the boredom.

Chloe's voice brought Mel back to the present. She was getting impatient because she had asked him more than once why he went to see Claire and he still hadn't answered her. He seemed to have drifted off into a world of his own and her voice clearly startled him. She had been trying to convince herself he would have a plausible explanation, but his silence told a different story, and she was feeling uneasy. She'd had high expectations for this evening, but it hadn't gone to plan because whether she liked it or not there were still three people in their relationship, and she couldn't shake off the intruder. She was beginning to feel that she might be the intruder; Mel and Claire were still married and it seemed her reservations about meeting a married man might be justified after all. She would never accept second best, but she didn't know how she could convince Mel to love her more than he loved his wife.

Mel remained quiet. He knew she was waiting for an answer, but he couldn't give her the answer she was looking for because he didn't know why he had been to visit Claire either. Eventually he mumbled something about her wanting to give him a card, but it was a feeble excuse and Chloe deserved better. If he walked away now, she would be hurt, but if he stayed he would hurt her a whole lot more. She was far too good for him, and she made him feel special which is why it was so difficult to let her go, but it was the right thing to do, he was sure of it.

A card wasn't exactly the crime of the century, but Chloe still felt threatened by it especially as he hadn't mentioned it before now. He had obviously allowed her to get close enough to him to remove the phone from his jacket pocket without him noticing. She clearly didn't need Chloe's number; she must have been looking for something more from him, and it didn't take a genius to work out what that was. Chloe's mind was running riot with possibilities and she felt very isolated, like a single tadpole in a pond full of piranha fish she felt certain the happy times were about to perish.

The evening had been memorable but for all the wrong reasons. Claire filled Chloe's thoughts and Mel had the same dilemma. Claire might as well have been sitting there at the dinner table with them, because her presence was very much at the forefront of both of their minds. Chloe had deliberately left her phone at home because she knew that now Claire had started her vendetta she would probably continue with it, especially if she had been drinking, and even though she didn't yet know it, Claire had already achieved her goal. She had ruined the evening from the outset by planting seeds of doubt in Chloe's mind and those seeds would soon grow into a sharp prickly cacti, capable of inflicting deep wounds with scars that would never fully fade.

Chloe paid the bill and they went home. Under the circumstances Mel was merrier than she expected but it was his birthday and he'd had a few drinks to celebrate. On the other hand, Chloe was stone cold sober; she'd decided to drive rather than waste money on a taxi, a decision she was now regretting, as a few glasses of wine might have helped to lift her dark mood. When they arrived home she immediately checked her phone and as expected there was a single message from Claire directed at Mel which simply said, 'see you tomorrow when you come to collect your phone,' followed by two totally unnecessary xx and she knew she had lost him.

The atmosphere between them was unusually sombre, and Mel knew he would have to tell Chloe his decision soon.

He decided to sleep on it; firstly because he was too much of a coward to tell her tonight after all the effort she'd made and secondly because he couldn't deny that he'd like to make love to her one last time. He left earlier than usual the following morning so he could pick up his phone on the way to work. It was easier that way because he couldn't face seeing the pain in Chloe's eyes again. He hadn't wanted to hurt her, but he'd always feared he would and he felt ashamed of himself.' He had to know if he could work things out with Claire, as his wife she deserved that much, they both did, but he knew it had cost him dearly.

Chloe knew from his body language that this was goodbye, and she struggled to hold back the tears as she watched him drive away. She had pretended to be asleep when he left because she knew it would be easier than facing up to the truth. She wanted to fight for her man but there was no point; it seemed he had never been hers to win. They had met at the wrong time, but if they were truly meant to be together, he would find his way back to her. She didn't know whether it would be weeks, months, or years, but he would come back - she was sure of it.

The Next Few Months

Without Mel around, Chloe's life was incomplete. She tried hard to stay strong, but the days seemed pointless because she had nothing to look forward to, and she started to realise just how much she had come to depend on him. She had heard from him only once since the morning he left, and she strongly suspected that the reply had been from Claire not Mel. He had Claire now, but Chloe had no one to fill the empty void that his departure had left, so she had broken the rules by sending him a casual text in a moment of weakness. As soon as she sent it she knew it made her look like a desperate woman, but she couldn't help herself. The reply stated that he had worked things out with Claire and had made it clear they didn't need her behaving like a bunny boiler by intruding on their new found happiness. Chloe wished she could be happy for them and be more dignified about it - turning a failed marriage around deserved recognition - but she felt nothing apart from a deep sense of loss.

Claire had been furious when the text came through from

Chloe. Mel even showed it to her to confirm it was casual and innocent and not initiated by him in any way, but she was fuming and insisted he allowed her to respond to it personally. After sending the message she deleted Chloe from his contact list, and erased the message history so there could be no further communication, unless of course Chloe dared to try again. After what she'd written she thought it unlikely, but she needed rid of this woman once and for all. Her response had been cruel, hurtful, and needlessly vindictive, but now she had him back she planned to keep hold of him, until a better offer came along of course.

Mel was bereft. He had foolishly believed he could make his marriage work, but Claire was refusing to cooperate and to make things worse he hadn't taken a note of Chloe's number and now he had no way of contacting her again. He knew Claire's text would have been tactless and insensitive and he could almost feel Chloe's pain. He wished he had followed his heart because he hadn't made the decision to leave her lightly. He made a choice to be where he thought he should be instead of where he wanted to be and now, he had to live with the painful consequences of that decision. He made a plan to keep his phone with him day and night until she contacted him again. He was certain she would contact him one day, and he hoped it would be soon.

Chloe had no way of knowing that Mel no longer had her number and the last text message had certainly put her in her place, so she made the decision not to try to contact him again. No one had ever called her a bunny boiler before and she owed it to herself to be someone's priority; second best wasn't good enough. She thought back to happier times, and the memories they had made together, they were the one thing she had left that Claire didn't have the power to destroy. Frustratingly, she still couldn't contemplate moving on. It wouldn't be fair on other guys because she would compare them all to Mel in much the same way she had compared everyone with Pete in the early days. The only man she hadn't compared with Pete was Mel because there had been no comparison. Mel had made her feel more special than any other man including Pete and she knew she wouldn't feel complete until she found a love like that again. Somehow, she was going to have to put Mel to the back of her mind the way he had put her to the back of his, but it wasn't going to be easy everything reminded her of him. The pillow that sat in the empty space on the bed next to hers still smelled of his aftershave and even now she couldn't bring herself to put it through the wash. Her love for him was addictive but it was fast growing into an unhealthy obsession which she knew could ruin her chances of finding love again. With a heavy heart she logged back on to the dating site, but she found herself nit-picking and being unfairly judgemental of the guys on there. She'd been about to log out when she decided to take a second look... just in case someone caught her eye. No single profile stood out to her as being better than the rest, but because she was desperately lonely, she managed to convince herself there was no reason why she couldn't go out and have some fun with one or two of them, on a purely platonic level of course. On that basis she decided it wouldn't matter which one she picked first if the whole idea was to go out and have some fun again, without the worry of commitment. She was beginning to understand why some women became lesbians after failed relationships with men. Women understood each other far better than men understood women, but she had no plans to start batting for the other side just yet.

There were four guys who looked like they might be okay, so she added them to her shortlist before closing her eyes and picking one at random. Her mum picked lottery numbers in much the same way and Chloe thought internet dating was a bit like a lottery. Unfortunately, her dates had been a bit like her mum's lottery numbers because she was still waiting to find love and her mum was still waiting to be the next lottery millionaire.

The winning guy was Brian, a forty-eight-year-old divorcee who worked as a manager for a large waste removal company. They met for a lunchtime drink in a local pub and Chloe felt no physical or emotional connection with him whatsoever and quickly came to the decision that he was the most boring guy she had ever met. It seemed Hippo bags were as inspiring to Brian as fire extinguishers had been to John and, after an hour of debating the benefits of bag versus skip, Chloe wished she had one to bundle him up in. The only advantage he had over John was that he didn't take three hours to drink a pint. Chloe wasn't sure how but somehow, he managed to invite himself back for a cup of tea afterwards where he continued to point out the many uses of hippo bags. Norman didn't seem to like him, and Brian clearly wasn't a dog lover either. Being a boxer, Norman, was naturally boisterous and bouncy, as well as ridiculously clumsy, and he managed to upset Brian several times by continuously standing on his feet. Brian took umbrage to this because apparently, he was a diabetic and was concerned that minor abrasions could develop into long term circulation problems. As a nurse, Chloe understood his concerns, but this was a boxer dog not a hippo standing on his feet, so she thought his concerns were a bit disproportionate.

Norman didn't understand what all the fuss was about. He'd been standing on the new human's feet in an effort to gain some attention because this stranger who had come in to his house, and sat on his sofa had completely ignored him, and at the very least he expected a pat on the head - although a belly rub would have been better. The conversation quickly dried up after Brian exhausted all the virtues of Hippo bags, and judging by the way Chloe and Norman were staring at him, he thought he might have outstayed his welcome. He quickly made his excuses and left before humiliating himself any further. He had fallen into the same trap with women before. They simply didn't understand business in the same way as men, so he was going to have to think of a different chat up line in future, because once again he had failed to impress. He wondered if any ladies would share his passion for fly fishing instead.

With Brian gone Chloe used the same technique as before to select her next date. It would be difficult to find another man as boring as Brian, but she thought it was probably safer not to assume anything.

Patrick was seven years her junior and worked for the police force. He wasn't a high-ranking officer like the vile detective chief superintendent Alan, so she hoped he would be a little more humble and unpretentious. As Alan had been the most arrogant man she had ever met, the odds of Patrick being a more regular kind of guy were well above average. He was a uniformed community support officer and Chloe did like a man in uniform.

Patrick suggested meeting in a trendy wine bar close to the local clubs and nightlife. As a general rule, she avoided such places because they were always full of youngsters, and she was old enough to be the mother of most of the customers, but Patrick was younger than her and he had never been married so she assumed it was more typical for a single guy to frequent this type of venue. Chloe had never dated a toy boy before but the prospect of it exhilarated her. She felt more alive and invigorated than she had in a long time and was determined to do everything possible to make sure she blended in with her younger compatriots.

Patrick suggested they meet outside the venue, which was a relief to Chloe because she was a bit short sighted and was worried about not being able to find him in a crowded room, or worse still tapping the wrong guy on the shoulder and then having to apologise. When she arrived, there had only been a group of teenagers and a solitary man standing outside the bar, so he was easy to recognise. She would have recognised him anyway because he was incredibly tall, and for once she was glad she had worn her heels. He greeted her warmly and his soft Irish accent made her legs tremble. The bar was packed and extremely noisy and there was loud music playing which made it difficult for her to hear him properly. She was keen to hear more of his sexy voice so after one drink, she boldly suggested they moved on to somewhere a bit quieter.

As they were both quite hungry they found a quiet table in a local restaurant with outstanding views over the sea that stretched out towards the illuminated silhouette of the Isle of Wight.

It was a romantic setting and Chloe had to remind herself that this was their first date. He was an attractive man, but she was totally captivated by his voice which she could happily have listened to for many more hours had they not run out of time. Chloe wondered why he had never married. He told her he had never met the right woman which seemed a reasonable enough explanation but she couldn't help wondering if there was something else, perhaps he was just extremely choosy when it came to women. His family still lived in Ireland, but he said he had little or no contact with them. He didn't elaborate further, and Chloe didn't like to ask too many questions, although she believed something bad must have happened because she thought Irish families were usually very close knit.

Patrick certainly had a few skeletons in his closet which became difficult to hide if he dated a girl long term. He rarely instigated a second date and relied heavily on one-night stands to avoid making plans for the future as there could never be a happy ever after. His family were ashamed of him, and he was disgusted with himself which is why he had moved to England to make a new start away from everyone who knew him. The pressure he'd put on his parents had very nearly destroyed their marriage and his dad made no secret of the fact he was glad to see the back of him. His mum was a gentle Irish woman with strong maternal instincts, and she fought hard to keep the family together, but he took advantage of her good nature and eventually his father disowned him. Without his father's knowledge his mum continued to maintain contact with him and sent food parcels every month to keep him going. She hated lying to her husband, but at the same time she loved her son dearly and despite everything she couldn't bring herself to turn her back on him completely.

Patrick came to this part of town because of the casino. He was addicted to gambling and lived for the thrill of the next win. He was a risk taker and even when he was on a winning streak he didn't know when to stop and always came away empty handed. He had stolen from his family time and time again to fund his habit, and understandably they'd had enough, but he did miss them terribly, especially his mum who he loved dearly. Eventually, his mum stopped sending him money because she knew he would just whittle it away, so she consoled herself by making lots of homemade goodies and parcelling them off to him once a month. He was in denial, but his mum could read him like a book, even though his dad naively believed he had turned a corner by moving to England and getting a job. She was a good woman and she loved her husband too much to shatter his beliefs, but she knew one day he would find out and then there would be hell to pay.

Patrick lived in a small flat provided by the police, and his rent was automatically deducted from his wages. His parents were delighted but nonetheless surprised when he secured a job with the force because they firmly believed with all his problems, the only long-term lodgings he would find would be the inside of a police cell. His poor credit rating meant he was unable to rent from an agent or private landlord without a guarantor and unsurprisingly no one was prepared to back him. This is where it had all gone wrong in the past with previous girlfriends. He could hide his addiction up to a point, but once it got to the stage where they wanted to move in, his cover was blown and they didn't hang around for much longer after that. He was his own worst enemy, but his desire to gamble was stronger than his desire to seek help, and as time passed, he became more isolated from family and friends. There were times when he hated himself for what he had done, and for the misery he had caused the people that loved him, but by now he was an accomplished risk taker, and he was convinced that one day it would be his turn for the big win and then all his worries and financial problems would be over. Like a perfect gentleman he escorted Chloe back to her car and they made arrangements to meet again. He'd had a nice evening and she was good company as well as easy on the eye, so perhaps another date wouldn't hurt. He'd just about scraped enough cash together to pay the bill without breaking into the wad of notes stashed in his jacket pocket. He waved goodbye to Chloe and headed straight for the casino. He had a good feeling about tonight and was feeling confident when he put all the money on red number sixteen. Chloe was his lucky charm; he felt sure of it, and tonight was the night he'd been waiting for. As the croupier spun the wheel he waited in anticipation as the ball went round and round in circles before finally settling on black number thirty-three. He watched helplessly as his money was taken away, and as he got up to leave he consoled himself that he would have better luck next time. Chloe was puzzled when she saw Patrick heading back towards the bars and clubs in her car mirror. It was late, and most of them would be closing soon, so it seemed rather odd. She decided to put it to the back of her mind and try not to overthink the situation, after all her plan was to have some fun and nothing else.

Patrick had suggested cooking a meal for her next time because it would save him money and give him time alone with her. He couldn't cook but that didn't matter because he had a whole stack of tasty home baked meals in his freezer courtesy of his generous mother. It would be enough to impress Chloe and she would never find out he couldn't cook anything more than beans on toast; like all the other women he had met from the dating site, she wasn't going to be a long-term prospect. Chloe was looking forward to the meal. It was unusual for a guy to offer to cook for her and she always thought food tasted better when she hadn't had to cook it for herself, with the exception of Foie gras that was, which looked and tasted foul. He'd offered her a wide choice of meals and she was impressed with his extensive repertoire. She opted for the beef bourguignon because it could be left to cook on its own in the oven which would give them more time to get to know each other, and she was already secretly hoping she might get to know him a whole lot better.

It didn't matter to Patrick which meal she picked because they were all at his disposal, neatly packed away like readymade supermarket meals, but with all the taste and goodness of home cooking. All he had to do was defrost them and heat them up, before transferring them to one of his own dishes, and that would be enough to convince Chloe he had made an effort and spent hours slaving over a hot stove to impress her. He didn't see the point in making too much effort with women because as a general rule, they didn't hang around long enough to make it worth his while. His mum was keen for him to settle down with a nice young lady as she always put it because she was desperate for grandchildren, but as far as Patrick was concerned kids were not on his agenda now, or in the future. He hadn't told his mother this because she would be heartbroken, and he had already let her down enough. At her age she needed to have hope, and he didn't want her to let go of her belief that one day he would turn his life around and behave like the good catholic boy she had raised.

When Chloe arrived at the modest little flat, she was impressed with the effort he had made. There was very little furniture, but the minimalist look was all the rage these days and the table was nicely set for dinner. There was a delicious smell coming from the small kitchen area, filling the flat with the aroma of hearty winter comfort food and her tummy rumbled in anticipation. The food was warming up nicely in the oven, so he offered her a glass of wine as a pre meal appetizer. He didn't do starters because his mum didn't supply them, and from past experience a glass of wine was well received by the ladies. He sat down beside her on the sofa and watched as she sipped from her glass. Physically he was very attracted to her and with her job as a nurse she was exactly the type of woman his mum would approve of. It was all totally hypothetical of course because she would never get to meet his darling mum, but if things were different, and he hadn't screwed his life up he was certain they would have become good friends.

Chloe was pleased when he sat down next to her and

casually draped his arm around her back until it was almost touching her shoulder. He was chatty, and she was surprised to learn he was interested in history and was partway through the application process to join the Freemasons. She struggled to see why someone like Patrick would want to join the Freemasons because from what she'd heard about them they seemed a bit odd, and she didn't approve of their blatant discrimination against women either. It was all cloak and dagger type stuff shrouded in mystery and men who engaged in funny handshakes.

Patrick's father was a time-honoured Freemason with traditional values. His mother had never really got the hang of it and had eventually stopped asking about their 'goings on' because he always laughed at her and told her it was a secret. She'd once told Patrick she thought he was a spy for the government, and he had howled with laughter. They had been the good old days, and he wanted them back, but it seemed that ship had sailed, and wasn't coming back. Patrick wanted to make his father proud of him again and because Freemasons were expected to be of a high moral standing, he'd thought joining them might do the trick. He hadn't anticipated it being such a difficult and time-consuming process and he was becoming increasingly frustrated by his lack of progress.

Chloe was feeling hungry and was bored of listening to the history of the Freemasons. When she asked him a question about them, he refused to answer because he said nobody was allowed to give their secrets away, which she thought was rather childish of him. She didn't really want to know anyway and had only asked out of politeness. She hadn't expected him to go on about it for so long, and secretly hoped dinner would soon be ready so she could make her excuses and leave. Whilst attempting to stifle a yawn, she reminded him it might be a good idea to go and check on the dinner, but he didn't respond. He appeared to have gone into a trance like state and was gazing at the wall opposite like a dummy, with a fixed vacant stare. He'd only had one small glass of wine so she was certain he couldn't be drunk and when she checked the bottle, she saw it was only cheap plonk at 5.5%. She couldn't help feeling a bit miffed that he hadn't invested in a better-quality wine to go with their meal, and she wasn't surprised he was still single if he was that much of a cheapskate. Suddenly she felt his arm behind her go rigid followed by violent muscle contractions and then a full-blown seizure which caused him to fall to the floor. Her training told her he was probably safer on the floor and she quickly started moving objects out of the way to stop him from hurting himself. He hadn't mentioned anything about epilepsy, and he drove a car, so she had no idea what was going on. Her hand was shaking as she dialled 999 but the friendly call operator quickly calmed her down and kept her talking while the ambulance was dispatched.

There was a strong smell coming from the kitchen and smoke was pouring out of the oven which triggered the smoke alarms. The noise was ear-piercing, and the concerned operator asked if she needed the fire brigade too. She told her she didn't need the fire brigade, but she needed to switch the oven off and remove the charred remains of the now - cremated beef bourguignon. The operator said the ambulance had been dispatched but she needed the full address including the post code and Chloe couldn't even remember the house number without going to the front door to check. She glanced at Patrick. The seizures had stopped, and although he was still twitchy and unresponsive, he was breathing which was a relief because it meant she didn't have to start CPR;, it also gave her time to run to the front door and blurt out number thirty-seven to the patiently waiting call handler. She put him into the recovery position and waited for the paramedics to arrive. It only took about six minutes, but to Chloe it had seemed for ever, and when they arrived, she was so relieved to see them she had burst into tears. She wasn't prepared for all the questions, but she understood why they needed such a detailed history; the only problem was she couldn't answer any of their questions. What was his full name, what was his date of birth, who was his next of kin, did he have any significant medical history, what medications was he taking? It was only the second time she had met him how could she possibly know the answers to such questions? Somewhat feebly she told them his star sign was Libra so his birthday must be either September or October and they just gave her a blank look. She felt useless but at least she was able to answer their questions about the seizure which they agreed sounded very much like a grand mal fit.

Patrick was starting to wake up, but he was groggy and confused and despite his protests the paramedics insisted on taking him to hospital. Chloe felt a bit guilty leaving him to go alone, but she wasn't family, and she wasn't even his girlfriend, so it wasn't her place to be there with him. By now she was starving so she picked up some fish and chips and ate them on a bench on the sea front. It was chilly outside, but she barely noticed the goose pimples on her skin. Ship navigation lights twinkled out at sea and the sound of the gently lapping waves on the shoreline was calming and peaceful. The date had turned out to be a disaster, but she knew things were going to be much worse for Patrick because if he did have epilepsy he could lose his job, and at the very least, he was likely to lose his driving licence until the results of all investigations were known, and she knew that could take months. She reflected on the evening's events and wondered why her life couldn't be normal. What happened to the boy meets girl and happy ever after stories, and why did they only ever happen to other people and not her? She hoped Patrick would be ok, but she didn't want to hear from him again. They had nothing in common apart from a mutual physical attraction, but it was only lust, and she was glad now it hadn't gone any further. Her mind wandered back to Mel, and she knew for certain that what they'd had together was real, but Mel was supposed to be history, and she was cross with herself for allowing him back in to intrude on her thoughts. She took out her phone and re read his last message. It was cold and vindictive and not a message from the Mel she had grown to know and love, and her eyes filled with tears as the memories of what might have been ran down her cold cheeks.

There were only two guys left on her shortlist of potential suitors and one of them was another police officer. Her gut instinct was telling her to avoid him at all costs, but his profile suggested he was the kind of guy who wore his heart on his sleeve and for some reason it made her want to reach out to him. It seemed she was a sucker for lonely, needy guys but she hoped this one might be different, he seemed different from what he had written in his profile anyway, and she hoped that was a good sign. Tom was the same age as Chloe and widowed with two young daughters. Like Chloe he was forced to combine the demands of a stressful job with the needs of his children single handedly, but his children were much younger than hers, and his wife had tragically died when his youngest daughter was only two years old.

As a nurse Chloe had dealt with death many times, but no one close to her had ever died apart from the family dog, and that her broken her heart. She was only a child when it happened and despite her mum's protests, she insisted on going to the vets with her. He had been poorly for some time, but had deteriorated quickly, and her mum had told her it was time for him to cross the rainbow bridge and go to doggy heaven where all the other doggies would be waiting to welcome him. She hugged him close to the very end and saw the pain disappear from his eyes as he closed them for the very last time. Afterwards her mum had to drag her sobbing through the crowded waiting room while people looked on sympathetically. At the time she had been too young to understand, but she understood now, and although it still made her sad, she knew her mum had done the right thing for him.

In his photo Tom looked tall and rather stocky. She wondered if it was a recent photo because he looked younger than his forty-five years. She thought his kids might keep him young, although she was convinced hers had aged her since reaching the exasperating teenage years. His emails were light-hearted and at times entertaining. He seemed genuine and honest with a level of integrity that so many others lacked. He almost sounded too good to be true, which in itself was troubling, because from her experience if something seemed too good to be true, there was usually a very good reason for it. She scolded herself for being so cynical.

She needed someone to restore her faith in humanity and she needed to believe there were good people in the world, especially police officers because it was their duty to be honourable.

She arranged to meet Tom on the boardwalk at a local quayside boutique shopping and restaurant destination. There were plenty of bars and restaurants to choose from and the views over the marina were exceptionally pretty at this time of the year. There were also a few shops that sold unusual quirky gifts that she used to enjoy browsing around, but they were too expensive for her now. At one time she and Pete would go there every weekend to enjoy a meal and mooch around the shops together, but she hadn't been back since he left so it would do her good.

They had arranged to meet for lunch because the weather was glorious, and Chloe thought it would be nice to make the most of the opportunity of eating al fresco. The car park was huge, so she didn't have the advantage of being able to park up somewhere to try to catch an early glimpse of him, but seeing as she had forgotten to ask what car he was driving it was completely irrelevant anyway. She believed that people who took good care of their cars almost certainly took good care of their homes which probably meant they cared about their appearance too. Physical attraction was as important as an emotional connection because she would never consider having sex with a man she wasn't attracted to. It made her wonder how prostitutes got on when a seedy kerb crawler turned out to be a middle-aged balding man wearing a dirty raincoat and a toupee. Obviously, money was an incentive for these women, but Chloe decided she'd rather starve and live on the streets than give herself willingly to some dirty old man who couldn't get his kicks elsewhere. People accused her of being shallow and to a certain extent they were right, but she certainly wasn't the only woman in the world who believed chemistry and sexual compatibility were essential components of any relationship.

She made her way to the boardwalk entrance, but no one was waiting. She wasn't used to arriving first and generally tried to avoid it in case it made her look desperate. She checked her watch; he was only a couple of minutes late and there was probably a plausible explanation for it. Perhaps he was stuck in traffic or had problems with childcare, but he hadn't phoned to let her know, and that in itself was enough to irritate her. She was a stickler for good timekeeping but not everyone understood her obsession with it; she was working on developing higher tolerance levels, although in her experience there was rarely a convincing excuse for lateness. She thought about going back to her car but that would be futile because she would only have to come straight back, and if he was stood waiting, he would think it was she that was late and that would never do.

Tom hadn't meant to be late. He had meticulously planned this day but his babysitter had let him down at the last minute and he had resorted to bribing his seventeen-year-old niece with the promise of front row tickets to see some boy band in London. He fully intended to phone Chloe to let her know he might be a few minutes late but the optimist in him thought he might still make it on time if he put his foot down. He hadn't expected to run into so much traffic but he felt sure she would understand because she had children of her own, and she would know that when you had kids things didn't always go to plan.

This was his first date since his wife died of breast cancer three years previously, and he was badly out of practice. He hadn't dated in over twenty years, since the day he met his wife Julia, and he truly believed they would be together forever. He wasn't single through choice and when she became ill, he was convinced she would get better. Even when she was transferred to the hospice, he believed she would come home again, but he had been in denial, and saying goodbye to her was the hardest thing he had ever had to do. He didn't think anything could be more difficult than that, but telling his little girls that their mummy had gone to heaven and was now an angel looking over them had been even more heart breaking, especially when the eldest asked if she would be the angel sitting on top of the tree at Christmas. Children's perception of death was so very different to grownups, and as their innocent little faces peered anxiously into his he gave them a huge daddy bear hug and promised he would be there to look after them for ever.

Tom pulled into the car park ten minutes late. Considering the amount of traffic on the road he had made good time. He wasn't in the habit of breaking the speed limit, and he hoped the technology on his new sat nav hadn't let him down by failing to spot any of the speed cameras, otherwise this date was going to prove very pricey, especially as he was expected to foot the bill for the boy band tickets as well.

Chloe's patience was wearing thin, and she kept checking her watch obsessively every few seconds and tutting out loud. He was almost eleven minutes late and she was starting to think she had been stood up. As she looked up, she spotted a guy hurrying towards her from the car park. He was panting and out of breath by the time he reached her, and his face was flushed a deep red colour, beads of sweat were dripping unattractively from his forehead. Tom searched his pockets for a tissue to mop his brow. He could see from the expression on her face that she was annoyed he was late, and just to make a point she kept glancing at her watch. He apologised, but he could see she wasn't listening. She seemed to be staring at him and he wasn't surprised because he had been a bit economical with the truth in his profile and he could tell she was disappointed. He knew he had let himself go a bit since his wife died but he lacked the motivation to do anything about it. If he had been honest in his profile, he would never have been able to pull a girl like Chloe, but it wasn't real because he had lured her here under false pretences and now it looked as if he had humiliated himself even more.

Chloe wasn't sure how long she had been staring at him, but by the look on his face it had been long enough to make him feel uncomfortable and she felt ashamed of herself for being so judgemental. He was very tall which was a bonus, but he was as wide as he was tall, and he reminded her of the fat controller in Thomas the tank engine. His face was well rounded which gave him a youthful appearance but in medical terms he was morbidly obese and clearly unfit, which is why the short walk across the car park had caused him to break out in such a sweat. Tom knew exactly what she was thinking, and he didn't blame her. After Julia died, he sought comfort in food and once he started, he couldn't stop. He knew he was gaining weight because he was struggling to do his uniform up, but he didn't dare stand on the scales in case he broke them. He had a physical fitness test coming up at work and his boss had kindly taken him to one side for a chat because he was concerned he might not pass. If he failed, he risked losing his job but he lacked motivation to do anything and if it wasn't for his kids he would have given up long ago.

Chloe suggested they ate in a bar where most days a pianist played the shiny grand piano that stood proud in the window. There were empty tables outside, but Chloe thought Tom might expire if she forced him to sit in the sun. It seemed a pity as it was a glorious day, but she thought they could always go for a walk after their meal once he'd had a chance to cool down a bit. The pianist was playing a soft slightly melancholy tune and she couldn't help noticing how sad Tom looked. A waitress showed them to a small table for two and Chloe wondered if Tom would be able to squeeze his ample frame into the chair and unbeknown to Chloe, Tom was wondering the same thing. He had been humiliated in the past when he'd tried to ride a rollercoaster with his girls and was asked to step off because they were unable to fasten the safety belt. That alone should have been enough of an incentive for him to change his lifestyle and lose weight, but instead he binged on junk food and retreated back into his lonely man cave to lick his wounds. He promised Julia before she died that he would look after himself and find love again, but how could he possibly love someone else when he no longer loved himself?

Tom had a hearty appetite and there were several tempting dishes on the menu but as Chloe ordered a healthy Caesar salad, he felt obliged to do the same. He was hoping it might turn out to be the incentive he needed to push start his new healthy eating plan and turn his life around so Julia would be proud of him, and he surprised himself by thoroughly enjoying the salad. Unexpectedly Chloe found herself enjoying Tom's company. He was very knowledgeable on a wide range of subjects and once he relaxed, he had a great sense of humour. He wasn't the type of guy she would usually date but he was kind and caring and if he were to lose some weight she thought she could actually be attracted to him too.

After Julia's death Tom used his dry humour as a coping strategy to mask his sadness. Making other people laugh made him feel good about himself for a short while at least, and he had little else to offer women apart from about nineteen stone of total devotion. He knew instantly Chloe wasn't the right woman for him because he saw the disappointment in her eyes when he came running across the car park. Like most other women she couldn't see past his weight and if she couldn't accept him for the man he was now, why would he want her to be a part of his future. He also had his girls to consider, and she hadn't even asked after them. He wasn't looking for another mum for them because Julia would always be their mother, but they would soon get to that awkward age where they needed a mother figure in their lives, and he needed help with that part of their growing up. He made up his mind he was going to change, not for Chloe, or for any other woman for that matter, but for himself and for his two little girls who needed him. He was going to be the man that Julia had fallen in love with, and the man she was proud to call her husband. No woman would ever replace her, but one day he hoped he would be able to find the same kind of unconditional love that they had shared, and he knew that wouldn't be with the woman he was looking at right now. He was a good man, and she was an attractive woman, but it would end there. To her credit he knew she could easily have run the other way when she saw him coming, but she hadn't, and for that he was thankful, because having lunch with her had boosted his self-esteem and given him the confidence to make changes and move forward with his life.

During the meal she had laughed at his jokes but there were times when she seemed preoccupied, and on one or two occasions she had called him Mel. She didn't notice the slip up and he chose not to correct her because it was obvious to him that she was very much in love with this guy, and he hoped for her sake that one day they would be reunited. Life was too short for regrets; he was living proof of that. After the meal, Chloe suggested they took a walk along the quayside and Tom agreed because a walk would give him the opportunity to say what he needed to say away from the eavesdroppers in the restaurant.

The sun was shining and as they strolled along the quayside Chloe could feel the warm rays on her back. She'd only had one small glass of wine, but she was feeling a bit giggly and lightheaded. She glanced at Tom's huge frame next to her and she felt comfortable and safe but there were no fireworks, and she felt an unexpected surge of disappointment. Tom sensed her dilemma and knew the time had come to let her off the hook. He knew she probably didn't want to see him again, but it would spare her the need to invent an excuse not to. He took her gently by the arm and turned her round to face him, and for a moment Chloe thought he was going to kiss her, and to her surprise, she felt slightly disappointed when he didn't. To Tom's dismay she started to cry. She didn't know why she was crying but she was feeling rejected all over again and this time it was definitely her own fault. She had judged him on physical appearance alone, and even though he was right when he said he wasn't the man for her, his words cut deep into her soul because the man who was right for her had made it clear he didn't want her anymore. Tom hugged her because he understood loss and rejection better than most. He didn't know why she was so unhappy, but it was obvious to him that she was in a bad place right now and he suspected it had something to do with a man called Mel. Chloe needed that hug more than Tom realised, and she knew she would always be eternally grateful to him for teaching her a very important lesson. Somehow, he had managed to dump her, yet at the same time he had restored her faith in humanity, and it took a very special person to be able to do that. He had let her down gently because he was a big man with a big heart and one day another lucky lady would have the honour of becoming his wife, but it wouldn't be her. Meeting Tom had forced her into a different way of thinking. She had always been too quick to judge, which is why she had ostracised the majority of Pete's family, but if she wanted to find happiness she knew she would have to change, she just wasn't sure how to do it. She had put up protective barriers for so long, and on the one occasion when she let her guard down, she had been left badly hurt.

There was only one guy left on her short list so she decided to start a new search and see if there were any fresh faces among them. As she scrolled down, the same old familiar faces stared back at her so she assumed they must be as unlucky in love as her. She promised herself she wouldn't judge, but looking at some of their profiles it was hardly surprising they were still single. When she'd written her own profile, she made sure she put time and effort into constructing a well written synopsis of herself, because she wanted to attract the right type of man, but that theory had already been blown right out the window given the standard of her suitors so far. She had no idea why she was still making excuses for Mel, but somehow it made it easier for her to believe he hadn't deliberately set out to hurt her. He was obviously confused and had used the dating site as bait to win back his wife, and she had been the unlucky guinea pig used in the experiment. His conduct had been far from exemplary but deep down she still loved him, and she wasn't ready to write him off as one of the bad guys just yet.

While she was scrolling, a message popped up from a local guy called Steve. There was something about him that seemed familiar but she couldn't pinpoint what it was; although the town was quite small and it was possible she had seen him around somewhere. He was completely bald, but that didn't put her off as she secretly thought bald men were quite sexy, providing they didn't try to cover it up with one of those ridiculous looking toupee things. Steve lived no more than a mile away from her with his dog and two pet snakes. She wasn't keen on snakes, but they were better than spiders, so she tried not to dwell on it too much. She reflected back to the time when she'd had a horrifying experience with an entire army of banana spiders on the 'Weeki Wachee' river in Florida while attempting to navigate 7.4 terrifying miles in a ridiculously flimsy Kayak. She and a friend were away on holiday together and it was their last day, so the river trip was meant to be a relaxing experience, mingling with the wildlife, and watching the manatee swim in the clear shallow waters. There was no mention in the brochure of doing battle with spiders the size of dinner plates, and when the ordeal was finally over, she had demanded a full refund from the grinning yank standing on the riverbank. Of course, she hadn't got it because somewhere in the small print it said to expect spiders at certain times of the year, and it just happened to be that time of the year, and after that she vowed never to leave England again.

Steve suggested they meet up for a walk in the woods with their dogs which seemed harmless enough. Norman loved his walks, and he loved having other dogs to play with so it was a plan that would suit everyone. Steve said his dog was friendly, but it didn't look very friendly when he got it out of the car. Norman was franticly wagging his little stump of a tail and Steve's dog was growling menacingly at him. Steve said it was okay because his dog was just being protective, but Chloe decided to err on the side of caution and keep Norman on a lead just in case. The woods were lovely at this time of year and the trees provided shelter from the warm summer sun with their expanding canopy of green foliage. A small stream meandered gently through the woodland winding its way through the trees before disappearing underground somewhere. During the winter months the stream was full to the brim and the water flowed forcefully but today only a small trickle lined the dry, rocky bed. Norman usually made a beeline for the stream and was tugging frantically at his lead. He loved prancing around in the water, pouncing hectically on floating leaves and Chloe was certain that if he were a kid, he would be the class clown. Steve's dog appeared to have lost interest, so she decided to let Norman off the lead. As predicted, he headed straight for the water so they decided to stop for a bit and sit down on a nearby bench where she could keep an eye on him.

Steve hadn't said much about himself, and she still hadn't worked out why he seemed so familiar. She asked him about his hobbies, and he told her he was a car enthusiast and owned an authentic American police car which he entered into competitions and took to shows around the country. He had the NYPD uniform to match and ideally he was looking for a female partner who was willing to dress up so they could play cops and robbers together. Chloe hated dressing up even as a kid, so there was no way she was going to indulge his fantasy and dress up now. She could just imagine what her kids would have to say about it, and she knew she would never be able to live it down. She had seen the car around town because he used it for school prom nights, and for the occasional hen or stag do, but she couldn't help thinking he had to be a bit of an anorak to be doing the full 'Starsky and

Hutch' thing at his age.

He hoped she would share his enthusiasm, but her silence suggested otherwise. He knew she liked cars because he had admired her shiny black BMW in the surgery car park on a number of occasions, but now it was all beginning to feel a bit awkward. He should have been used to it by now because other women had reacted in much the same way as Chloe, and some had even gone as far as accusing him of being some kind of kinky sex fiend which is why he always worried about mentioning it. As far as he was concerned, he came as a package complete with car and uniform, in much the same way as most women came with kids and a string of ex's who had broken their hearts.

Norman broke the silence by bounding enthusiastically back to Chloe which caused Steve's not so friendly dog to growl again. He'd had enough of the stream and was ready to move on to the next adventure. Chloe felt much the same. It was time to continue her journey and when they reached the entrance, she and Steve said their inevitable polite goodbyes to each other before walking off in opposite directions.

Chloe sighed as she walked away and glanced down at Norman trotting contently by her side. She gave him a playful pat on the head and he responded with an approving lick of her hand. He really did love his human and their daily walks together were the highlight of his life, but he could tell she was sad on some days, and that made him feel sad too.

Her 'just have a bit of fun' strategy didn't seem to be working and, with just the one guy left on the short list, Chloe wasn't feeling very optimistic. His name was James, and although she didn't yet know it, he would broaden her horizons and open her mind to a whole new world which would force her to reflect on her decisions and make a difficult choice.

James

James was the same age as Chloe, and an Aquarius too, which according to her astrology book made them compatible. The book was written by someone who went by the name of 'Mystic Mabel' and according to her kids, it was nothing but a load of twaddle. Chloe knew she should have ditched it long ago, but her mum had brainwashed her with her superstitious beliefs all of her life and it was difficult to ignore.

James lived in the north of the county, which she reasoned was far enough away in case he turned out to be another sociopath. He worked as a head gardener for the National Trust and lived with a ginger tom cat aptly named Garfield due to its love of food, after he chose to adopt him as his human. She liked the idea that the cat had adopted James, and not the other way around, because in her experience cats were extremely fussy creatures and from the sound of him, this cat had chosen well.

James thought himself to be a good person, but he was unlucky in love and had never found the right girl to marry him. He had proposed to a girl once when he was in his early twenties, but she had turned him down because she said they were too young, and she wanted to travel and see the world. A few months later he found out she was shacked up with some American Indian tribe in Alaska, and in the years that followed no one else came along. There was a time when he'd wanted a family of his own, but he felt he was a bit too old and set in his ways for that now. He was happy to settle for a good woman and his cat, even though he considered himself to be more of a dog person. Ideally, he was looking for a woman around the same age as himself and he knew she would probably already have children, but the idea of a ready-made family didn't put him off, and he rather liked the idea of having some little people around to spoil.

He'd turned to internet dating after exhausting the club scene. He'd had some fun and met plenty of young ladies to boost his ego, but most were fashion conscious bimbos, young enough to be his daughter, who spent the majority of their time in the toilet giggling with their mates, and reapplying their lippy, and that wasn't what he was looking for.

In her emails, Chloe had mentioned a liking for the outdoors, so he thought it might be nice to meet up at a local heritage site and beauty spot. It was slightly more local to her than it was to him, but he didn't mind driving, and as an employee of the company he could get them free entry to the picturesque house and gardens. He planned to surprise her with a picnic on the lawn and he hoped he might impress her with some of his homemade treats. He enjoyed cooking and had become something of a dab hand in the kitchen after inheriting his late mother's cookbooks. He had very nearly given them all away to a charity shop but changed his mind at the last minute and decided to try out a few of the recipes, discovering that he was surprisingly good at it.

Chloe hated cooking and always found it a chore. She only ever made a real effort at Christmas when her mum came for dinner and expected a traditional meal with a fresh turkey and all the trimmings. Pete had always helped with the cooking but now he was gone she relied on take outs and ready meals, and if it wasn't for the kids she knew she would probably live on little more than cereal and chocolate milk shake. She approved of James's idea of meeting at the heritage site. Although it was only a few miles from her home, she had never been there before, and it was something that had been on her to do list since the kids were little.

Chloe was tall for a woman but James's six-foot six muscular physique positively dwarfed her and she was instantly attracted to him. James considered himself lucky to have a job that kept him fit and well-toned because it meant he didn't have to waste time and money going to the gym. He'd had a trial run at the gym a few years back for something to do, but he'd immediately felt out of place in his jogging bottoms amongst all the Lycra-clad gym goers and he never went back. James was equally impressed. He liked tall girls, but they seemed to be in short supply, and at least when (and if) they kissed, he wouldn't have to stoop down and strain his back. He was keen to start exploring the gardens so impulsively he took her by the hand and she didn't pull away. She could already feel an emotional connection with him, and like Tom, the portly police officer, there was something about him that made her feel safe.

James had worked in these gardens many times and was proud of the manicured lawns and colourful flowers which were refreshingly fragrant at this time of the year. Hidden among the blooms was a man-made pond which James and a few of his co-workers had dug themselves. It had taken days of blood, sweat and tears but the finished product, which also boasted a small waterfall, blended skilfully with the environment, and was now a haven for nature and wildlife. A few benches had been strategically placed so visitors could take full advantage of the pond and listen to the soft sound of the water drizzling from the waterfall onto the rocks below. It was a romantic spot and a place where James had seen many lovers embrace and exchange passionate kisses. James hoped that one day he would find his soul mate too, so he could bring her to this exact same spot and ask her to marry him. He looked wistfully at Chloe and wondered if sometime in the future she might turn out to be that woman. He hoped so, but she had taken a long time to respond to his first email, and he couldn't help wondering if she had been holding back – he hoped her heart didn't belong to someone else. Chloe was captivated by the splendour and tranquillity of the gardens. She hadn't felt this relaxed in a long time and she took a moment to immerse herself in the beauty around her. James gave her a friendly nudge to get her attention and bring her back to the present. He could see she was preoccupied, and he somehow suspected she'd experienced deep sadness at some stage in her life, but it was too soon for him to start asking questions.

James was holding up a wicker basket and pointing to a

spot he had earmarked for their picnic and Chloe's emotions got the better of her. She couldn't believe a man would go to so much effort to make a date so special for her, and although she tried hard not to, she started to cry. James hugged her gently at first, and then more fiercely as she sobbed agonisingly on his shoulder. He wanted to protect her, and although he still had no idea what had happened to her, he knew it must have been something very bad. Long after her tears were spent, she continued to cling to him. She found comfort in his touch and took pleasure in the smell of his freshly laundered tee shirt, which was by now sopping wet, having taken the brunt of her tears. As she lifted her head off his shoulder, he softly cupped her face in his hands and searched her eyes for answers. He planted a gentle kiss on her forehead and within minutes they were kissing passionately on the picnic rug that James had carefully laid out, oblivious to the stares from stunned passers-by. With the ice well and truly broken, the tears were quickly forgotten, and they spent the rest of the day laughing and frolicking around like any other loved up couple. The physical attraction between them was undeniable, but it was early days still, and Chloe convinced herself it had to be lust. She didn't want him thinking she was easy; she'd got carried away in the moment and that's all there was to it. His kiss had aroused her physically, but her mind had already wandered back to Mel, and she felt guilty for betraying him. James thought he'd sensed some hesitation after their kiss and, although brief, it had planted a little seed of doubt. He felt sure he could love her…if only she would let him. James sensed her hesitation and change in mood, and he knew the moment was lost. He knew he could easily love her if only she would let him but he was competing with an unknown entity and that left him at a distinct disadvantage.

Mel was feeling sorry for himself. It had been several months since Claire had sent the spiteful text message from his phone and there had been no word from Chloe since. He didn't know why he was surprised, after all Claire had made it clear she wasn't to make contact again, but Chloe was no shrinking violet, and despite her strong- minded spirit, he knew she had enough pride not to make a fool of herself. Claire had relaxed her control over Mel's phone because as far as she was concerned the game was over, but she was drinking more than ever and was too wasted most of the time to even care. There had been no winners in Claire's little game, and Mel had been a complete fool to think he could make their marriage work. His ignorance had cost him dearly and he had lost the one person who truly loved him. He'd thought about driving over to Chloe's house many times, but he was afraid of rejection. He knew there could even be another man in her life by now, but he preferred not to think about it because winning her back was all that mattered.

It was Saturday night and Chloe was looking forward to spending it with James. He had invited her over to his house for dinner followed by a film of her choice, and she was feeling optimistic about the evening ahead. She liked thrillers and had chosen a creepy one so she could snuggle up close to him on the sofa during the scary bits. She vowed to overcome the hesitation she'd showed after their kiss at the heritage site, and after all the effort he'd made, she wanted to make it up to him; she wasn't ready to tell him about Mel yet. She didn't know if it was possible to be in love with two men at the same time, but if it was, she had read somewhere that she should choose the second one, because if the first one had been good enough, it wouldn't have been necessary to go looking for a second one in the first place. On paper it looked straightforward, but this wasn't a Mills and Boon textbook romance, although she wished she was guaranteed a similarly predictable happy ending. She desperately wanted her own happy ending, and if the theory were true, then it wasn't too far away with James, but perhaps it wasn't as easy as that when her heart still belonged to Mel... although sometimes she really wished it didn't. She took a final look in the mirror before leaving. She was no supermodel, but she was stylish and still in pretty good shape for a woman approaching middle age. Mel's loss was most definitely James's gain, providing she could rid herself of the guilt when he tried to get close to her again.

James was thrilled when Chloe accepted his invitation to dinner. He was worried he might have gone too far by kissing her on their first date, but it had seemed so natural, and to be fair she had responded with more enthusiasm than he had anticipated. He loved spontaneity, and preferred not to plan anything, but he wanted tonight to be perfect so he had it all planned down to the very last detail. James lived no more than ten miles away from the evil Alan, and Chloe shuddered at the memory of him and wished now she had been brave enough to report him to the police. She had been at her most vulnerable, and he'd preyed on her naivety by telling her the police wouldn't believe her story, although it seemed obvious to her now that he had said that to protect himself. She had kept quiet to protect herself, and the remains of her dignity which he had destroyed over the course of one terrifying weekend. He should have gone to prison for what he had done to her, although she would have been more than happy to see him surgically castrated without an anaesthetic first. He was a dangerous man, and as far as she knew he was still free to rape and terrorise other women who her silence had failed to protect. For a moment she felt guilty, and mentally chastised herself for being so pathetic and weak. It wasn't too late to come forward now, her counsellor had told her that there was no time limit when it came to reporting sexual offences such as rape,, but she couldn't face the whole world thinking the same as Alan, that she was nothing more than a cheap and dirty tramp who had naively expected a weekend away for nothing. If it had got as far as court, and somehow she doubted that it would, she felt certain the jury would vote in Alan's favour and believe she was nothing but a cheap prostitute holding a grudge. She couldn't face more humiliation, so she decided not to go through with it. She'd put it to the back of her mind... until now that was. Being less than ten miles from his home was too close for comfort, and she found herself nervously scanning every car on the road for his unmarked police car. If one tried to stop her, she didn't know what she would do, but she knew she wouldn't stop just in case it was him. It was of course unlikely to be him because he was far too busy solving murders and other major crimes like rape to mingle with the traffic cops, and she cringed at the irony of the situation. A flashing light followed by an impatient siren suddenly caught her attention, and she was relieved to see it was just an ambulance coming from the opposite direction. She was too nervous for her own good and made up her mind it was time to get a grip on things again and take back control of her life.

James lived in a small modern mid terrace house which was ample size for him and the cat. He hoped to be able to move one day to somewhere more rural, but for the time being the house served its purpose and was close to work and local amenities. If and when he moved, he wanted a house with a big garden big enough for a dog. He knew Chloe had a dog called Norman who sounded fun, but a bit crazy, and like his owner, he was looking forward to getting to know him. If it wasn't for Garfield who hated dogs with a vengeance, he would have suggested Chloe brought him along tonight but he feared poor Norman would not fare well if he was unlucky enough to be confronted by his cat whose Jekyll and Hyde personality was activated at the very sight of a dog.

James saw Chloe's car pull up outside and he felt the butterflies in his stomach. He used to get the exact same feeling as a young boy when he came downstairs on Christmas morning to find heaps of presents under the tree from Santa. He had believed in Santa until he went to secondary school where he became the laughing stock of the class. Kids could be cruel, and he had never been able to completely forgive his mum for not putting the record straight earlier. When the doorbell rang, he couldn't resist greeting her with an enthusiastic bear hug which momentarily took her breath away, although she was secretly delighted to feel loved and wanted again. She needed love, but thoughts of intimacy brought back horrific memories of the rape, and it also brought back painful memories of rejection, first by Pete and later by Mel. She wondered if she was destined to live the rest of her life as a frigid spinster, but she knew the past was no place to live, and maybe James could provide the ticket to her future, if only she would let him. She had definitely made progress; for months she had been in denial and blamed herself for allowing so many bad things to happen to her. She didn't think she could ever forgive Alan, and she would certainly never forget, but she was working towards acceptance as a way of moving forward with her life.

Chloe was feeling hungry and the dinner smelled good. Homemade lamb stew with dumplings was on the menu and James wanted it to be perfect. He handed Chloe a glass of wine while he finished off in the kitchen and she settled down on the sofa with one of the plumpest cats she had ever seen. Garfield wasn't used to sharing his end of the sofa with anyone else, but he was prepared to compromise providing she continued to indulge him by softly stroking his head. As she moved her hand to his chin, he got the distinct whiff of dog, and he leapt off the sofa hissing and spitting with his hair standing up on end ready to do battle. After looking around and realising there was no dog, Garfield strolled off into the kitchen to find James. He liked the smell of what was in the oven, and he looked at his empty bowl in disgust. James always spoiled him which is why he'd chosen him as his adoptive human, and he knew if he hung around long enough a few tasty morsels would find their way into his bowl. Meanwhile in the lounge, Chloe was thankful to have escaped the unprovoked attack from the possessed moggy without a single scratch, and was glad now she had chosen to have a dog.

James called from the kitchen. The dinner was ready, and he was keen to show off his culinary skills. Garfield was sitting patiently by his empty bowl feigning disinterest, but he knew his adopted human James wouldn't forget about him. Chloe thought of Norman. He was a terrible scrounge and had no table manners whatsoever. If he was with them now he'd be sitting right next to her, drooling impatiently, and staring sadly at her with those puppy dog eyes of his, waiting for the leftovers. Norman loved mealtimes. Ever since he was a puppy the kids had discreetly fed him their unwanted sprouts from under the table. Unfortunately for them the sprouts exacerbated his colitis and after numerous visits to the vet, the kids were ordered to eat them themselves which they claimed was nothing short of child abuse.

The meal was delicious and put Chloe's cooking skills to shame. At school they called it domestic science and Chloe hated it because her dishes never turned out the same as everyone else's and there was always an enormous pile of washing up at the end of it too. Chloe was eternally grateful to the inventor of the dishwasher because it meant she no longer had to be a slave to the kitchen sink, but James's kitchen wasn't big enough for a dishwasher so they would have to wash up together, which Chloe thought might be fun. Under normal circumstances Chloe would never have described washing up as fun, but she'd had a few glasses of wine and was feeling a bit tipsy, and she thought she might tease James by indulging in a spot of playful mischief with the soap suds. James was delighted to see Chloe so relaxed and was more than happy to oblige, and before long they were both covered in foam and bubbles. Garfield looked on in disgust. He was usually fed by now and he didn't appreciate all the joviality. He'd had to move from his favourite spot because he was getting covered in water, and no self-respecting cat deliberately wanted to get wet. Within minutes, all was forgiven because James popped a few chunks of left over lamb into his bowl. He'd sneaked in a few vegetables too, but Garfield had no intention of eating them. James often tried to mix in some veg, but he was strictly a fresh fish and meat only type cat, and if James wanted him to hang around, he'd do well to remember that fact.

The after-dinner plan was to retire to the lounge to watch a film, but after the frolics at the sink Chloe was feeling surprisingly amorous and was ready to take things with James to the next level. James wanted that too, but he needed to be sure it was what she really wanted and not just the drink talking, so somewhat reluctantly he suggested they had a coffee instead. Chloe tried hard to hide her disappointment. She had foolishly misjudged the situation and could guess what he was thinking. The alcohol had gone to her head and made her a bit playful, but she knew what she wanted, and it certainly wasn't coffee because she only ever drank tea anyway. James was already back in the kitchen putting the kettle on. Maybe she would drink coffee just this once. She hoped the caffeine would reach her brain quickly and prompt her to say something more sensible. She had been a bit reckless because he hadn't mentioned anything about her staying the night, yet she'd already drunk too much to drive. It had been wrong of her to assume and now she was faced with a dilemma. James returned to the lounge with two steaming mugs of coffee. The night was still young and things had moved faster than he'd expected. He liked to warm up slowly, but it seemed Chloe was on fast boil, and there was no need to rush. By the looks of it they had all night - he couldn't possibly allow her to drive home -,but he didn't want to take advantage, so he thought it only gentlemanly to offer her the use of his spare room for the night. Chloe's reaction was a mixture of frustration and relief. At least she no longer had to worry about driving home, but she feared her impulsive act of premature promiscuity may have driven James away from her forever. It was her own fault; the alcohol had loosened her inhibitions, and, as a result, she had unintentionally turned the perfect evening with a lovely man into an audition for an episode of 'Loose Women.'

James was secretly hoping she wouldn't take up the offer of the spare room. He was only wanting to slow the pace down a bit, but instead it had ground to a complete halt. The silence between them was uncomfortable, but he had a plan up his sleeve and was quietly confident that the evening could still be salvaged. He reached for the scrabble board, it had never let him down yet, and if his thinking was correct, they would soon be back on track.

Chloe hadn't played scrabble for years and had become bored with it after her mother insisted they play it every day during the school holidays. Her private school education had enhanced her vocabulary in more ways than one, and it wasn't long before she had become an unforgiving opponent. Chloe thrived on a challenge, and her competitive mind had no room for losers. She hadn't predicted they would end up sitting in front of a scrabble board together, but this was an unexpected opportunity to redeem herself and she intended to make the most of it. Hopefully, James had been a boy scout because that way he would 'be prepared' for anything, and she planned to annihilate him. James smiled to himself because this was unlikely to be like any other game of scrabble she had played previously. Words could be fun, and they could also be extremely powerful, and he planned to use this game to his advantage. He hadn't been brave enough to open up and tell her how he really felt, but he could spell the words out on the board, and he hoped they would speak for themselves. It was a bit risky, but he was certain she had a sense of humour and he hoped she would feel safe enough with him to join in the fun. Under normal circumstances James would never have dreamt of cheating but these were exceptional circumstances, and he needed the advantage of a head start. To him it wasn't about winning the game, it was about winning the heart of a woman who he thought he might grow to love. If his plan was to work, he needed to go first so he sneaked a quick glimpse into the bag of letters in the hope he might find one of the two blank tiles… he was in luck. According to scrabble rules, a blank tile beats the letter A when drawing for the first player so Chloe couldn't beat him unless she managed to draw the remaining blank tile which he thought was unlikely to happen. Chloe liked to go first because the first player automatically benefitted from a double word score, so she was disappointed when she drew the letter T out of the bag, and things went from bad to worse when James drew miraculously drew a blank tile. She was sure she had seen him peeping into the bag, , and was ready to demand a reselection, but she didn't think James was the type to cheat so she had let it go. When she was a kid, she would sulk for hours if she couldn't go first, but on this occasion, she decided to be more gracious about it. She had already shown herself up once with her overly suggestive after dinner behaviour, and she didn't want him thinking she threw tantrums like an immature schoolgirl too. It was only the first round after all, so there would be plenty of time to catch up. James was delighted his plan had worked. All he needed now were seven letters to make a meaningful word, and as luck would have it, he had the letter X to help boost his score. In the centre of the board, he spelled out the word 'sexy' which, with the double word score, credited him with a whopping twenty-eight points. Chloe paid little attention to the word because her goal was to win, and in order to get ahead she needed to exceed his score. She had her eye on the letter X; using that would gain her an additional eight points, and that could make the difference between winning and losing the game. Her letter selection wasn't to her liking, but she was determined to use them resourcefully, so she used the existing X on the board to spell out the word 'exact' to equal James's score. James used Chloe's letter C to spell the word seduce which only gave him nine more points, and then Chloe added a D to it to make the words seduced and drunk which added a hefty thirty-eight more points to her score. James wasn't sure if her choice of words were purely coincidental, or whether she had cottoned on to playing his version of the game. Although it was only worth eight points James decided to test the water by using the letter K to make the word 'kiss' to see how Chloe would respond. They were still in the early stages of the game which he knew could go on for hours unless there was a good reason to stop. A physical kiss would be much more fun and, as an added bonus, he felt pretty confident it wouldn't just stop there. Chloe hesitated briefly. She could feel her cheeks burning, and as he moved closer, she could feel his warm breath on her skin. As he gently stroked her unruly hair away from her face their noses brushed softly together, and her body tingled with anticipation. They had kissed before on their first date at the heritage site, but today something was different. She suspected he was falling in love with her and given time she thought she could probably love him too, but he deserved more than she was able to give right now. It would be grossly unfair of her to expect him to wait with no guarantee of the happy ever after he so desperately wanted. He made her feel safe, and in her mind, she could almost imagine them growing old and grey together, but he would never be her fairy tale prince; her heart still belonged to another man. Chloe felt a pang of guilt. Mel wasn't worthy of her love, and he didn't justify a place in her heart. She had tried hard to let him go, but she knew she hadn't tried hard enough because she always found an excuse to keep his memory alive, and in the meantime, she had let this lovely man believe they could have a future together. It hadn't been deliberate, and alcohol had played a big part by addling her already confused brain, but somehow, she had to make amends, and sleeping with James wasn't the solution and would only complicate matters more. She craved love and affection, and James was offering it to her on a plate, but it would never be enough, because as much as she hated herself for it, she was still in love with Mel.

James was the right guy for someone, but he wasn't the

right guy for her, and she owed it to him to tell him the truth even though she knew it wasn't what he wanted to hear. She tried to reason that it was better to tell him now than in six months' time but even with the best intentions the truth hurt, and Chloe knew she would never forget the sad haunted look in his eyes when she told him it was not going to work and that it was over between them.

She laid awake in James's spare room most of the night. Her heart ached for him, but she convinced herself her decision was for the best. Tomorrow was another day and although it had been over three months since Mel had walked out of her life, she had to try one more time before she could accept their relationship was doomed and over for good. She felt both excited and apprehensive at the prospect of hearing from Mel again but mentally she prepared herself for rejection. If he had wanted her, he would surely have made contact by now, and she risked getting herself branded as a homewrecker or worse still, a resentful bunny boiler. She had to know one way or another, and like her mum always told her, 'Only sticks and stones could break her bones.' She didn't agree with the next part of the rhyme because words could hurt her very much, and Mel's last words to her had not only hurt her but had broken her heart too. She looked at his last message again,, Mel was a bit of an idiot but he wasn't cruel, and she strongly suspected the message had been sent by Claire. There was only one way to find out, but she would have to pull on her big girl pants and be brave to know for sure.

James was awake in the room next door. His gut instincts had been right, but he hadn't expected it to end so abruptly, and he certainly hadn't been ready for it to end tonight. He respected her honesty, but letting her go wasn't easy. He hoped this Mel guy was worth all the heartache although he already suspected he wasn't, but this was something Chloe needed to find out for herself. It would have been easy for her to keep her options open and string him along for a bit longer while she waited for her prince charming to make up his mind, and he was grateful she'd spared him that ordeal. At the very least she needed some closure so she could move on to the next chapter in her life because it seemed to him, she had been stuck on the same page for too long now.

The following morning Chloe and James exchanged an uneasy goodbye at the door. It couldn't have been more different to the enthusiastic welcome from the previous evening, and she felt sad for what might have been. They behaved like two embarrassed strangers, and although James closed the door behind her with a heavy heart, he also believed he had dodged a bullet. She had promised him she would keep in touch, but James suspected it was just something to say at a time when words failed them both. He didn't think he wanted her to stay in touch, after all he still had his pride, and much like her he wasn't prepared to settle for second best either. As he waved goodbye to her from the window, he hoped she would live her dream, but only fairy tales had happy endings, and from what she'd told him, although Mel was good at playing the role of Prince Charming, she was never going to be his Cinderella.

An Old
Flame Reignites

Chloe was feeling tired during the drive home. She had been awake most of the night, but the initial adrenaline rush had been replaced by feelings of apprehension and anxiety, and a familiar fear of rejection was starting to creep back in. She made a choice which seemed right at the time, so why did it suddenly feel so wrong now? She tried hard to convince herself that it was normal to feel this way, and her anxiety was because she was moving out of her comfort zone back into unknown territory. James had been her comfort zone, and if she had been brave enough to let him in, she felt certain he could have been her rock too. Why did she always tread the most difficult path? It seemed she was her own worst enemy when it came to men, although other aspects of her life were equally problematic at times too. A life with James could have been cosy like being wrapped up in a comfy duvet, but instead, she had chosen to lie on a bed of nails, and she had no one but herself to blame for the consequences. The only thing that could make things right now was a successful reunion with Mel. She had sensed James's misgivings about Mel, but he had been too much of a gentleman to tell her. If she and Mel could work things out it would help validate her decision to leave James, but she no longer felt as brave as she did last night, and her tired and tormented sleep- deprived brain was flooded with doubts. Chloe decided she had to get some sleep before contacting Mel just in case she changed her mind when she woke up. She didn't think she would, but making major decisions when you were tired was nearly as bad as making major decisions when you were angry, and she didn't want to let her heart rule her head. She would have to do it before he finished work though, because otherwise she might have Claire to deal with and that would be catastrophic.

Chloe slept for a few hours, but it was a fitful sleep plagued by vivid dreams and sporadic episodes of tossing and turning. Claire featured heavily in her dreams which Chloe thought was probably a bad omen. She had never met Claire, but something was telling Chloe that she wouldn't go down without a fight, and she briefly wondered whether she was a strong enough opponent. People thought she was tough because she was good at wearing a hard outer shell, but she wasn't as tough as everyone thought; although it would never do for Claire to know that. She picked up her phone and stared blankly at the screen for what seemed like an eternity but realistically was probably no more than a few minutes. She had come too far to back out now, and her hands were visibly shaking as she cautiously typed out what she hoped Mel would see as a light hearted casual message. She quickly pressed the send button before she had a chance to change her mind, and then panicked and switched the phone off because she was afraid she might not like what he had to say. She knew she couldn't leave her phone switched off for ever, but she would need some Dutch courage before switching it back on, and she decided a large glass of wine wouldn't go amiss.

Mel was in a meeting at work when he felt his phone vibrate in his pocket. He was in no hurry to check it because Claire was in the habit of sending him malicious drunken texts when she surfaced from bed around lunch time, and he wasn't in the mood for dealing with her right now. He knew he should check it just in case it was urgent; Claire had recently been diagnosed with alcohol related liver disease and was in fact quite ill. Claire however was in denial and had proceeded to hurl verbal abuse at the alarmed doctor who had sensitively tried to address her drinking habits again. He would check it later. He needed a few more hours to hide away and take refuge from the barrage of abuse that Claire was likely to hurl at him. Work was his safe haven, and it was also the only place where there was any element of normality left in his life. He frequently joined in with the daily banter when his work colleagues were talking about their wives and girlfriends because it reminded him of the life he had shared with Claire before she chose vodka over him. He thought he had perfected the art of deception as far as his work colleagues were concerned, and his make belief world had almost become real to him. He was careful to avoid work social events, but with three kids there was always a plausible excuse for his absence. However, with the imminent retirement of his business partner he was going to have to devote more time to the company and this would include his presence at corporate events. Mel tried to put it to the back of his mind because just the thought of taking Claire to the work Christmas party filled him with horror. There wouldn't be many other wives capable of drinking the men under the table, but he knew Claire would be in her element. With Chloe it would have been so very different, and he knew he would never have had to worry about her showing him up. Sadly, it looked like Chloe was gone for good, but her memory lived on in his heart, and he knew he would never forget her. He'd been convinced she would try and make contact with him again, but as the days grew into weeks and the weeks grew into months, his hopes of a successful reunion with her had started to fade. In some ways her silence was a blessing because with Claire's worsening health problems he wasn't in a position to just walk away, and he couldn't expect Chloe to shoulder that responsibility too. Their marriage was over, but there was no one else to take care of her, and whether he liked it or not she was still his wife, and he still felt responsible for her. If Chloe made contact it would create a huge dilemma, but at least he would have someone to share the burden with.

Chloe was disappointed. She had sent the message over an hour ago and had received a delivery report, but Mel still hadn't responded. She willed her phone to beep or ring but it remained frustratingly quiet, and she was certain that meant one of only two things, and neither possibility was good. Either Mel really did hate her, or Claire had got hold of his phone again and was busy plotting her revenge. She wondered if Claire had insisted he changed his mobile number, but her message had definitely gone to someone and she was grateful now that it hadn't been a bit saucy or suggestive, just in case whoever it was got the wrong idea.

Her cheeks flushed a dark shade of crimson as she looked back at some of the past text correspondence with Mel. She had considered deleting the messages just in case she ever lost her phone, but to delete them would be like deleting him, and how could she just erase someone who had impacted on her life so profoundly? She smiled broadly; whenever she thought about Mel her imagination ran riot. She had a vivid imagination courtesy of his adventurous demands in the bedroom department. He had certainly taught her a thing or two about sex and there definitely was no room to be coy. Prior to meeting Mel she always thought sex was a bit overrated, and during the early stages of their relationship she had felt self-conscious at times, but it wasn't long before she was a willing participant; she was even able to surprise him with a few ideas of her own. She no longer had any hang ups or inhibitions where sex was concerned because she was utterly and totally in love with him, and she believed he was in love with her too. He had taken away the demons from her past and she was confident he held the key to her future, at least she'd thought he did until the day he went running back to his wife.

In her mind she'd had everything planned down to the last detail, even venturing into bridal shops to choose a gown for their anticipated big day. She had managed to find an elegant vintage style ivory dress with a lace overlay, which made her feel feminine and girly. Encouraged by the enthusiastic sales assistant, and without really thinking, she had stupidly put a deposit down on it. She had been certain that Mel was going to propose to her, but when it became evident that he wasn't, she was forced to come up with some feeble excuse and lost both her deposit and the dress. The greatest loss of all though was most definitely her pride and her self- esteem.

Mel's meeting had finished, and he was out having a late lunch with his coworkers when he suddenly remembered his phone had vibrated a few hours earlier. As he reached for the phone in his pocket it began to ring, and he sighed loudly when Claire's name flashed up on the screen. He prepared himself for the familiar torrent of abuse because he hadn't responded to her earlier message, and as usual she didn't fail to disappoint him. It was obvious from her slurred speech she had already found the vodka bottle that he had tried to hide from her. He knew hiding the bottle made her angry, but he felt useless, and it was the only thing he could think of to protect her from herself. She had already lost her job at the surgery following complaints from patients who didn't appreciate being treated by an alcoholic nurse in a room that smelled like a brewery. Her employer had no choice but to act quickly to avoid allegations of clinical negligence, which realistically had only been a matter of time. Nevertheless, it had been a sad end to what had been a successful nursing career. Claire had been a good nurse, and nobody wanted to see her profession end on such a sour note. Claire had resented losing her job and responded to her dismissal by bombarding her ex-employers with malicious emails and hurling insults about them on social media. Things went from bad to worse and she was struck off the register which meant she would never be able to practice as a nurse again. Mel didn't seriously believe that Claire would ever be capable of practising as a nurse again, but Claire was convinced everyone was ganging up on her and wanted to put in a no win no fee claim for unfair dismissal. Eventually he managed to convince her that making such a claim would be futile. She had overstepped the mark and breached the NMC code of conduct and whether she agreed with the decision or not, there was no going back.

Claire was indeed a bitter woman. Since losing her job her days were empty and she was stuck at home alone with only a bottle of vodka for company and now that was empty too. The frustration infuriated her and without thinking she threw the bottle at the wall causing it to come crashing back down splintering shards of glass all over the floor. To make matters worse she had stepped on the glass and cut her foot and now there was blood everywhere. She was far too drunk to clean it up herself so Mel would have to come home and sort it out which was the reason for her call. She also needed another bottle of vodka and it was Mel's responsibility to keep her stocked up, so she wasn't best pleased to find he'd neglected his duty. Mel had been forced to take her car keys away from her fearing that she would kill herself or someone else if she got behind the wheel of a car. He was right of course, but there were days when she thought death would be the best solution because there was nothing left for her to live for anymore. She thought of Mel at work laughing and joking and leading a normal life with his work colleagues and she despised him for it. She hated having him at home too because he either criticised her continuously for her drinking or sat blankly staring at that wretched phone of his. She knew what he was thinking, or rather who he was thinking about, and now she regretted deleting that number. She had enjoyed playing games with Chloe. It had given her back some control, and it had been fun watching them take the bait. After he came back, she'd quickly lost interest in having him around, but she wished now that she hadn't been so impulsive.

Claire's ill-timed call had distracted Mel and he put the phone back in his pocket without bothering to read the message. He quickly made his excuses to the lads at work and left before she had the opportunity to ring him again. He thought he had managed to hide his complicated home life from his employees, but he had disappeared so many times of late they knew he was covering for something, and he remained blissfully unaware of the fact he was the main subject of all the workplace gossip. He was the boss, and he was a good man, but they were the labour force and although they were concerned for him they didn't think he would appreciate them asking too many questions and intruding too deeply into his personal life.

Mel dreaded going home and with each passing day the feelings of dread increased. Claire was a liability and not safe to be left alone, but he had to work to pay the bills and seven bottles of vodka a week didn't come cheap either. He hated himself for buying them for her. At one time he had refused to buy them anymore, guilty that he was simply fuelling her addiction. It had been naïve of him because it wasn't until he witnessed the devastating effects of Claire going cold turkey, that he realised it wasn't the solution. He tried to avoid using the same shops when buying alcohol in a vain attempt to hide Claire's drinking problem from the neighbourhood although it seemed it was too late for that now; he was increasingly aware of the gossip mongers and their knowing, sympathetic looks. Today he had to get home quickly because during one of her many tantrums, she had managed to injure herself and he needed to find out the extent of the damage. He fully expected another trip to the emergency department where Claire was already well known among the staff, and he felt ashamed. In the early days, their marriage had been good and their friends saw them as the perfect couple - how he longed to be able to turn back the clock. He didn't know specifically what had changed in the beginning neither did he recall the exact moment it had happened; things had crept up on them almost silently and had quickly spiralled out of control. They both had stressful jobs and at weekends it was the norm to let their hair down and party all night which usually involved consuming large quantities of alcohol. Their weekend lifestyle helped to ease the pressures of the working week, but neither of them thought they had a problem. He couldn't remember when Claire had started drinking during the week, but what had started out as one or two evenings, had quickly escalated to a full seven days. He often came home from work to find Claire drinking a glass of wine while cooking the dinner, and then pouring herself another to accompany the meal. She always had a plausible excuse about needing to relax after a stressful day at work, and he thought little of it until he started getting phone calls from the school because Claire had forgotten to pick up the boys, and they were worried because she wasn't answering her phone. It was all downhill from then on, and it wasn't long before Claire substituted wine for vodka because its odour was easier to conceal. As Mel drew closer to home, he stopped at the local shop to pick up another bottle of vodka. He didn't have enough time to drive to a shop further away, and he knew she would go berserk if he dared to go home without one.

When Mel opened the door, he was shocked to find that his home resembled a crime scene. Claire was lying crumpled on the kitchen floor bathed in a pile of her own vomit, surrounded by shards of blood-stained glass with several small abrasions on her bare feet. She was breathing, but despite his rigorous attempts he was unable to rouse her, and a feeling of panic started to rise in his throat. Instinctively he dialled 999 and while he was waiting for the ambulance to arrive, he noticed there seemed to be far more blood than he would normally expect from a few minor foot wounds. On closer inspection he could see the blood was mixed with the vomit, a serious complication of her chronic liver disease that the hospital consultant had warned her might happen if she continued to drink. Things were bad enough before this happened, but now they were really bad, and he had no one to turn to for help. Claire's alcoholism and erratic behaviour had ostracised them both from friends and apart from the boys, there was no other family to speak of that Mel could rely on, and they were going to need him to be their rock. He willed the ambulance to arrive quickly so someone else could take control of the situation. It was only minutes before he heard the familiar wail of sirens but it had seemed like hours and for the first time in years Mel sobbed his heart out like a small child.

The ambulance crew turned out to be his temporary rock. Claire was their priority but a team of three had turned up, and one of them took Mel aside for a chat and gave him a much-needed shoulder to cry on while the other two attempted to stabilise Claire in the ambulance. Mel wasn't sure why he was crying, but he thought it was probably with relief. He had shouldered the responsibility of caring for Claire single handedly for far too long now and he was at breaking point. As his confused mind attempted to interpret the different emotions, he wished Chloe was with him. As a nurse, Chloe would know what to do and she had a clever knack of saying the right thing.

Claire was rushed to the emergency department of the local hospital, but it soon became clear that she was going to need transferring to a more specialist unit in London. The consultant led Mel into a private room for a quiet discussion about her condition. He spoke softly but his words revealed the harsh reality of the situation. Claire was dying, she had lost a lot of blood as a result of severe scarring on her liver, and it was touch and go whether or not she would survive. They would do what they could for her, but he warned him the outlook was bleak. It had all happened so quickly, and it was too much information for him to take in. He didn't understand the medical jargon, but it didn't really matter because he had only heard a few of the words, and he was still trying to digest them. Someone handed him a cup of tea but he couldn't remember drinking it. The consultant had told him to prepare for the worst. but Mel hadn't uttered a single word in response because in reality he had already lost Claire a long time ago.

After a few hours, the medical team agreed that Claire's condition was stable enough to be transferred by ambulance to London, but Mel did not go with her. He had to get home to clean up the mess before the boys got in from school. If they arrived home before him and found the house in that state, they'd think he had murdered her or vice versa. Regrettably, they were the innocent victims of their parents' shattered marriage and had witnessed disturbing outbursts of physical and verbal abuse on a daily basis. It had become worse since Claire lost her job, and although Mel had tried hard to protect them, they were clearly traumatised by it all. His eldest son was away at university but the other two were busy studying for important exams at a local secondary school. They were bright boys, but the youngest boy Joel had got in with the wrong crowd and was becoming disruptive in class, and the school wanted to schedule a meeting with both Mel and Claire to discuss possible reasons for his out of character behaviour. The school had made it clear that they wanted to see both parents together and Mel was fast running out of excuses for their non-attendance. Under no circumstances could he ever consider taking Claire to the school - their unruly son's behaviour wasn't a patch on hers - and he feared that after a confrontation with Claire, they might end up calling the Social Services or worse still the police. People were always telling him that every cloud had a silver lining, but as far as he was concerned it was just another cliche and he remained cynical. For some reason, his clouds always turned into violent storms that left him physically and mentally battered, and today's cloud had been very dark indeed, but if he was lucky, he might be able to use it to his advantage. Claire's unplanned hospital admission would give him some much-needed breathing space and get the school off his back for a while at least. He would be able to go in and explain to the teachers that Claire was critically ill in hospital and apologise profusely for their son's inappropriate behaviour in class. They would make all the right noises and naturally he would be distraught, so it would be insensitive of them to ask probing questions at such a difficult time. He also knew it was certain to win him the sympathy vote and buy him enough time to straighten things out at home. The welfare of his boys had to be his number one priority and keeping Claire away from the school gates was in everyone's best interest. He tried not to dwell too much on the possibility that Claire would not find her way back from this. The boys had lost their mother in much the same way as he had lost his wife, and he had been playing the role of both parents for months now. He believed he had failed as a husband and a father and in many ways, it would be easier for him and the boys to move forward if Claire didn't come back. Instantly he felt ashamed, she was his wife and the mother of his children, and they had loved each other once, but as he looked around at the shambles which had once been their cherished family home, he knew that love didn't live there anymore. He gagged as he began the arduous task of clearing up the glass and the puke. He didn't like vomit at the best of times, but it had been there a good few hours and its stench was nauseating.

He glanced at the vodka bottle that he'd brought earlier and suddenly felt very angry. He wasn't to blame for their destructive relationship, it was the booze that had poisoned their marriage and wrecked their family unit. He picked up the bottle and impulsively went to throw it at the wall but stopped because he had nothing to gain from it. Throwing the bottle wouldn't solve anything, it would just create more mess and there was more than enough of that for him to clear up already. By the time the kids came in the floor was scrubbed and the only smell was that of a lingering disinfectant. It smelled more like a clinical room in a hospital than a domestic kitchen, but at least it was clean, and the evidence all gone. Explaining to the boys that their mum was in a hospital more than fifty miles away was difficult enough without revealing all the gory details to them. They were of course old enough to know the truth, but Mel figured that some things were better left unsaid, especially if it risked causing more trauma to an already damaged child. Sometimes being a little economical with the truth was a necessity. Tomorrow he would talk to the school as planned and give the boys an impromptu day off. If Claire was well enough, he would take them to visit her, but at this moment in time her fate remained unclear, and only time would tell if she would live to see another tomorrow.

Chloe was wishing she had never sent the message. No response was almost as humiliating as a rebuff, but Mel's silence spoke volumes. It had been more than five hours now and Chloe silently scolded herself for her moment of madness. Despite her reservations, she'd had a good gut feeling when she sent the message and she felt certain he would be pleased to hear from her. She decided in future she would count to ten before making any decisions, although with her track record adding another zero and counting to one hundred would probably be a safer option. Pete had always said how much he loved her spontaneity and impulsive nature but evidently, he hadn't loved it enough to stick around after their incompatibility became blatantly clear to everyone, everyone except Chloe that was.

Mel was contemplating ringing the hospital. The boys were in need of reassurance, but he couldn't promise he would be able to give them the answers they wanted to hear. He had deliberately stalled for as long as possible and the boys had bought his excuses up to a point, but now they were growing impatient, and he couldn't put it off any longer. Somewhat reluctantly he reached for his phone and saw that he had one unread message. He remembered his phone vibrating in his pocket earlier in the day when he was in the meeting, but he had assumed it was Claire and forgotten to actually look at it. On closer inspection he saw that it was an unknown number although something about it seemed oddly familiar. Immediately he thought of Chloe, but that was just wishful thinking. He almost didn't open it because if it wasn't her, he knew he would be disappointed, but he still believed in miracles, and even though he wasn't normally a religious man he believed the lord had answered his prayers from time to time. He hadn't had anything to smile about for a very long time but now he was grinning from ear to ear, because finally a ray of sunshine had burst through the dark clouds, and he was certain it wouldn't be long before his darling Chloe would be back in his arms again.

Mel read her message over and over again until it finally sank in that it really was from her. He had waited for this moment for so long it almost seemed surreal, and he wanted to savour every word. The message was brief and polite but that didn't surprise him after the last message Claire had sent to her from his phone. Without wanting to be too arrogant he was confident she was just testing the water to see if it was safe to wade in a bit deeper. He didn't blame her for being cautious but her tenacity made him love and admire her all the more. The boys were staring at him inquisitively. He was supposed to be phoning the hospital to ask after their mum who was fighting for her life and instead, he was sitting there grinning like a Cheshire cat. For a brief moment he felt guilty, and he was glad the boys weren't able to read his thoughts. He had been thinking about another woman, a woman they had only heard about from Claire, but Chloe wasn't just another woman, she was much more than that and he hoped one day they might understand.

Chloe had come into his life and showed him how to love again. He hadn't planned to fall in love with her, but she was such an easy person to love and it had been years since Claire had given him the warm and fuzzy feeling he felt when he was with Chloe. He had been naïve in thinking there was a chance he could work things out with Claire, their marriage had run its course, but he still clung to the hope that they could turn it back round. He looked at the message from Chloe again. It was casual, perhaps more casual than he would like, but he hoped it was a sign that she was willing to give him a second chance.

Mel rang the hospital and spoke to a senior nurse who was looking after Claire on the high dependency unit. She had been given two units of blood, but she needed more because her blood pressure remained dangerously low. The nurse described her condition as critical but stable and said they would have a better idea in the morning once they had her next set of blood results. She promised to phone him if there was any change overnight and Mel thanked her and said that unless he heard otherwise, he would contact them again first thing in the morning. He would decide tomorrow if taking the boys to visit her was a good idea. He knew they needed reassurance, and so far, he had been of little comfort to them, but he doubted they would find solace from seeing her in her current state.

The boys knew about Chloe, and it seemed Claire had made a good job of poisoning their minds, and as a result, Chloe was like a cancer to them. As far as they were concerned, she was a homewrecker, and much to Claire's delight the mere mention of her name provided an outlet for their anger and hostility. Unfortunately, it was all one sided and they seemed oblivious to their mother's misdemeanours so Mel always bore the brunt of the blame. As far as the boys were concerned Chloe was history, and for the time being at least it was going to have to stay that way.

Mel was feeling anxious because it had been several hours since Chloe had sent the message and he didn't want her to think he was ignoring her. He knew he had treated her badly and he wanted to make amends. He decided to send a quick message back to her now and phone her later to explain the reasons for the delay. He couldn't wait to hear her voice again so later couldn't come soon enough, but he had to be certain the boys were out of earshot because now wasn't a good time to reintroduce Chloe back into their troubled lives. Like most teenagers they usually spent their evenings hanging out with friends or glued to their phones on social networking sites, but today they seemed unusually clingy and although he understood their reasons, it was starting to irritate him. He knew he was lucky to have a second chance at love so he couldn't afford to allow his brainwashed teenagers to get in the way. He paused briefly before simply writing the words, ' I love you Chloe' and quickly pressed the send button. He had waited far too long for this moment, a moment that he truly believed would never come, so it was time to wear his heart on his sleeve and make his feelings for her clear.

Chloe had almost given up on hearing from Mel. She had wasted the entire afternoon

pacing around anxiously like an expectant father, and there was still no word from him. She had so many things to do, but since sending the text she had been unable to concentrate on any task for more than a few minutes. Eventually she decided to forget about the housework and sat down to watch some trashy afternoon film on TV instead. Her eyes felt heavy and before long she found herself dozing off on the sofa. She woke with a start after hearing what she thought was the doorbell, but when she got to the door no one was there and that was when she remembered her phone still sitting on the arm of the sofa right next to where she had been sleeping. It was her own fault for selecting a ring tone that sounded much the same as the doorbell but because she was a bit of a technophobe, she had never got round to changing it. It certainly confused poor Norman who frequently ran to the door expecting a visitor only to be disappointed to find no one was there.

The message could have been from anyone, but she instinctively knew it was from him, and her heart thumped loudly with apprehension as she picked up her phone. She couldn't bring herself to look at it straight away in case it was another rebuff. She thought she would be used to rejection by now but for some reason it never seemed to get any easier. She had been waiting months for this moment and had rehearsed it over and over in her head, but this was no longer a rehearsal, it was a real thing, and it would either fill her heart with joy or shatter it into tiny little pieces. She had to do it, she had to open the message even if it was humiliating. She had instigated all this so she would have to be brave and face the consequence. As she opened the message, she closed her eyes and said a silent prayer. She wasn't in the least bit religious, but a prayer wouldn't hurt, and if there really was a God now was the time for him to work his miracles. When she opened them again and read the text, she suspected Claire was up to her old tricks once more. Why on earth would Mel say he loved her when she hadn't heard from him in months? She was tired of playing games and refused to give Claire the satisfaction of becoming her victim for a second time, so she decided to ignore it. She could picture Claire having a good laugh at her expense, and she wasn't going to take the bait. Two could play that game and she consoled herself with the belief that if karma truly existed, one of these days Claire would get her comeuppance.

It was Mel's turn to feel disappointed. He had expected a rapid response to his heartfelt message but instead it had met with a stony silence. He was angry with himself for being so pushy. Maybe she did only want friendship and the message was her way of letting him know she'd successfully moved on, but had no regrets. The thought of there being another man in her life was unthinkable, but he had no intention of giving up now and vowed to do whatever was needed to win her back, even if that meant giving her some space. Under the circumstances there was no immediate hurry for them to get back together, but he needed to know she still wanted him as much as he wanted her, and providing he could keep Claire out the way, they would have the rest of their lives to iron out the creases. He decided to ring her as planned to reassure her he meant what he said.

Chloe was staring at her phone still mulling over the words. She was ninety nine percent certain it was Claire who had sent the message, but the one percent doubt was enough to stop her sending back a malicious response. She had never met the woman, yet she already despised her because Claire had what she wanted, and she was a bad loser. Claire might have met him first, but he didn't come with a lifetime guarantee of happiness. Over the years Chloe had got used to hand me downs, courtesy of her mother's passion for charity shops, and she'd thought Mel was the equivalent of a human preloved item whose owner was reluctant to let go even though she had no use for it anymore.

The boys had gone out and Mel finally had the opportunity to ring Chloe. He was desperate to hear her voice again, but he didn't know what to say about Claire. He knew he would have to tell her the truth; they couldn't have a future together based on lies and deceit, and he wanted a future with her more than anything else in the world. He didn't know how she would respond, but as a caring, kind-hearted woman he hoped she would be able to show some compassion for Claire's predicament. Claire's behaviour had been deplorable, but the booze had made her mentally unstable, and he knew she couldn't be held wholly responsible for her erratic and unpredictable behaviour. He couldn't blame the drink for all of her actions because he knew she could be manipulative, but it had pickled her liver and frazzled her brain cells, reducing her to a pitiful shadow of her former self. He hated himself for thinking it but in some ways, it would have been easier if he hadn't come home early that day. If he hadn't, Claire would almost certainly have choked on her own vomit and died alone in a drunken heap on the kitchen floor. She had been dead to him for a long time now, but he knew that was no excuse for having such dark thoughts about the woman he was once proud to call his wife, and for a brief moment he felt ashamed of himself. There was no guarantee that Claire would pull through, but even if she did, he thought her recovery would be short lived if she didn't stop drinking, and Claire didn't want to stop drinking. He didn't know how he and Chloe would be able to make a life together with Claire in the background, but he would find a way; the alternative option of a life without her was unthinkable.

Chloe was still staring at her phone when Mel rang. She had been waiting to confront Claire since the day Mel left, but she still couldn't believe the nerve of this woman. She had obviously become bored waiting for a response and decided to provoke her with a phone call instead. Chloe wanted to ignore it, but curiosity got the better of her. She answered abruptly ready to do battle with her love rival, but immediately softened at the sound of Mel's anxious voice. For a moment she was lost for words because she couldn't believe it was really him but when he repeated the words, " I love you

Chloe," her eyes filled with tears and all thoughts of Claire were temporarily forgotten.

Claire

Claire had been an inpatient in the specialist hepatology unit for just over two weeks now, and Mel had only been to visit her twice. On the first occasion he'd brought the boys along, but the second time he turned up alone. The boys were in denial and had somehow managed to turn a blind eye to all the drips and drains and had gone home believing she would get better. Claire didn't want to frighten them and remained surprisingly positive during their visit, even though she knew the long-term outlook was bleak. The doctors had spoken to her at length about her condition and emphasised the importance of making healthy lifestyle changes. They told her the only chance of a cure was a liver transplant, but unless she agreed to stop drinking, they would not consider putting her on the transplant list. They wanted to send her to a residential alcohol rehabilitation unit for twelve weeks at the other end of the country to dry out, but she stubbornly refused to go, and they had reached stalemate.

More than anything Claire wanted to go home. Mel had

been unusually quiet when he visited and she was certain he was up to something, and she couldn't find out what it was from her hospital bed. She was also fairly certain there was a bottle of vodka there somewhere with her name on it, and as soon as they let her out, she fully intended to find it. Mel had only gone back for a second visit because the doctors had asked to speak with them both. The addiction unit miles from anywhere, was the answer to his prayers and it would get Claire out of his way for a full twelve weeks and give him a chance to concentrate on rebuilding his relationship with Chloe. He was frustrated by Claire's blasé attitude, after all she was a mother, and even if she didn't care about him anymore, the boys still needed her. The doctors shared his frustration and shook their heads in dismay, but there was little else they could do because they believed she still had capacity to make her own decisions. Mel on the other hand didn't agree and argued that the alcohol had messed with her brain. He was keen to make a 'best interests' decision on her behalf, but the doctors had refused, and he didn't push too hard just in case they suspected he had ulterior motives.

Claire was told she would have to remain in the hospital because they were trialling a new drug on her which could buy her time given that her liver damage was irreversible. Claire blamed the new drug for her increasing agitation even though the doctors explained it was primarily due to the extensive organ damage and abrupt withdrawal from alcohol. The medical team focused on keeping her adequately hydrated with intravenous fluids, but the only fluid Claire wanted came in a one litre glass bottle and she made that blatantly clear to everyone. She begged Mel to smuggle a small bottle in for her, and when he refused, she became physically and verbally abusive towards him and the doctors had no choice but to sedate her. Mel had since spoken to the doctors alone, and they had mutually agreed that home wasn't a safe environment for her, not for the foreseeable future anyway. This gave him some much-needed respite, but he had no idea how long it might last, so he knew he would have to use the time well. His absence at the hospital was already raising questions from concerned staff, but he no longer cared what anyone else thought, because until they had tried walking in his shoes, they had no right to pass judgement.

Claire was becoming increasingly disruptive, and her violent outbursts were alarming staff and other patients. She had also taken to spitting out her medication and pulling out cannulas used for intravenous drug therapy. She hurled torrents of abuse at the doctors and reduced some of the nurses to tears with her derogatory verbal remarks. Her plan was to provoke them so they would let her go home. When that failed, she insisted on signing a self-discharge form, but her plan backfired, and she found herself detained under the mental health act instead. As her next of kin Mel was involved in the decision and Claire vowed to get her revenge.

Mel presented a strong well-rehearsed case to the multidisciplinary team and was able to provide credible reasons as to why it would not be appropriate to care for Claire at home. They had sectioned her as a last resort, but they had no choice given that she was still critically ill and in need of round the clock medical care. It always helped to have a family member on board when difficult decisions had to be made about a loved one, but Mel had made their job surprisingly easy by choosing the path of least resistance. In fact, he had made no objections whatsoever and had shown little emotion as he explained about the need to keep his business on track, and the importance of the boys having a quiet, stable home environment prior to sitting their exams. Mel also knew that the home nursing team wouldn't last more than five minutes in Claire's company, and he couldn't cope with her on his own, especially as he still needed to convince Chloe he was serious about her.

A Second Chance

Chloe was still inwardly digesting Mel's words. They were the words she had been waiting to hear for so long, but she was feeling apprehensive. Actions spoke louder than words and if he truly loved her, he needed to prove it. She wanted to be able to trust him again but after everything that had happened it was going to take time. Mel seemed to be in a rush but she needed to protect herself, and she wasn't about to enter into a relationship with him again without a proper safety net of some kind. There were boundaries which she was reluctant to cross and the biggest boundary of all was Claire. Mel tried to explain about the vile text message sent by Claire shortly before she deleted Chloe's number from his phone for good. Chloe thought his excuse for not getting back in touch with her was pretty lame given that her number would still be on a bill from his network provider, but Mel claimed he hadn't thought of doing that because he didn't get itemised bills anymore. Chloe had told him she needed a man who was willing to make an effort and fight for her, and Mel still had a lot to do to convince her he could be that man. He had also told her about Claire's illness which had taken its toll on him and the boys and for a moment she felt sorry for her. It seemed Claire had lost everything, and Chloe wondered if it was unethical to start shagging her husband again while she was critically ill in a hospital bed. She knew it was ridiculous, but she couldn't help feeling partially responsible, after all she had wanted payback. If this was karma, she decided it really was a bitch. Immoral or not it seemed Claire was safely out the way, and they had a few weeks to themselves so it would be a pity not to make the most of it.

Mel was delighted when Chloe agreed to meet up with him. He knew he had a lot of making up to do and was keen to get started. Chloe was initially a bit hesitant and insisted they take things slow, but he knew deep down she was crazy about him, and with an extra-large helping of his gracious charm he was sure there would be room for manoeuvre. They agreed to meet in the car park of a country pub that had become a firm favourite of theirs. It was a bit out of the way and frequented mainly by locals, but they had fitted in easily with the regulars and Mel thought the home cooked steak and ale pie was the best he had ever tasted. He had arrived early but today food was the last thing on his mind. He watched anxiously as car headlights approached then drove on by before disappearing into the distance. He tried hard to ignore the niggling doubts in his head that kept trying to convince him she might have changed her mind.

Chloe was stopped in a layby about half a mile away from the pub. She hadn't changed her mind, but she wanted to play it cool and it wouldn't do any harm to make him sweat a bit longer. She had waited months for this moment, and if he was as serious about her as he claimed, an extra five minutes or so would be of little consequence. She quickly checked her reflection in the mirror on the sun visor and made a few adjustments to her hair before driving on. She still looked pretty good for a woman of her age and she could afford to be choosy. Unfortunately, she had a habit of making bad choices, but she hoped her run of bad luck was about to change. She was a bit of a tease and always enjoyed the thrill of the chase, but could also become easily bored. Mel had never really been hers because he already belonged to Claire, and she wondered if that was what she found so fascinating about him. She thought she loved him, but then she thought she might just be in love with the idea of loving him. It was certainly a lot easier to love him when she couldn't have him and that worried her. Only time would tell; she wasn't going to make it easy for him to walk back into her life. There was a rocky road ahead of them, and with Claire still very much alive, it was likely to be covered in crazy paving.

Mel was nervously clock watching. She was only five minutes late and he suspected there would be a genuine reason for it, but he was becoming increasingly anxious. Five minutes could easily have been five hours - it felt like an eternity - and he understood how Chloe must have felt when she was waiting for him to respond to her message. After the way he had behaved, he wouldn't blame her for not turning up, but he didn't think she was the type of woman who would hold a grudge; unlike Claire revenge was not part of her makeup. A siren wailed in the distance somewhere and for a moment he panicked in case she'd had an accident before putting the thought to the back of his mind. For a brief moment his mind wandered back to Claire and an unexpected pang of guilt engulfed his conscience. He had hardly given her a second thought and he knew that was wrong on so many levels. He had played a large part in keeping her confined to a hospital bed although from what he'd heard he'd done her a favour; according to the staff she had calmed down and was responding better than expected to the treatment. He hadn't been to visit her again because she didn't want him there and that suited him - the feeling was mutual. Another car was approaching and when it slowed down to turn in to the car park, he immediately recognised it as the car that belonged to his beloved Chloe and his heart jumped with joy.

Chloe was struggling to control her emotions because the moment she saw him standing there, her plans to remain calm and casual deserted her. She didn't know whether to laugh or cry, but in the end, it didn't matter because she ended up doing both. Mel literally swept her off her feet, and as they clung to each other he kissed her so fiercely she didn't think she could ever let him go again. She felt safe in his arms, but then she had always felt safe with him, even before they officially met in person. First, she fell in love with his photo, and then, after hearing his voice, she fell in love with him all over again. Meeting him in person outside the tapas bar simply sealed the deal. She was smitten from day one, and he felt exactly the same way about her. They were meant for each other, and her only regret was that they had not met sooner so they could have loved each other for longer. Despite everything, he had nurtured her through some difficult times and to a certain extent he had restored her faith in men. Mel had been there for her in the dark days that followed the brutal sexual assault at the hands of Alan. So far, she had spared him the full gory details of what Alan did to her that night, but she would tell him one day when the time was right. She hadn't thought she could ever be intimate with a man again after that fateful weekend, but Mel was always so loving and gentle and sensitive to her needs that she felt able to put the past behind her. She still had flashbacks and occasional night terrors, but they were occurring less frequently now, and her counsellor had warned her that they were to be expected. She thought the old adage about time being a great healer was a bit of a cliché, but she was starting to believe it was true providing she didn't try to expedite the process. She had been keen to hurry it along, but her counsellor kept reminding her there was no time limit on grief, and that had since become one of her favourite phrases to use when she was counselling patients at work.

The plan was to have a quiet drink and a bite to eat in the pub. They had a lot of catching up to do, and not all of it merited a public audience. They could go somewhere more private afterwards because they would need some alone time but right now the only thing on the menu was food and an ice-cold beer. Mel knew he had gained weight over the past few months, and he hoped Chloe would still fancy him. He convinced himself she would have more of him to love, but he knew he should do something about it if he wanted her to stick around. He'd always thought he was punching above his own weight when he met Chloe, and he wanted her to be as proud of him as he was of her. He had got into the habit of comfort eating at work and business lunches gave him the perfect excuse to indulge in his favourite foods. Claire had stopped cooking meals in favour of vodka which she drank morning, noon, and night as a substitute for food, so most evenings he and the boys ended up with a takeout. As a result, his weight had spiralled out of control, and he stopped going to the gym because he got fed up with Claire constantly accusing him of going there to meet other women.

Chloe immediately noticed that Mel had gained a bit of weight, but she felt no need to mention it because it wasn't something that mattered to her anymore. She secretly liked the idea of grabbing his love handles during a moment of passion anyway. She briefly thought back to Tom, the portly police officer with the heart of gold who she had cruelly judged because of his weight. His compassion and empathy had taught her a lot about herself, and she didn't like the person she had become. She had a lot to thank him for because he had shown her the important things about a person were on the inside, and not every oil painting was beautiful. Meeting Tom had helped her to become a better person, and for that she would always be grateful.

Mel was starving but being conscious of his expanding waistline he told Chloe he was going to order a salad. Chloe laughed at him because she knew he loathed salad, and he didn't argue when she suggested he opted for a helping of his favourite pie instead. With a cheeky smile and a glint in her eye she couldn't resist reminding him that there would be plenty of chance to work it off later and he blushed openly as the bulge in his trousers started to compete with his expanding waistline. Chloe was relieved that he was still attracted to her. She had been worried that things would be different between them a second time around, but it seemed they were on track to pick up where they left off. For the time being it was just the two of them, but unbeknown to Chloe it wouldn't be long before her resilience would be tested again because against all the odds, Claire hadn't given up the fight. Claire was the elephant in the room, and they had avoided talking about her. She had always been the third person in their relationship but tonight wasn't about her, and neither of them wanted to let her spoil what had been a lovely evening together. Claire was a major problem and they both knew they couldn't ignore her for ever, but for the time being out of sight meant out of mind, although for Chloe that wasn't completely true. Loving Mel was a huge gamble, and she knew the odds were stacked against her. Mel lit up her life, but she knew Claire had the power to cast a dark shadow over her happiness and propel her back to the gloomy black hole that Mel had rescued her from. She couldn't go back to that place again, but fighting Claire for a second time wasn't going to be easy. She knew that if she lost him again her world would collapse, but she was a born risk taker and failure wasn't something she was accustomed to.

Chloe hadn't been surprised at the reaction from her kids when she'd told them about Mel. She understood where they were coming from because they were the ones who'd had to pick up the pieces after he unceremoniously dumped her the last time, and as far as they were concerned, he was a total loser. Chloe was desperate to prove them wrong, but she knew this second chance of love didn't come with any guarantees, and she couldn't pretend otherwise. She tried to convince herself that it would be easier this time because she knew what she was up against, but something was telling her it wasn't going to be straightforward. If he messed up again, she told herself she would gladly return him to Claire as damaged goods. She had nothing against preloved items providing they were fully functional, reliable, and not showing signs of too much wear and tear. If Mel couldn't step up to the mark and be the man she needed him to be he would have to go back, it was a simple as that. She was kidding herself of course; she had already invested too much time and energy into their relationship to give up now.

The stress of the past few months coupled with Claire's illness was starting to take its toll on Mel and Chloe joked he was ageing prematurely. He was physically and mentally exhausted, but it was nothing a bit of TLC from Chloe couldn't remedy. He knew there was going to be some difficult times ahead, but with Chloe by his side he was sure he could get through them. Much to everyone's surprise, Claire's condition had improved sufficiently enough for the hospital staff to start talking about discharge plans on the understanding she attended regular outpatient appointments and continued to cooperate fully with the mental health team and alcohol intervention services. Apparently, she had agreed to stop drinking and was already in receipt of counselling, but Claire was an expert in manipulative behaviour and knew exactly what to say to get what she wanted, and Mel feared the worse. Claire couldn't believe how easy it had been to dupe them into believing she could change. Inwardly she was seething, and her only goal was to get out of hospital. When she did, she planned to push every boundary and make Mel pay for what he had done to her. Mel reckoned she would be home for no more than five minutes before she fell off the wagon again. He felt ashamed for thinking it, but it many ways it would be easier for him if she did start drinking again. He was almost tempted to leave a few bottles of vodka within easy reach because he knew she wouldn't be able to resist them. Her liver damage was already irreversible, so it was only a matter of time before the meds stopped working and the alcohol seized control of her frail body once more to speed up her inevitable demise. There was a time when he would have done anything to save her, but he no longer felt any remorse in wishing he hadn't come home early that day. If he had ignored her message and stayed at work, nature would almost certainly have taken its course and Claire would no longer be his problem. Understandably, it would have been traumatic for the boys if they had come home from school and found her in that state, but they would have got over it because kids were naturally resilient. Claire was a liability and all the time she was still breathing, their lives would essentially be on hold, and he hated her for it.

Mel and Chloe left the pub hand in hand and decided to take a drive out to a nearby country park in Mel's car to have some time alone. Chloe often walked Norman in this park because it was quite remote, and he could run free for hours in the vast expanse of woodland chasing squirrels up trees without wreaking havoc on other walkers. The park was completely different at night. There were no cars in the carpark and it was dark and eerie outside. Under normal circumstances she would never choose to come here at night, and she was glad Mel was there to keep her safe. As he stopped the car, she locked the doors just in case there was an axe murderer hiding behind a tree waiting for his chance to kill them both. She had an overactive imagination and had clearly been watching far too many horror movies as the light from the moon was casting creepy shadows from the overhead trees, causing her imagination to run riot. Mel sensed her unease and put his arm around her shoulders to reassure her. Her body tingled with desire at his touch and the sexual tension between them was undeniable. She had promised herself that this time they would take things more slowly but sometimes promises were made to be broken. Like most women she liked the idea of chocolates and flowers and good old-fashioned courtship but now she craved adventure and the excitement of having wild unadulterated sex in a car in the middle of nowhere filled her with anticipation. She hadn't had nookie in a car since she was a teenager. Dairy Lane had been a favourite spot for her and Pete because it was a no through road with nothing but a small dairy farm at the bottom of the road. One day the farmer had come along in his tractor and caught them at it and Pete was forced to speed off completely naked. They had laughed about it for months after but had never dared to try their luck in that leafy lane again. In those days they didn't have a choice. Both sets of parents were strict with traditional values and it was considered to be improper for a woman to entertain her boyfriend in her bedroom alone. Even when she and Pete got engaged Chloe's mother was insistent they sleep in separate bedrooms at opposite ends of the landing - according to her it wasn't appropriate to sleep together in the same bed until they were married. It was an old house, and the floorboards creaked so there was no sneaking out in the middle of the night for a quick kiss and cuddle either, but they'd had fun trying.

They could have driven back to Chloe's and enjoyed the luxury of her king-size bed with its soft memory foam mattress and bright red satin duvet cover. Red was her favourite colour, but her kids thought it looked like something a prostitute would choose, and flatly refused to let her buy a matching bright red lampshade in case passers-by got the wrong idea. Going home would have been nice. She had reached an age where comfort was more appealing than adventure and decided she must be getting old. She was still a thrill seeker at heart, but the tables had turned at home and she couldn't face her kids' disapproving looks if she turned up with Mel then whisked him upstairs on the pretext that he was there to mend the longstanding leak in the bathroom. They were no longer children, they were young adults with opinions of their own, and they weren't afraid to express them. From a young age she encouraged them to be assertive and speak up for themselves so they didn't get bullied at school, but right now she wished they could be a little more tolerant. Mel had let her down before, and her kids told her he would do it again and that's what she was afraid of. She wanted to believe he could change, but she had her doubts. She feared that Claire would never allow him to love another woman and was likely to use every trick in the book to take advantage of her ill health and exploit his good nature in the process. The kids didn't agree he was a good person and had been quick to judge. They had a point, and his actions were difficult to defend; after all what kind of man shags another woman while his wife is critically ill in hospital, and what kind of woman goes along with it? A small part of her felt ashamed because it didn't look good on her either. They made it sound so sleazy and they were right, but they hadn't walked in her shoes and met with rejection time and time again. Love wasn't always black and white and one day they would find that out for themselves.

Chloe did her best to make the most of the time she and Mel had together. It was inevitable that things would change when Claire got home, and she struggled to shake off a nagging unease. They had good times together, but Claire's presence was always felt, a bit like a third invisible person, and Chloe couldn't help wondering if she would still be with them even if she was dead. Mel constantly tried to reassure her that Claire was dead to him, but she wasn't dead to Chloe, she was Mel's wife, his first love and her love rival as far as she was concerned Claire was the only thing that stood in the way of her future happiness.

Claire had been stuck in hospital for five long weeks, but they were finally preparing to discharge her. There were lots of boxes that needed ticking before they would let her go, and as far as Claire was concerned Mel was deliberately delaying the process by not cooperating with her request to visit. At first, she hadn't wanted him to visit but now he was her ticket to freedom, and she needed to get him there as quickly as possible. The hospital was concerned there wasn't enough support for her at home, and it seemed that was the only thing stopping them from letting her go. Mel's absence at visiting times had become noticeable, and the fact that he hadn't even bothered to phone was also a cause for concern. Claire tried making excuses for him by saying he was working away but she knew they weren't that gullible and the raised eyebrows among the staff spoke volumes. Claire had already guessed who was distracting her husband and she intended to do something about it at the earliest opportunity. She found it difficult to believe he could love another woman and had been naïve in thinking they were exclusive. Her erratic behaviour had pushed Mel into the arms of other women before, but he had always come running back, up until now that was. She had been wrong to think Chloe was nothing more than a passing phase, and she was curious to find out what was so special about her. She would find out for sure, but for the time being her priority was to get Mel to focus his attention back on her so she could return home and take back control of his life.

Mel could no longer afford to ignore Claire because her consultant had phoned him personally to discuss her discharge plan. He had been abrupt on the phone, and his tone of voice had made Mel feel a bit like a naughty schoolboy. The consultant had made it very clear he wasn't interested in their marital conflict, and the only reason for his call was to ensure Claire would have the necessary emotional support at home, and he needed Mel to confirm she would be discharged back to a safe environment. He described Claire as weak and vulnerable, but Mel knew different. Claire was a devious predator who would stop at nothing to trap her prey, and he feared for the connection that he and Chloe had worked so hard to rebuild together. Much like a Jenga tower he was afraid their world would soon come crashing down and he would be forced to pick up the pieces all over again.

Claire's Homecoming

Chloe was feeling unusually emotional and vulnerable. She had been dreading this day for weeks, but Mel hadn't been able to postpone the inevitable discharge date any longer. They had avoided talking about Claire and made the most of every single precious moment together but her presence was now in the forefront of both of their minds, and they couldn't ignore it any longer. The hospital was insistent that Claire would need someone at home with her initially, so Mel had arranged to take a few weeks off work. Chloe couldn't help thinking what a terrible waste of precious leave it was, and she suspected Claire had engineered the situation to her advantage.

She struggled to accept Claire as Mel's wife because it was the title she herself wanted, and one day she was certain she would have it. Over the past few weeks Mel had mentioned marriage to her several times so she assumed he had plans to divorce Claire when the time was right, unless of course Claire really did die and then there would be no need for messy divorce proceedings. She repeated his name to herself over and over again, and the more she said it the more she liked the sound of it, and the more convincing it all became. Mrs Chloe Elizabeth Richmond had a good ring to it and before long she got completely carried away and had got a piece of paper to practise her new signature. There was no denying she was annoyed that Mel had agreed to spend the entire two weeks with Claire, but he had assured her he would be in touch every day and with a bit of help from their smart phones, there was nothing to stop them from indulging in a bit of cybersex to keep the mood alive. Chloe had never considered using technology for sexual gratification before, she thought it sounded dirty and sleazy and reminded her of men in dirty raincoats, but with Mel it would be exciting, and would help to remind him what he was missing out on. They'd had sex at every opportunity since getting back together and each time it got better and better. She wondered if it would be the same over the phone but like her mother always said, 'practice makes perfect,' although she quite clearly hadn't been referring to cybersex when she said it. Chloe smiled when she thought of her dear mum. She had always been very conservative with her attitude to life and proudly told everyone that she raised Chloe to be a lady, or at least that's what she thought anyway. Chloe was surprised she never found herself in one of those Swiss finishing school type places where she could continue to learn the social graces necessary to prepare her for society. Cybersex was unlikely to be a feature of any self-respecting debutante, and she knew her mother would be thoroughly disgusted if she knew her one and only daughter indulged in such filth.

Mel arrived at the hospital with a feeling of unease. He

had deliberately been ignoring Claire for weeks in order to satisfy his own selfish desires, and now he had to face the consequences. He had already endured a humiliating grilling over the phone from Claire's consultant, but the worst was yet to come, because today he had to face Claire, and when it came to Claire, he was a total coward. He made his way slowly up the stairs to the hepatology ward on the third floor. He chose to take the stairs because it was the longer route and he needed as much time as possible to prepare for the impressive display of fireworks and verbal abuse that was, without a doubt, heading his way. In some ways, it might work to his advantage if Claire kicked off because the hospital might think twice about letting her go home with him, but he suspected Claire knew better than that and would wait until they were alone before launching her attack. The prospect of being alone again with Claire filled him with dread and he wondered how long it would be before she finally tipped him over the edge. The liver cirrhosis hadn't killed her yet, but it had caused enough damage to ensure she would never make old bones. His desire to be back in Chloe's arms was so strong he momentarily thought back to his original idea of putting temptation within easy reach of Claire at home. He had put the bottle of vodka at the back of a kitchen cupboard, and it would only be a matter of time before she found it. He would of course plead ignorance when she started drinking again, but he couldn't knowingly lie to the boys who he knew would never forgive him for being so reckless. If Claire wanted to start drinking again, she would find a way, he was certain of it, so he decided to compromise and avoid bearing the brunt of the guilt. He wouldn't deliberately make it easy for her to find, but he wouldn't make it too difficult either. He would leave it where it was at the back of the cupboard with a few carefully chosen items in front of it so only the top of the bottle could be seen. She was likely to spot it quickly, because she had the eyes of an eagle and didn't like to miss an opportunity. It wouldn't be long before she fell off the wagon again, and he would be able to run back and propose to his beloved Chloe as a lonely widower, as opposed to a cruel, ruthless divorcee who ditched his wife at a time when she needed him most.

Mel strolled on to the ward with an outer confidence that didn't reflect his inner turmoil. His stomach told a different story altogether, and the perpetual somersaults were making him feel nauseated. He loathed hospitals at the best of times and as he entered the ward, he was greeted with the familiar whiff of leftover food. It reminded him of school dinners which his mother had always insisted he ate every day despite his pleas for a packed lunch. When he first met Claire, she'd worked on a busy medical ward which frequently smelled of a pungent disinfectant used in abundance to disguise the foul odour of bodily fluids, that as far as Mel was concerned should only be found in a morgue or a toilet. When she came home from work he could smell it on her uniform, and he wouldn't let her near him until she had showered. Claire always teased him about his OCD as she liked to call it and for a brief moment he smiled; it had been a long time since he had been able to remember the good times they'd had together.

Claire was all packed up and ready to go. She had been watching as he entered the ward, and she had to admit he was still as handsome as he was on the day they first met. The years had been good to him, and apart from a few silver streaks hidden among his dark curly locks little else about him had changed. Unfortunately, the same couldn't be said about her. The alcohol had taken its toll and she was grossly undernourished with sagging yellow skin and sunken eyes. When she first met Mel, she had played hard to get because she knew she could afford to. Back then, she could have had any man she wanted, but she had chosen Mel and she had chosen well because they'd had many happy years together. She wasn't sure when it had all started to go wrong but she guessed it was around the time she started drinking. She'd thought she could control it, but vodka had the same irresistible urge for Claire as chocolate had for other women. The trouble with chocolate is that one piece is never enough, and for her, the same applied to vodka, one glass wasn't enough and before long she craved it more and more. Her cravings could only be satisfied by another glass, and then another and so it went on. Excess chocolate only made you fat and spotty, and the consequences were reversible, but excess alcohol destroyed lives, turning its victims into social outcasts with tragic outcomes, and she was one such victim. As Mel approached, she attempted a half-hearted smile. She still loved him even though she had told him countless times that she didn't. She wanted to hate him, but she couldn't because he was her first true love, her only love, and a devoted father to their three wonderful boys. Someone once told her there was a fine line between love and hate and she thought she understood that now.

Mel deliberately cleared his throat to catch her attention.

He had been standing at the foot of her bed for a good thirty seconds, but she seemed deep in thought and appeared not to have noticed him. Claire was momentarily startled. She had watched him walk into the ward but had been so busy conjuring up memories of the past she had failed to see him standing there. She stared at him softly for a moment before reminding herself that she was supposed to hate him. It was his fault she had been locked up in this place for so long, and to add insult to injury he hadn't even bothered coming to visit her because he had been too busy entertaining his fancy woman. Mel thought she didn't know what he'd been up to, but there was a time and a place for everything, and this was neither the time or the place to let the cat out of the bag, and besides, she didn't want to give him an opportunity to make up some lame excuse for his absence.

Mel was taken aback by Claire's appearance. She looked fragile and gaunt and could have passed for a woman at least thirty years older. His once beautiful wife who should have been in the prime of her life was looking like an old age pensioner, and his heart went out to her. He still loved her – although he hated her at times too - but not in the way a husband should love his wife. He cared for her because she was the mother of his children and he thought he probably loved her more like a brother would love a sister. When she looked at him, he could see the hatred in her eyes so he quickly looked away again, and it saddened him. It was still hard to comprehend how two people who had once been so very much in love could now despise each other so much. If he had looked long enough and met her gaze he would have seen past the hate, and acknowledged the love she was trying so hard to deny.

It was going to be a difficult homecoming for both of them but somehow, they were going to have to learn to live together again until alternative arrangements for Claire's care could be made. He had no idea what he was going to do because he had been too afraid to let on to Chloe that there was no backup plan. Claire's parents were elderly and in poor health so they couldn't be expected to take care of her, and although the boys were old enough to help take some of the responsibility, it wasn't right of him to expect them to take on the role of her carer. Like all kids they needed some stability in their lives, and he knew were looking forward to their mother coming home. Mel knew they secretly hoped that he and Claire could work out their differences so they could be a proper family again, but he hadn't told them about Chloe's reappearance in his life. He had tried to tell them about her being back in his life on a number of occasions, but his cowardly fear of being judged by them had stopped him at the last moment. Claire had rejected him, and he was over that now, but he couldn't face rejection from his children as well. Chloe hadn't reacted well to the situation so he promised her he would tell the boys about her once their exams were over. He had stalled for as long as he could, but their exams were now done and dusted, and he was fast running out of excuses; he didn't think he could put it off any longer. He knew Chloe's own kids hadn't taken the news well, but she was a stronger person than him, and hadn't allowed their criticisms to spoil her happiness.

Claire had a plan and now was as good a time as any to execute it. Her plan involved lulling Mel into a false sense of security which would ultimately lead to his downfall. She could never forgive him for what he had done, but he had always been gullible, and she knew she could coax him into believing just about anything. Her body was frail and weak but contrary to popular belief, her brain was still in good working order and she intended to use it to its full potential. She looked up at him standing nervously at the end of her bed and smiled warmly. He smiled back at her and for a few seconds she remained silent because it was that daft lop-sided smile of his that she had fallen in love with all those years ago. If her plan was to work she had to sound convincing so she reached for his hand and with her sweetest voice she said to Mel, "Come on darling it's time for us to go home."

Home Sweet Home

It had been a strange journey home in the car. Claire chatted continuously about anything and everything and Mel wondered if she had undergone some sort of personality transplant during her stay in the hospital. According to Claire the addiction counselling had shown her the error of her ways, and she was ready to make a fresh start, and she wanted to prove it to Mel by arranging a renewal of vows service at the church where they were married. Mel was totally unprepared for this and was completely baffled by such a random suggestion. He hadn't bargained on marrying Claire again because he intended to marry Chloe, and he was pretty certain she was going to say yes when he popped the question. They had talked about marriage a number of times over the past few weeks, and although he hadn't proposed to her yet, he had it all planned out in his head and he could tell she was getting excited about it. He wanted the proposal to be creative and truly unique and after a lot of thought he'd come up with what he thought was the perfect idea. Chloe was an avid reader and had a copy of every novel from one local author in particular. He planned to buy a hardback copy of her latest book and ask the author to sign it and write the words, "Will you marry me? love Mel," on the inside cover. He would take her to dinner at the tapas bar where they first met and keep the champagne on ice ready to celebrate in style after he slipped the beautiful diamond and aquamarine ring he intended to buy on to her slender finger. Aquamarine was Chloe's birthstone and Mel thought the pretty pale blue tint would complement her soft eyes which had captured his heart from the moment they first met.

Once they were home Mel fully expected to do battle with the courts and divorce solicitors, but Claire had only been home five minutes and it seemed she wanted to marry him again and go through with a farcical second wedding. She wanted a big party afterwards followed by a honeymoon in her favourite location on Italy's stunning Amalfi Coast where she had holidayed with her parents as a child. They'd had no choice but to stick to a strict budget for their first wedding because they were busy saving up to buy a house. It hadn't seemed important to them at the time because their love for each other was all that mattered. Their honeymoon had consisted of a weekend in Bognor Regis. The location was irrelevant because in those days they hadn't been able to get enough of each other, and they had hardly stepped outside the bedroom of their modest seafront budget hotel. This time Claire had it all planned out and was already talking about designer dresses and expensive hotels, and as the sole wage earner Mel wondered where she thought the money was coming from to pay for such extravagances. He was lost for words which was just as well because Claire didn't give him an opportunity to talk. His mind wandered back to his darling Chloe, and he knew without a doubt he could never go through the motions of marrying Claire again. He wanted a divorce but now wasn't the time to tell her just in case it intensified her ridiculous overly ambitious plans and ideas.

Claire knew exactly what she was doing, and she was thoroughly enjoying watching him squirm. She had sensed his revulsion when she mentioned renewing their vows and that had been enough to confirm her suspicions about Chloe. She had already got rid of the damned woman once, and now it looked as if she would have to do it again. She didn't want to marry Mel again any more than he wanted to marry her, but she had no intention of letting him off the hook just yet, because that would give him the green light to go running back to his mistress. She had only said it to wind him up and as usual it had worked a treat. Mel had always been so predictable which made him easy to manipulate, but after a while the simplicity of it all had bored her and fuelled her desire to seek physical and emotional stimulation from other men outside of their marriage. She didn't even feel remorseful; if Mel hadn't been such a boring husband she would never have needed to seek male attention elsewhere. Unfortunately, her adulterous activities had given her a bit more than she had bargained for and some recent investigations at the hospital had revealed a nasty case of genital warts. She was told they were extremely contagious and would need treating at a sexual health clinic on her discharge from hospital prior to indulging in any form of sexual activity. They were unsightly but not painful and Claire had a devious plan up her sleeve which involved postponing treatment until they had served their purpose. If she played her cards right, she could get her revenge on Chloe by making sure she received a gift that kept on giving, and it would serve her right for trying to steal her husband. She would get them treated at a later date; she didn't want them to spoil her chances of finding love again, but right now she had more important things to think about.

In order for her plan to work she would have to get Mel relaxed and in the mood for some impromptu marital relations, and she knew the only way she could do that was to get him drunk. For a brief moment it saddened her to think that the only way to get her husband to make love to her was to get him drunk, but it no longer mattered because it wasn't about making love anymore, it was just going to be a mechanical act with a single purpose. She knew Mel was a bit of a lightweight when it came to alcohol so it wouldn't take much to get him sloshed and then the deed could be done. She had no idea whether there was any alcohol left in the house, but if there was, she was going to find it. She was pleased when he made no attempt to stop her from going into the kitchen to find something suitable to celebrate her homecoming, although his apathy confirmed her belief that he really didn't care anymore and she felt disappointed, but she brushed her feelings aside; there was no room for emotion if her plan was going to work.

Claire convinced herself that one small glass would be okay even though the hospital had made it perfectly clear that it wasn't. She hated the counselling sessions because they were always so bloody patronising and she thought they treated her like a silly little girl. She often became angry with them, but they ignored her tantrums and eventually she realised it was easier to comply than it was to resist. They treated her like a child, but she wasn't a child, she was an irresponsible adult who was still capable of making decisions about her own life, even if those decisions were to the detriment of her own health and wellbeing. In the end she only agreed to stop drinking to shut them up and to get them off her back, and it seemed to work. In hindsight, if she had done as she was told sooner, she might have got out of that dreary place a few weeks earlier, and she silently chastised herself for being so stubborn. She told them time and time again she could stop drinking any time she wanted if she put her mind to it, but they didn't listen to her, they never listened to her, and she despised their interference in her life. Even when they told her the damage to her liver was beyond repair and a transplant was her only option, it didn't give her enough incentive to stop drinking; alcohol was her only pleasure left in life, and no one had the right to take that away from her.

Mel sat motionless in the lounge while Claire clattered around in the kitchen cupboards searching for the elusive bottle of vodka. The banging and crashing and verbal expletives suggested she was becoming increasingly frustrated, and he was sorely tempted to find it for her, if only to stop her from destroying the kitchen altogether. In the end he resisted the temptation to help her find it. He wanted to keep his conscience clear so he could plead ignorance and avoid taking the blame should she end up in the emergency department in another drunken stupor. After about ten minutes there was a triumphant shriek of delight from the kitchen which confirmed that she had finally found it and he breathed a sigh of relief. He had no intention of joining her for a drink, after all he had nothing to celebrate, but there was no reason why a glass of vodka couldn't cheer up a nearby houseplant which had definitely fallen victim to recent neglect. A few minutes later Claire marched victoriously into the room carrying two large glasses of vodka topped with a dash of orange juice which she joked would help to boost her vitamin C levels. She held up her glass to toast their new-found happiness and knocked it back in one go before returning to the kitchen for a top up. Mel took the opportunity to quickly empty the contents of his glass into the flowerpot and when Claire returned, she looked pleased and headed straight back to the kitchen to refill his glass. He pretended to take a sip, but as soon as she turned away from him, he lost no time in emptying the second glass into the same flowerpot. He wasn't sure if he was imagining things, but the plant seemed to look better for it, and then he remembered Claire jokingly saying that vodka stopped plants from wilting early, and if that were true, he wondered why it didn't have the same effect on people. Chances were the plant would be dead by the morning but at least he would be sober and wouldn't have to worry about doing something he might later live to regret. He knew he was a bit of a lightweight when it came to alcohol but that was because Claire drank the contents of every alcoholic beverage in the house before he could get a look in. He'd become accustomed to going without a lot of things, but he didn't miss alcohol in the same way he missed the love and companionship that came from being part of a couple. Meeting Chloe had filled the empty void in his life, but she had made it blatantly clear that she wanted to be more than just his bit on the side, and he only had two weeks to sort it out. She hadn't been happy when he told her he was taking two weeks off work to be with Claire when she came out of hospital, but fortunately she had agreed to a compromise, and right now the thought of talking to Chloe on the phone every day was the only thing keeping him sane.

Claire hadn't had a drink for weeks and the alcohol was going to her head. She felt dizzy and was struggling to focus and she couldn't keep her eyes open a moment longer. She'd only had two large glasses of vodka, but it usually took about two bottles for her to feel this bad. She was taking a lot of medications so she convinced herself that the alcohol had reacted with one of the drugs and after a short snooze she would be as right as rain again. Mel watched her stagger up the stairs and into the bedroom mumbling incoherently and for a moment he felt remorseful. He had been in this situation many times before so it was no great surprise to find himself here again, but he hadn't expected it to happen so soon. Claire had behaved exactly as he wanted so why was he feeling so guilty about it? He knew he should have got rid of that bottle when he had the chance instead of just hiding it away in the cupboard, or at the very least he should have tried to stop her from drinking it but he hadn't, and it was too late now because the boys would be home soon and he had to get rid of the evidence. He would tell them she was sleeping because she was tired after the journey, and they would have no reason not to believe him. He knew how much they had been looking forward to her coming home and he didn't want them finding out she was as pissed as a newt already. As their father he was supposed to protect them, but instead he let them down time and time again, and he felt ashamed of himself for being so weak. It was futile, but all he could do for now was wash up the empty glasses and tip the remainder of the bottle down the sink. He knew he wouldn't be able to hide it from them for long because once Claire got started on the drink there was no stopping her, although realistically he knew he was just trying to delay the inevitable.

After clearing up, Mel had about half an hour to spare before the boys came rushing home from school, and once again his thoughts turned to Chloe. He desperately wanted to call her just to hear her voice, but she would be at work, and he had promised to wait until the evening for a longer, more intimate chat with her. Talking to Chloe would make him feel better, she had a way of making things right even when, like now, they were clearly all wrong. He decided to text her just to let her know he was thinking about her. They had only been apart for a day, but he was already missing her and he wondered how he could possibly keep it up for another two weeks.

Chloe was at work but she couldn't stop thinking about Mel. It was only day one and she was already jealous of the time he was spending with Claire. She tried telling herself that she was being ridiculous, after all Claire was a sick woman, but there was still that niggling doubt at the back of her mind that served to remind her she was nothing more than his mistress. It had become something of a contest between her and Claire with Mel being the ultimate prize, and there were days when she wondered if he enjoyed being torn between two lovers. The unexpected text from him mid-afternoon helped to alleviate some of her doubts because at least it meant he wasn't being kept busy by Claire. She hadn't expected to hear from him so soon, and she secretly hoped it meant things weren't going to plan his end. She had only given him two weeks to sort things out and she hoped he would get on with it sooner rather than later, but it was reassuring to imagine that Claire was being her usual uncooperative self. The text itself was plain and simple but he told her he loved her, and then signed it off with ten kisses. For a brief moment, all her doubts melted away and she smiled to herself as she typed out a suitable response. She replied by sending him two smiley faces and four coloured hearts; for one-upmanship she added an extra ten kisses to make out she loved him twice as much as he loved her, although she hoped that bit wasn't true.

Mel crept quietly up the stairs to check on Claire before the boys got in. True to form he found her crashed out on the bed fully clothed and snoring loudly. From past experience he knew she would remain comatose for many more hours to come, but he also knew the first thing she would want when she woke up was another drink, and there would be hell to pay if she didn't get it. The sound of the front door opening and two giggling teenagers calling out to them forced him back down the stairs. Although their youthful banter was unlikely to wake her, he couldn't afford to take the chance. There was no alcohol left in the house, and right now there was no contingency plan either. His explanation to the boys was so plausible he almost believed it himself. He told them she was tired because some of the medications she was on were likely to make her drowsy, and because it had been a long day for her; luckily, they bought it. Now they were home he needed to pop to the shop to get something in for dinner, but he was also going to have to buy a replacement bottle of vodka just in case Claire became more irrational when she woke up. He knew what he was doing was wrong, and he didn't know how he was going to explain it to the boys, but it was all about self-preservation, and only someone in the same situation would be able to understand his motives. He wondered if Chloe would understand. As a nurse he suspected she would be disgusted with him for allowing it to happen, although on a personal level maybe she would feel differently. He was disgusted with himself. He'd been unwillingly placed in a no-win predicament and he wondered if his boys would ever be able to forgive him when they found out he was nothing more than a cowardly supplier. He was no better than a drug dealer feeding her addiction, the only difference being he wasn't getting paid for it. By the time he got back from the shop the boys were chatting away happily at the kitchen table doing their homework oblivious to the catastrophe that was about to transpire. As he unpacked the shopping bag, he realised he had forgotten to buy the vodka and swore loudly causing the boys to look at him inquisitively. He quickly mumbled an excuse under his breath, and they settled back down to do their homework.

Claire's chronic alcoholism had become a family disease because one way or another it had affected each and every one of them and stressed their family unit to breaking point. The boys had coped remarkably well under the circumstances given that they had witnessed events that many adults would struggle to deal with. AA hadn't worked for Claire because she refused to acknowledge she had a problem. Mel had continued to attend long after Claire had left because it gave him an opportunity to meet other people in the same boat as him, and it gave him a safe environment to express his emotions which could be extremely unpredictable. There were times when he became angry, not just with Claire, but with the entire universe. At other times he would just sit back quietly and listen feeling reassured to know he wasn't alone in a world that had suddenly become a very lonely place. Sometimes he would cry but it didn't matter because he was allowed to openly shed tears without fear of retribution. If he cried at home Claire would mock him for not being a man, but in the group environment no one judged him and for that he was grateful. He hadn't told Chloe he had cried at the meetings in case she thought crying made him a less of a man like Claire did, but he would tell her one day because she had a right to know what kind of man she was going to marry. Marrying Chloe was still a long way off but the group had encouraged him to find something positive to focus on, and now he finally had, he was terrified of losing it. When Claire lost her job he had to stop going to the meetings because as the sole wage earner he found himself working later and later to make ends meet, and there simply weren't enough hours in the day to fit everything in. He missed the group camaraderie and the chance to have some adult conversation, and it hadn't been long before a dark cloud of loneliness enveloped him once more. Meeting Chloe had changed all of that, but she had come into his life at a time when he was at his most vulnerable, and he knew he had come to depend on her in much the same way as Claire depended on alcohol.

He pretended to the boys that he would try and wake their mother up for dinner even though he knew she would still be out cold. He tiptoed silently up the stairs to briefly check on her before hurrying back down having done nothing more than peep motionless through the gap in the bedroom door. Joel was disappointed because he was keen to tell her about his achievements in the school athletics team, but Mel managed to convince him that his mum would be in a better frame of mind if they allowed her to wake up naturally, and luckily Joel agreed with him. He had said it for purely selfish reasons, because he wanted to enjoy the peace for a little while longer, and because he needed time to prepare the boys for the storm ahead, although he still had no idea what he was going to say to them. They'd had no reason to doubt her when she told them she was off the booze for good, and like most kids they thought their lives would go back to normal, so this was going to be a major shock to them.

Claire loved the boys but after the first two were born she desperately wanted a girl and it was obvious when Joel was born that she was disappointed. Joel was a difficult baby and it had taken her months to bond with him, but to Mel's relief she'd eventually relaxed, and they had settled down to a hectic, testosterone-driven family life. The boys were all sports mad but Joel 'exceptional talent on the sports field fed Claire's competitive nature and she soon realised she was far more at home on a muddy football pitch with a bunch of grubby boys than she ever would have been at ballet classes with the little girl they never had. Joel idolised Claire, which is why he had gone off the rails at school when her drinking problem escalated. He'd reverted back to silly childish attention seeking behaviour, but Mel knew he wasn't really a bad kid. His behaviour had just been a cry for help from a young boy desperate to win back his mother's love. Joel had never lost her love of course but he was too young to understand what was going on, and had mistakenly thought her drinking problem was because he had done something bad. Mel glanced over and witnessed the anguish in his young son's eyes. Joel was a sensitive boy who didn't cope well with stress. After the temporary glitch at school, he'd worked hard to redeem himself and Mel was concerned that Claire's presence back in the house would confuse him again. He hoped Claire would stay asleep because he needed to phone Chloe to relieve himself of the burden he had unwittingly managed to inflict upon himself.

He had wanted to be honest with her and tell her what he'd done, but he knew only a complete moron would allow his alcoholic wife access to a bottle of vodka after being discharged from hospital, and she had every right to be angry with him. He hated lying to her, but he couldn't face being judged by the one person who had never judged him. He was guilty as charged, and whether he liked it or not, he was going to have to face the consequences of what he had done all by himself. He told the boys he was going to the study to make some business calls. They were both engrossed on the X-Box playing computer games so they responded with a brief grunt which suited him because it meant they would be unlikely to disturb him. He had been thinking about Chloe all day and couldn't wait to talk to her again although he knew he would have to be careful not to give too much information away about Claire. Chloe was sure to ask after her, so for the time being he had invented a slightly different version of events that sounded plausible and would help to reinforce his good character.

Chloe was willing her phone to ring although realistically she knew it was still a bit early for Mel to call. They had agreed he would ring every night after Claire had gone to bed, but as it was still only 7pm she knew it was highly unlikely she would be tucked up in bed just yet. Nevertheless, it was frustrating because now Claire was home from hospital Chloe couldn't just ring him when she wanted to, just in case the wretched woman was within earshot. Her brain had been working overtime all day, and visions of Mel playing happy families with Claire and the boys was playing havoc with her already tormented mind. She had been tempted to phone him on a number of occasions throughout the day, but they'd agreed to follow a set of rules and she didn't want to jeopardise their relationship by sabotaging the plan. She was busy daydreaming, and she jumped when the phone rang. Earlier than expected, Chloe was pleased that the call meant Claire was in bed and Mel would be able to concentrate on her. Her mood softened at the sound of his voice, although she thought she picked up an uneasiness in his tone. He was talking so quietly she could barely hear him, and she had to ask him to repeat himself several times over. She listened patiently as he prattled on about his day and about Claire going to bed early because she was a bit overwhelmed by the homecoming, and it all sounded extremely plausible... so why wasn't she buying it? He repeated over and over again how much he loved her, and she could feel the emotion in his voice which sounded as if it might break at any moment. She wished she could hold him to reassure him, but she felt helpless, and for a brief moment she pitied him. Suddenly there was a loud shout from Joel, and Mel had no time to say anything more to her. He managed to utter a quick apology and dropped the phone down on his desk before rushing off to see what all the commotion was about.

Chloe sat with her phone in her lap for at least an hour afterwards hoping he would call back, but there was nothing. She wanted to call him, but they had made a pact, and she had sensed an urgency that suggested she wasn't his main priority right now. She wondered if she would ever be his priority, and for a moment she felt bitter. He would tell her when he was good and ready but pangs of jealousy were already creeping in, and she didn't think she could survive another two weeks of not knowing.

Claire had woken sooner than expected and provided Mel with a temporary reprieve. He had sensed Chloe's misgivings when he told her the reasons for Claire's early night, and he realised now that he had probably talked about it in too much detail to make it sound convincing, after all Chloe was hardly likely to be interested in Claire's bedtime routine. At least he had managed to avoid the web of lies he had invented to get him off the hook. She would find out soon enough but now wasn't the time. He wondered if there would ever be a right time, but more than anything else, he hoped she would understand.

The Next Two Weeks

Mel opened the study door to find Joel tentatively helping Claire down the stairs. She was stumbling wildly all over the place, and slurring her words incomprehensively making it difficult for Joel to understand what she was saying. He thought he heard her mumble the word vodka and looked questionably at his dad for some much-needed reassurance. This wasn't the reunion he had been looking forward to so much with his mother, and Mel knew he couldn't conceal the truth from his sons any longer. They were innocent victims caught in the middle of their warring parents, and they deserved better.

Mel recalled the day his sons were born. He had been so proud of his boys and proud of Claire too, but in their teenage years when the boys were at their most vulnerable, they had let them down badly as parents. Under the circumstances, it came as no surprise when their eldest son Lewis chose a university as far away as possible at the other end of the country, leaving Jack and Joel to fend for themselves in a home that mimicked a war zone. Joel, the more sensitive of the two boys had gone through a rebellious phase at school, but that was over now and much to everyone's relief he seemed to have settled back down again. Joel was so like Claire; he was an opportunist and liked to push boundaries, but he didn't have a bad bone in his body. Both boys had always shown remarkable resilience in the presence of adversity but the fear on Joel's face told a different story now, and Mel feared this might be the trigger to tip him over the edge again.

Claire slid unceremoniously from Joel's arms into a heap on the sofa. Still semi-comatose, she looked like a vagrant from the streets with her tangled hair and stale breath, and once again Mel wondered how they had reached this alien place. The fun-loving intelligent woman he had married and once loved so dearly, had long gone and been replaced by a boozy unrecognisable monster for whom he was still responsible, because whether he liked it or not, she was still his wife. Claire needed him now more than ever and the boys needed at least one parent to be a good role model, so for the time being Chloe was going to have to take a back seat. Chloe knew the score with Claire, and he hoped she understood that he had to be there for his boys; but she would wait, he was certain of it.

For a brief moment no one said a word. It was an awkward silence and Mel could see the pain in the inquisitive eyes of his confused sons. They needed answers but he couldn't give them the answers they wanted to hear. The truth was going to hurt them, but covering up the cracks with more lies would destroy them, and he couldn't risk doing that to them. Finally, he had an opportunity to unburden himself, but before he had a chance to speak Claire stirred from her drunken stupor and demanded he fetch the remainder of the bottle of vodka, and with that both the boys fled. Briefly their eyes met, and Mel could see the hatred in them as she screamed at him to fetch the bottle, but there was no more vodka, because he had emptied it down the sink, along with all his hopes and dreams of a new life with Chloe. The front door banged shut, and he watched sadly as his boys walked down the road with their rucksacks on their backs and their heads hung low. He knew where they were going because they had been there many times before, but more importantly he knew they would be safe. Angie was a retired nurse, and an ex-colleague of Claire's. She lived nearby and had kindly taken the boys under her wing when Claire first started drinking. She always provided a bolt hole for them, and her home was everything a home should be, a safe haven filled with love and laughter, so it was no surprise the boys had made a beeline for her door again. Mel needed a bolthole too, and there was only one place he could go. It would mean leaving Claire to her own devices, but he suspected she would eventually go back to sleep. The worse that could happen would be if she found her way out onto the street. It had happened before and one of the neighbours had called the police who in turn had called an ambulance which, much to Claire's disgust, had carted her off to hospital. Like most neighbours they could be nosey which was hardly surprising given the circus show they had witnessed over the past few years, but at least he knew someone would be looking out for her. He grabbed his keys and left, leaving Claire alone uttering profanities to herself. Her eyes were already closing so he suspected she would shortly be passed out on the sofa anyway. He was glad the boys weren't around to hear her, although he feared the damage was already done. He would check with Angie that the boys were okay, and then make his way to Chloe's. Chloe wouldn't be expecting him, but it would be a nice surprise for her after the disappointing phone call, and he didn't anticipate any objections from her. Angie wouldn't ask questions; she knew the score with Claire and she wasn't the sort of woman to indulge in malicious gossip. Angie was the earth mother type of woman whose natural instinct was to heal and nurture. She could never say no to anyone in need and was well known for taking in the local waifs and strays, although they were usually the four-legged kind. Before she retired Angie was a surrogate mum to everyone at the surgery, always ready with a box of tissues and a shoulder to cry on, and her departure left an empty void in the hearts of many people. Angie always looked out for Claire even though Claire didn't appreciate it, and frequently referred to her sarcastically as, 'Saint Angela.' A few weeks after Angie retired Claire was sacked from her job, but Angie had stuck around to help pick up the pieces of their shattered family life even though she didn't have to. Claire may not have been thankful, but Mel most certainly was, and in his mind this humble, unassuming woman was every bit a saint.

Although it was only round the corner, Mel took the longer route and drove slowly to Angie's house. He needed time to think about what he was going to say to the boys, although deep down he knew there were no words that could bring them comfort right now. As he drew up outside, Angie was waiting at the door as if she were expecting him. For a moment Mel was anxious and felt obliged to look away. He had taken advantage of her good nature for months now, and there was every chance she'd had enough of being treated as an unpaid carer. She had retired to spend more time with her own family, not take on someone else's, but he couldn't afford for her to bail out on him just yet. He needed to get away even if it was for just the one night, to lay in the arms of his beloved Chloe, and forget about Claire. The two-week pact that he had made to spend time with Claire following her discharge from hospital was now terminated, and he knew Chloe would be pleased because she had protested bitterly about it; not that he could blame her.

Mel looked back over to where Angie had been standing but she was no longer there; she had made her way over to the car and was gesturing him to wind down the window. Mel flashed Angie an awkward smile as he wound down the window. Deep down he was consumed with guilt, but he needed her and was unashamedly prepared to say or do anything to keep her on board. As it turned out he needn't have worried too much because as usual Angie's main concern was for the welfare of the boys. She explained they were upset and didn't want to see him just yet and Mel could sense her disgust as the relief showed in his eyes. He would happily have spent time with the boys - he wanted more than anything to be able to comfort them - but where could they go right now? Home was totally out of the question and he understood enough to know that much of their anger was directed at their mum – he was just the unfortunate whipping boy. He wondered if Angie knew about Chloe. He had been careful to keep details of his private life secret, but Claire had always said that Angie could read people like a book and right now he felt as visible as an open page.

He briefly considered checking up on Claire before making his way to Chloe's. It usually took about an hour to drive there providing the traffic wasn't too heavy and given that the rush hour traffic was gone he anticipated making good time. In the end he decided there was no point going back home; Claire would probably be asleep again by now, and if she wasn't sleeping they would only end up arguing, and he didn't want to waste his energy. He wondered if he should phone Chloe first but that would spoil the surprise, and he wanted to surprise her; even though she claimed she didn't like surprises. He turned the radio up loud and found himself singing along to, 'I'd do anything for love,' and then laughed at how appropriate it seemed.

Halfway through the journey he decided he would ring Chloe after all. He had been searching for an excuse to phone her anyway and had managed to convince himself she would prefer to know he was coming – he suspected she'd even touch up her makeup - although in his eyes she always looked beautiful. One of the things he loved about Chloe was her inability to recognise her own beauty. She was a beautiful woman inside and out, yet she never believed she was good enough. He knew she had taken it badly when Pete left, but he felt certain there was more than just a failed marriage to blame for her lack of self-worth. There were times when she seemed unusually quiet and deep in thought, but he didn't like to ask questions as it seemed an intrusion of her privacy. He assumed she would tell him when she was good and ready. There had been times when he thought she had come close, only to change the subject at the last minute. It was frustrating because he wanted her to trust him, but trust was a two-way process, and he knew he hadn't always been completely straight with her either. He made up his mind there and then, that tonight was the night he was going to be honest with Chloe and let all his skeletons out of the closet, and he hoped she might feel able to do the same. He reached into his pocket for his phone but it wasn't there, and then he remembered he'd left it on his desk after Claire's resurgence had forced him to abruptly end his call to Chloe. It didn't really matter, it just meant reverting back to plan A and paying Chloe a surprise visit after all. She would be thrilled to see him, he was sure of it, and with Claire out cold at home there would be no one to disturb them. Mel started to whistle. He only ever whistled when he was happy, and he was happy because everything was going nicely to plan. It used to irritate Claire when he whistled, and even though she wasn't there with him he whistled even louder as if to make a point, and it felt good.

Claire was fuming. Mel had left her all alone and had already broken his promise to the medical team that he would be there to care for her. She had a pretty good idea where he was heading, and she intended to make him pay for deserting her. As she swung herself round on his office chair, she giggled menacingly to herself. She loved playing games, and she finally had an opportunity to play her favourite game again, courtesy of her dumbass husband's careless blunder. She looked at the phone in her hand and smiled as he began typing out a message before pressing the send button. All she had to do now was sit back and wait for the party to begin.

Chloe

A
s expected, the road was quiet and Mel was making good time. Providing there were no traffic incidents on the M25 he would be with Chloe in about half an hour and his stomach turned somersaults in anticipation of seeing her again. He could see blue lights moving quickly in his mirror behind him and automatically checked his speed to make sure they weren't after him. He already had six points on his licence and having attended a speed awareness course for a relatively minor disregard of the speed limit only three months earlier, he knew he risked losing his licence if he was caught speeding again. Two police cars and an ambulance raced past and to his dismay the traffic started to slow down; within minutes the motorway was at a compete standstill. The traffic and travel news on the local radio station temporarily interrupted Chris Rea's, 'The road to hell,' just as he entered the M25 slipway, and he cursed himself for not taking the longer, but more scenic route along the less busy A roads. There were reports of an accident involving an overturned caravan on the southbound carriageway with tailbacks of

more than three miles already. By the sound of it he was going to be there for a while, and to make things worse the damned radio was now playing 'you can't hurry love.' Mel hated caravans and the idiots that towed them hogging the roads and slowing down the traffic, and now he had a reason to hate them even more.

Chloe was attempting to pass the time by watching a film on TV, but she couldn't concentrate. She kept looking at her watch, she thought Mel would have phoned her back by now, and she was becoming increasingly frustrated because his stupid two-week rule meant she couldn't ring him. It was all the more infuriating when he knew how anxious she became when she didn't hear from him, and if he loved her as much as he claimed to love her he would have made an effort to ease her mind instead of allowing it to run riot with ridiculous visions of a reconciliation with Claire. She knew it was unlikely that they would be rolling around in the bed together given Claire's state of health, but she was feeling insecure, and she needed some clarification from him that all was still well. It always amazed Chloe how time seemed to stand still when you were waiting for something, yet at work there were never enough hours in the day to finish everything that needed to be done. She checked her watch again and as if to prove a point, only five minutes had passed since she last looked at it; she decided to run a bath. A bath would help to relax her, and she would be able to indulge herself in the soft perfumed bubbles while listening to some of her favourite tunes on the radio. As she lowered herself into the luxurious foam her phone beeped to indicate that a text message had come through. She decided to leave it a few minutes to allow the warm water in her jacuzzi bath to massage her tired body. When her divorce came through, she had decided to treat herself to something special. She had only ever enjoyed the luxury of a jacuzzi bath in posh hotels, and to have one of her own was at the top of her wish list. It had been an extravagant treat and something she couldn't really afford at the time, but Pete's departure had left her bereft and she had bought the bath as a consolation prize. Her phone beeped again to remind her she had an unread message and Chloe smiled when she saw it was from Mel.

Mel was becoming increasingly frustrated stuck in a queue of traffic on what really was the road to hell. Twenty minutes had passed, and nothing had moved. Blue lights were flashing up ahead and people were starting to get out of their vehicles to protest amongst themselves. The north bound carriageway had also slowed due to the foolish rubberneckers gawping at the whole fiasco. Chloe would be wondering why he hadn't phoned yet, and he swore loudly for leaving in such a hurry and forgetting his phone.

Chloe had stopped smiling. She was staring at her phone in total disbelief and kept re reading the message just to be sure she wasn't imagining it. The message was malicious and cold, and despite the warm bath water the content sent an icy chill through her entire body. She read the words over and over again, "I'm sorry Chloe but Claire needs me and I've realised I still love her." The phone beeped for a second time and this time the message made her feel nauseous. "Last night I wanted her and the sex was amazing." Chloe remembered back to the messages Claire had sent previously, and tried hard to convince herself that Claire was indeed the perpetrator once more. Mel wouldn't do this to her, she was sure of it, but he had gone back to Claire once before; what was there to stop him from doing it again? Mel loved her, he told her so every day, but he had cut the last phone call short, and she had an inkling he was hiding something from her. She needed to calm down and stop overthinking the situation. This is what nightmares were made of and if it was Claire playing games, she certainly knew how to exploit her vulnerability. All of a sudden, the bathroom door eased open a few inches and Norman cautiously poked his head through. He loved bath time - so long as it wasn't his bath time - and he had been waiting patiently outside the door for an invite to come and chase the bubbles. His human had usually called him in by now and he was missing out on his favourite game. He sensed her sadness and gave her a comforting lick on the chin, and despite her sorrow, Chloe couldn't resist giving him a hug. Her hands were all soapy and wet and she laughed briefly as he quickly backed away. She loved Norman, and she was a sucker for those doleful eyes and big slobbery chops of his. Having Norman around was like having a continuous infusion of happy pills. He could remedy almost anything, but he couldn't change the one thing she desperately wanted, and that was to make Mel love her more than he loved Claire.

Claire's game wasn't going to plan. She had sent the texts to get a reaction from Chloe, but it had been more than twenty minutes since she had sent the last message, and there was still no response. She was getting bored of waiting now, and it seemed like she was going to have change her strategy and move to plan B. Plan B was going to take a lot of nerve, and ideally she would have liked a few drinks first, but there was none left in the house because by the looks of it, her stupid husband had tipped the remains of the bottle down the sink before he left. She had found the empty bottle in the bin, and out of sheer frustration had been tempted to throw it at the wall again, but then she remembered what had happened the last time she did that, and she didn't want to end up being the centre of attention in the emergency department again. She had been down this road before when she had tricked Mel into believing she wanted to change, and she had survived by finding alternatives. There had been many occasions when Mel had accused her of mixing with unsavoury characters as he liked to call them, but they'd had their uses and had been full of useful tips and information. This one particular tip of theirs was worth its weight in gold and had turned out to be a life saver on more than one occasion. Mel was blissfully ignorant about the cheap supermarket brand, alcohol substitute which was an everyday item on their weekly shopping list, and even though the mouthwash burned her throat as it went down, it was a quick fix, and it wasn't long before she felt back in control. She made herself comfortable in Mel's leather-bound swivel office chair and scrolled down his list of contacts. She stopped when she reached Chloe's name and mischievously changed her name to hussy before calling her.

Chloe was surprised to see Mel was calling her. Although she was almost sure he hadn't sent those texts, she wasn't ready to speak to him just yet so she decided to ignore the call. She assumed he was on a guilt trip and was looking for an opportunity to explain himself or to ease his conscience, but she didn't need to hear the, 'it's not you it's me' storyline, because she had heard it all before. The phone went to voicemail, but he didn't leave a message. Instead, her phone rang again and again until she was eventually forced to answer it out of sheer frustration. As she put the phone to her ear, she felt ready to explode, but before she had a chance to speak a woman's voice interrupted and Chloe was somewhat taken aback when Claire calmly said, "You must be Chloe and I believe you are shagging my husband."

The blue lights were still flashing but the traffic on the motorway was slowly starting to move. The wretched caravan had been moved to the hard shoulder and there was a recovery vehicle there now too, but there was still a lot of debris to clear from the road, and the police had only been able to open one lane. The local radio station said the tailbacks stretched for approximately ten miles and Mel reckoned he was probably somewhere in the middle of it all. By the time he got to Chloe's it would be time to go to bed but that wasn't necessarily a bad thing because there was a lot of making up to do. Mel grinned to himself, he liked the idea of making up, and by all accounts he was pretty good at it. He'd had no complaints so far anyway, and he was quietly confident there wouldn't be any in the future. He knew he was lucky to have a woman like Chloe in his life, but it worked both ways, and he sincerely hoped her gratitude extended in his direction too. She had seemed a bit shy with him in the bedroom department at first, but he'd put that down to nerves. Claire always said he had the gift of the gab and could sweet talk any woman into bed. He liked to be adventurous, but at the same time he believed in being gentlemanly and sensitive to his woman's needs. He certainly wasn't a wham, bam, thankyou mam type bloke, and he had seen Chloe's confidence increase in the bedroom significantly during their time together. Thoughts of Chloe had successfully distracted him from the motorway chaos, and it wasn't until he heard the sounds of horns honking behind him, that he realised the traffic was on the move again. Providing there were no more incidents he could be there in half an hour. He whistled contentedly as his foot hit the throttle for the first time in more than an hour.

Claire was slurring her words and was unquestionably under the influence of something. It made no sense to Chloe whatsoever. Where on earth was Mel, and why had Claire got his phone? Chloe had mixed emotions. In one way she was relieved that Mel hadn't been responsible for sending those vile messages, but on the other hand she felt an unexpected surge of empathy for this vulnerable woman whose husband she was unashamedly 'shagging.' Claire did most of the talking, and Chloe was happy to let her talk; she wondered if Claire might not have many friends left that she could talk to now. She knew how addiction drove people away, and she suspected Claire might in fact be very lonely. Chloe obviously didn't count as a friend, because that would just be weird, but she had been told many times by people that she was a good listener, and she might even gain a few extra brownie points with Mel if she played the good Samaritan to his soon to be ex-wife. When it came to friends of her own, Chloe had very few that she considered to be true friends, although she had lots of acquaintances. Much of it was her own fault, because instead of embracing Pete's family and extending her network of friends, she had chosen to belittle them all, and as a result she had missed out. Obviously, she would never admit that to

Pete because that would involve acknowledging she was wrong, and she was far too proud to do that. It wasn't just her though who had missed out, the kids had missed out on spending time with their aunties, uncles, and cousins, and reluctantly she had to admit that Pete had missed out too. He was always the guy stuck in the middle trying to keep the peace, and eventually it had got too much for him, and he'd chosen to walk away. She didn't blame him anymore, and life without him had become easier now she wasn't so angry. She knew it was too late to turn back the clock, but it wasn't too late to change and build a more positive future for herself and the kids.

Once she started talking Claire found it hard to stop, even though her throat burned hideously with every word thanks to the ingestion of an entire bottle of acidic mouthwash. Usually when it got this bad, she could soothe it by drinking some milk, but there was only about an inch left in the carton in the fridge and it wasn't enough. She knew most of what she was saying was complete and utter drivel, and even though she thought she despised this woman for stealing her husband's heart, she sensed an unexpected kinship with her. She never thought Mel would fall in love with another woman, but after talking to Chloe, Claire had some inkling of why he had chosen her. It was her own stupid fault of course; she had goaded him mercilessly because she was bored, but it had spectacularly backfired on her, and now everything was out of control including her dependence on alcohol. Deep down she had known she had a drinking problem long before it became obvious to everyone else that she was in fact an alcoholic. She hated the term alcoholic because it suggested a lack of self-control, and for a long time, she had kidded herself into believing she could stop drinking. For a while she'd managed to cover her addiction well and was able to disguise her dragon breath with the use of copious amounts of toothpaste, peppermints, and mouthwash. She felt in control for a short time, but now her problems had spiralled out of control again and the mouthwash was becoming a dangerous, but extremely effective substitute for booze. She didn't dare tell anyone about it because there were days when that was all that was left in the house to fall back on, and it had become her only safety net. She had once been a well-respected, educated woman with a good job as a registered nurse and she knew the risks she was taking, but she couldn't stop, and although she pretended otherwise, she was both ashamed and terrified at the same time.

It was all very odd because Chloe was feeling the same affinity and some of what Claire was saying seemed to make sense. Claire was confident that under different circumstances they would have been friends because they shared some common ground. She was of course referring to their nursing backgrounds, but they also shared Mel, and both women claimed exclusive rights to him. Claire asked Chloe if she loved Mel and she replied without hesitation that she did, and Claire wept openly because although she hadn't shown it lately, she loved him too. Why had this woman who she wanted to hate so much chosen her husband to love? She sobbed openly down the phone to Chloe, and instinctively Chloe wished she could wrap her arms around her and give her a hug and tell her everything was going to be okay, even though she knew it wasn't. Without warning the phone went dead, and Chloe was left staring at the blank screen. She still had no idea where Mel was and why he wasn't with Claire, but the sound of Claire's distressed sobs haunted her, and her own problems faded into insignificance. She had stolen another woman's husband, and she was no better than the busty Brazilian bimbo who had lured Pete away from her. If anything, she was worse than the Brazilian bimbo because Claire was sick and unable to care for herself. She thought about her own wedding vows 'in sickness and in health, until death do us part' and she wondered if there was any meaning to them at all for Claire and Mel. She wasn't sure why, but she felt she should call Claire back just to check she was okay. She wasn't wholly responsible for all of Claire's problems, but she was partly responsible for stealing her husband, and for that she needed to take accountability. Mel had to be there somewhere with Claire surely, and Chloe hoped he had found her, because from the sound of it she wasn't safe to be left alone. As she pressed the redial button, she waited anxiously for Claire to answer, but the phone rang and rang before eventually going to voicemail. She wondered whether she should leave a message, but that seemed too much of an intrusion, and she doubted Claire would appreciate a welfare call from the woman who had just told her she was in love with her husband.

Chloe came from a broken dysfunctional family, and now her kids were forced to do the same. Worryingly they regarded divorce as the norm, and Chloe worried that their own chances of building a traditional family unit in the future were less likely as a result. Mel's kids would suffer the same fate, but for them it could be much worse because Claire's illness meant they might lose their mum for ever. At least Chloe's kids could still visit Pete if they wanted to, although skyping or face timing him seemed their preferred method of contact for now. Apparently, it was the modern way of doing things, but she had no doubt that if he were to offer them an all-expenses paid trip to South America they wouldn't say no. She had heard on the grapevine that Pete and the Brazilian bimbo planned to marry there sometime next year. She hadn't been surprised by the news because they were engaged after all, but if karma truly existed, she secretly hoped he might contract malaria or get his manhood chopped off by a crocodile somewhere in the Amazon. She hated the idea the kids might go but he was still their dad and despite everything that had happened, they still needed him as a role model, even if he wasn't a very good one. It seemed neither of them had been the best role models but it was never too late to change, and Chloe vowed there and then that the time had come for her to change because, whether she liked it or not, life wasn't all about her.

Norman's ears had pricked up and he was doing that funny head tilt of his that always made Chloe smile. A car door slammed shut and he went rushing to the front door. Chloe wasn't expecting any visitors, and she didn't really want any because she was still feeling unsettled about Claire. Where the hell was Mel anyway? The doorbell rang and Norman was wagging his tail furiously, eager to be the first to greet the unexpected guest. Chloe sighed, she wasn't in the mood for company, and if it was those bloody Jehovah's Witnesses again asking if she believed in life after death, she wouldn't be held responsible for her actions. She opened the door and Mel stood there with that impish grin on his face that usually made her giggle and go weak at the knees, but today it just irritated her. She wasn't keen on surprises and two within the hour was two too many as far as she was concerned. On a more positive note, Mel was alive which meant that Claire hadn't killed him, and Chloe could finally stop worrying about where he was. He would have to go back though, because she was still very worried about a woman she had never met, a woman who she feared was a danger to herself, a woman who was home alone, and without any support from the man she so clearly still loved.

Chloe loved Mel but the unexpected call from Claire had helped to confirm her fear that he had never really been hers to love. He had been nothing more than a short-term loan, but she had paid a hefty price for him, and the time had come to give him back to Claire. She expected him to argue when she told him he had to go home, but he seemed to understand and for a brief moment, she thought she saw a hint of relief behind the sadness in his eyes. As she closed the door behind him tears filled her eyes, and it wasn't long before memories of what might have been, flowed down her cheeks and plopped on to Norman's cold nose. Letting him go had been the right thing to do, but it certainly didn't make the pain any easier to bear.

Moving On

Allowing Mel to walk away was one of the hardest decisions Chloe had ever had to make. As she watched him drive away for the last time, she had to stop herself from running out and calling him back, but it was time to stop her heart from ruling her head and she knew she had to let him go. She had done the right thing, for Claire at least, but there was no great moment of triumph, just an empty void, and a dull ache in her broken heart. She'd thought love would be enough, but she knew now that it wasn't. She only had herself to blame, after all she had relied solely on a romanticized version of love and turned a blind eye to all the warning signs and red flags that she had religiously obeyed in the early days of her internet dating journey. She wondered if she would ever see him again, but deep down she knew that she wouldn't and she tried to convince herself that it would be better that way. There was no point in moping around, it was like people said, 'life goes on,' and she was never going to win the sympathy vote for dating a married man. People were always so quick to judge, and she wasn't ready to hear all the, 'I told you so's,' from well-meaning acquaintances just yet. She wished she had someone close to confide in, a friend to talk to, so she could free the heavy load that was weighing her down, but there was no one that she could trust to keep her secret. Suddenly, a cold nose nuzzled its way on to her lap. It was Norman reminding her that she did have a friend, and her secrets would always be safe with him.

Mel had mixed emotions. It had been a long and frustrating drive to Chloe's, and he hadn't expected to be on his way home again just yet. He'd sensed something was wrong the minute Chloe answered the door, and after she told him about the phone call from Claire, he felt an unexpected surge of panic. He wasn't sure why alarm bells were ringing because he had been down this road with Claire many times before and she had always been okay. Claire was tough, a natural born survivor, but she was also a bit of a drama queen and would do anything to draw attention to herself. He was annoyed because she had spoiled his surprise and ruined his plans for a night of uninterrupted love making with Chloe. When he left, Chloe made it sound like she wouldn't be seeing him again. He wasn't sure if she'd actually dumped him, but he managed to convince himself she was just overreacting and was quietly confident that in a day or two everything would be back to normal between them. He needed her, and he wasn't about to give up on her just yet, so to keep her sweet he was going to have to think seriously about getting that proposal out of the way sooner rather than later. He was happy with his plan, a ring on her finger would change everything, he would go shopping tomorrow and buy the ring, and all would be forgiven.

When he pulled into the driveway he was surprised to find the house in total darkness. He assumed Claire had gone back to sleep which would be typical now she'd stirred up a whole lot of trouble between him and Chloe. As usual, it seemed Claire had got her own way and that infuriated him even more. He knew it was his own damned fault for leaving his bloody phone behind, but it hadn't occurred to him that Claire would be in any fit state to get her grubby little hands on it. He hoped she was asleep, because he wasn't in the mood for another showdown with her tonight, and chances were by the morning, she would have forgotten about the whole thing anyway. He tiptoed quietly up to the front door and turned the key gently in the lock to avoid waking her. The house seemed cold, but it was chilly outside, and the heating was set to timer and had gone off hours ago. Even though it was dark inside he decided against turning on any lights. He would quickly check on Claire and try to find his phone before taking himself off to the spare room for the night. It was quite late, and he wondered if Chloe would mind if he called her. She had never worried about him phoning late before and he didn't like the way things had been left between them; he was eager to put things right. He crept slowly up the stairs trying hard to avoid the creaky boards which were always a huge giveaway when their eldest son Lewis, who was now at university, had rolled in late from a night out. Those creaky boards had caused endless family rows but mending them was still a long way down Mel's 'to do' list. At the time he'd deliberately avoided repairing them because there was something reassuring about hearing Lewis come home and knowing he was safe and sound, but now as his foot touched one of them, he quietly cursed himself for not doing something about it sooner.

Unexpectedly the bedroom door was wide open. Claire hated sleeping with the door open so he assumed she must be more sozzled than usual. He listened by the door for her breathing but could hear nothing. When she was pissed, she usually snored like a wart hog but there was no sound at all. He peered cautiously around the corner. The bedroom curtains were still open, and a streetlight reflected dimly onto the empty bed. Mel checked the other rooms but there was still no sign of her. There was a strong antiseptic smell coming from the bathroom, but a quick glance revealed nothing more innocuous than a small hand gel dispenser and an empty bottle of mouthwash. He tried not to panic. There had to be an easy explanation for this. She was probably asleep on the sofa, and he hadn't thought to look downstairs first. Keeping quiet was no longer a priority, he had to find Claire, so he switched on all the lights and raced quickly back downstairs. He darted from room to room in blind panic before remembering the study, the place where he had left his phone, and the only place left in the house where Claire could be. As he approached the study the door was ajar, and he could see his portable work lamp was still on. He called Claire's name softly before opening the door. There was no response from her, and instantly he knew why. A rough outline of a broken heart had been sketched on the blotting paper in front of her, and Claire was slumped lifelessly over the desk, with her face drenched in a pool of blood and vomit. His phone was still in her hand, and he knew instantly that she was gone.

She had died alone without giving him a chance to say a

proper goodbye, and the last words she had heard were Chloe's. He hated himself for what he had done, and for a brief moment he hated Chloe too because it should have been his last words she heard, not hers. She was his wife and he had let her down. They had grown apart, but he should have been there for her like he promised when they made their vows together. He turned round and walked despondently back to the hallway to grab the landline. When the operator answered and asked which service he wanted his mind went blank. It really wouldn't matter if they sent the pope because the outcome wouldn't change. He managed to blurt out the words, "My wife is dead," before dropping to the floor and sobbing uncontrollably. Within minutes sirens were wailing, and a whole host of emergency services were dispatched to the doorstep. A kindly paramedic explained gently to Mel that Claire was long gone, and under the circumstances it would be futile to perform CPR, and he hoped they wouldn't think badly of him for feeling just a tiny bit relieved, because it meant Claire wouldn't suffer anymore. Claire had truly suffered, and those people who had been ignorant enough to comment that her illness was self-inflicted, clearly had no understanding of the power of addiction. Her illness had left her physically and mentally scarred, and although it was clear she was never going to make old bones, she deserved to die with dignity.

Mel needed someone other than himself to blame, and he looked no further than Chloe because she was the last person who had spoken to Claire. Claire's body was taken away in a private ambulance and the police said the coroner would be informed because her death was unexpected which meant he would have to delay making funeral arrangements until after the postmortem. Mel hadn't thought that far ahead but the idea of a postmortem made him feel incredibly queasy. He needed to tell the boys, but it was getting late, and Angie would have them tucked up in bed by now with a steaming mug of hot chocolate each, blissfully unaware that tomorrow their lives were going to change forever. He thought about phoning Angie just to warn her, but she was such a decent person, and he didn't want to burden her unnecessarily. The only person he didn't feel guilty about troubling was Chloe; she was just as responsible as he was for Claire's sudden passing, and he didn't see why he should let her get off Scot-Free. Chances were, she knew a lot more than she'd let on and he wanted to know exactly what she'd said to Claire. She'd told him she was worried because the phone suddenly went dead, but now the only thing that was dead was Claire, and he was convinced she was hiding something from him. It was going to be a long night pacing a house which reeked of death, but sleep was out of the question, and the strong silhouette of the moon outside indicated that daybreak was still several hours away.

Chloe was tired but sleep evaded her, and although her body craved sleep her mind refused to shut down. Something didn't feel right and it worried her, but oddly enough it wasn't thoughts about Mel that unsettled her. She found herself remembering the phone conversation with Claire over and over again. She was certain she hadn't said anything out of turn, but maybe she shouldn't have admitted she loved Mel in case it was a step too far. She had blurted it out without thinking, and now she wished she'd answered a little more sensitively, because it was obvious Claire still loved him. She hadn't meant to upset her, but she didn't want to lie to her, and she wished now there was something she could do to put things right. She wanted Claire to know that she was someone she could talk to, and she hadn't expected her to just hang up the way she did. She wanted her to know about her reservations about dating a married man, but Mel had told her they were separated and, in the beginning, she'd had no reason to doubt him. He'd given her the impression that divorce was inevitable and it would only be a matter of time before everything was finalised. By the time she'd realised how complex the whole situation was, she was head over heels in love with the man. She wanted Claire to know she wasn't just some Jezebel who had deliberately stolen her husband away from her, but Claire hadn't given her a chance to explain, and she hated the way the call had ended. The busty Brazilian with no morals might have stolen Pete from under her nose, but she wasn't that kind of person, so why did she feel like the bad guy? She decided to get up to avoid overthinking the situation any longer. She had read somewhere that if you couldn't sleep you should get up and do something until you were tired enough to go back to bed. Norman was snoring loudly in his bed on the landing and lifted his head temporarily as Chloe walked past. She stroked his smooth silky head gently and whispered that it was still 'night nights' time and like a good boy he went straight back to sleep. Chloe wished she could sleep as easily as a dog and made up her mind that if there was such thing as life after death, she was definitely going to come back as a dog. Oh god why was she thinking about the afterlife; those damned

Jehovah's Witnesses who kept knocking on her door had a lot to answer for. She put the kettle on to make a cup of tea. Caffeine wasn't going to help her sleep, but she was past caring; she felt strangely uneasy about something, and she knew she wouldn't sleep until she found out what it was. She looked at the clock. It was gone midnight and she thought it was probably a bit late to ring Mel now. A few weeks ago, she wouldn't have thought twice about ringing him in the middle of the night as they often talked well into the early hours of the morning, but as she dithered the decision was taken out of her hands, because much to her surprise, Mel was ringing her.

Mel was emotional, and he seemed very angry about something. He was crying and shouting at the same time, and what he was saying made no sense whatsoever. Chloe tried to calm him down, and asked him to speak more slowly, but that only seemed to anger him more. She had never seen this side of Mel before and it frightened her. She thought he must have taken something because what he was saying couldn't be true. Surely Claire couldn't be dead, and if she was, how could it possibly be her fault? She'd only spoken to her a couple of hours ago, and although she'd seemed sad, she was very much alive. Mel was still ranting and raving, and nothing she said seemed to calm him down, and she briefly wondered if he had killed her, and was looking for a scapegoat to take the blame for his crime. Deep down she knew Mel was no more a murderer than she was, and she knew he must be in shock. Slowly it dawned on her that she had been the last person to speak to Claire, which made her an easy target to blame. She understood that he was angry, but he was also consumed by guilt, and that was the only reason she could find to excuse his ridiculous accusations. The only thing she was guilty of was loving him, but that hadn't been enough, and now he had lost both of the women who had loved him. She wished she could reach out to him and give him a hug. This was no time for him to be alone, and she hoped someone would be there to pick up the pieces. He'd talked fondly about a woman called Angie who looked out for the boys, and she hoped this kind woman could find it in her heart to look out for him too. Chloe thought back to that fateful call and wondered if she could have done something to prevent such a tragedy, but deep down she knew there was nothing she could have done; Claire had already been living on borrowed time. Mel hadn't said how she'd died , and Chloe didn't like to ask, but she thought it was likely to be a natural progression of her liver disease.

Mel slammed the phone down out of sheer frustration without saying goodbye to Chloe. What on earth was he thinking accusing Chloe like that, and what must she think of him for making such heinous accusations? It wasn't her fault Claire had died, he knew that, but he needed someone to blame because he wasn't yet ready to face up to the truth. He would ring her again to apologise after the dust had settled, if indeed it ever did settle. He still had the heartbreaking task of breaking the news to Angie and the boys. Angie would always be there for them no matter what - as far as they were concerned, she was already their surrogate mother - but under the circumstances, he couldn't expect her to condone his behaviour. She would be right of course; he should have been there for his family, and that included poor Claire. Instead, he'd stuck his head in the sand hoping all his problems would go away. Chloe became a much-needed distraction, but he had never planned to fall in love with her. She was the hinge to his bracket, and he'd come to rely heavily on her for strength and support. Finally, there was Lewis who had absconded to the other end of the country just to escape the hell hole that should have been his home. He wasn't sure if Lewis would ever forgive him, but he hoped in time that he would and he hoped that one day he could make the three of them proud of him again and give him a second chance to be the father they deserved.

The results of the inquest came as a shock to Mel. He wasn't surprised to learn that Claire had died from extensive blood loss as a result of bleeding oesophageal varices, but the toxicology results showed a large amount of methanol and hydrogen peroxide in her system which the coroner said were substances commonly found in mouthwash and frequently used by addicts as a cheap alternative to alcohol when supplies of their regular alcoholic beverage had run out. This news was completely devastating to Mel who had thought he was doing the right thing by removing what he imagined had been the source of the problem. He had no idea how desperate she'd been, but it was all starting to add up now, and it accounted for the ludicrous amount of mouthwash she'd insisted on buying every week. He remembered the day he came home with a cheaper alternative to her usual brand, and she'd gone berserk. He couldn't understand why she would blow such a trivial matter out of all proportion, but now he realised it was because the cheaper brand had a considerably lower alcohol content than she was accustomed to.

The boys took the news of Claire's death better than he expected. They admitted to him that they never expected her to make it out of the hospital, and he regretted not taking them to visit her more often. They agreed to focus on the future and build bridges on the fragile foundations of what was left of their lives. He wondered how much the boys knew about Chloe, but her name was never mentioned, and as far as Mel was concerned it never would be. Once or twice, he thought about phoning her to say he was sorry, but deep down he knew there was no need to apologise because Chloe would understand. She had accepted him for who he was, and although he didn't appreciate it at the time, she had performed the ultimate act of kindness by letting him go. She had loved him enough to set him free, and for that he would always be grateful.

He scrolled through her messages for one last time before pressing the delete button. He had a terrible memory for numbers, but the memories engraved in his heart he would remember forever.

The End

Dawn was born in London, England in 1962 and her boarding school education taught her the resilience to withstand adversity and be independent from an early age. She qualified as a Registered General Nurse in 1986, and she indulges her passion for writing in her spare time. She currently lives in Portsmouth, Hampshire with her husband and two boxer dogs. Her writing style reflects her personality, and has been described as quirky and unique. Dawn is naturally competitive and she isn't afraid to push boundaries. Her books often contain challenging themes that will take you on an emotional rollercoaster ride that will make you laugh and cry, often at the same time.

Plenty More Fish is the authors debut novel. If you enjoyed this book, and you are keen to see where Chloe's journey takes her next, why not treat yourself to the sequel, *His Other Child* - there's a teaser chapter on the next page

His Other Child

Chloe

C hloe sighed deeply. She didn't know how long she'd been sitting at her desk, but it must have been a long time because her elbows were starting to burn as they rested heavily on the hard-wooden surface. She stared wearily at the blank computer screen in front of her and briefly allowed her eyes to close. Apart from the low-pitched drone of a vacuum cleaner in the waiting room, and the usual friendly banter from the cleaners, the surgery was silent, and she treasured these rare moments of peace. The white noise from the vacuum cleaner usually helped her to focus, but today it did nothing to soothe her troubled mind, and she knew she should probably go home.

She glanced at her watch and was alarmed to see that it was already 7.30 pm. It was Friday, and her shift had finished two hours ago, but even though the patients were long gone, she always found an excuse not to go home on time. She told Grant it wasn't uncommon for nurses to run late because patients had an annoying habit of presenting her with half a dozen different problems in their ten-minute appointment slot, and although she rarely ran late herself, there was no need for him to know that. There were always things that needed doing of course, like ordering more stock, or tidying up the doctor's rooms, because she liked to leave every room spick and span ready for her colleagues to start work again on Monday morning.

She grabbed her coat and headed for the door but couldn't resist taking one final glance around the room again just in case she'd missed something. It was cold outside, and her car windscreen was frozen solid, which meant she'd have another ten valuable minutes to herself while she allowed it to defrost before she could drive away. She turned the fan on full and cursed under her breath as a rush of cold air blew into her face, causing her eyes to smart. For a brief moment, she thought she might cry, and then silently scolded herself for being so feeble. She vigorously rubbed her cold hands together under the freezing fan in a futile attempt to thaw them out and practised her well-rehearsed excuses out loud until they were pitch-perfect to avoid arousing Grant's suspicions. She'd done this so many times now she was almost starting to believe them herself, but Grant was gullible, and for that she was grateful. As she grabbed the ice-cold steering wheel, her entire body shivered, and she hugged her jacket closer to her trembling frame in a vain attempt to warm herself up. She'd been adamant that she wanted a car with leather seats and a leather steering wheel, but on days like this, she wished she'd been able to afford to upgrade to a newer model which came with the luxury of heated seats and a heated front windscreen. The car was always too hot in summer, and too cold in winter, but it was still her pride and joy, and no one, not even Grant, could convince her to trade it in for something more comfortable.

She could feel her phone vibrating in her pocket. It wasn't the first time it had rung, but she deliberately ignored it. She always kept her phone on silent at work anyway, and that was her excuse for not responding to Grant's calls. She knew he would be angry, and she didn't blame him, but every extra minute alone was precious, and she wasn't ready to face him, or that child of his just yet.

It was only a ten-minute drive home, but she reckoned she could get away with stretching it out to twenty with the poor weather conditions outside. Things were difficult at home right now, but she knew he'd never forgive himself if she were to rush and have an accident, and with a bit of luck, by the time she got in, that kid of his would be safely tucked up in bed. As she turned into the small cul-de-sac where they lived, she could see the curtains were still open, and the lights from the living room illuminated the outline of her husband pacing anxiously up and down in front of the window, holding their small daughter in his arms. She could see the television was on, and as she pulled onto the drive, another smaller figure joined him at the window, and she was disappointed to see that she was still up.

She'd promised Grant that she'd try to make more of an effort to bond with his daughter, but that promise didn't come with a guarantee of success, and it was at times like this that Chloe wished she had a superpower, so she could fast-forward the time to Sunday evening because that was when Crystal went back to her mother.

She met Grant after being introduced by a work colleague

who was keen to remove her from the internet dating scene for her own safety. After three years of disastrous dates, involving several official, and unofficial brushes with the law, and finally the heartbreak of a lost, unrequited love, she'd given up on internet dating anyway. Grant had come along at a time when she was vulnerable, and although it wasn't love at first sight for either of them, they formed a natural friendship, which had gradually turned into love. At least she thought it was love, but there were times when she had her doubts, and it was no coincidence that today was Friday, and those ugly doubts had resurfaced once again. After their first date, she'd left it almost two weeks before contacting him again despite constant reminders from the well-meaning work colleague who'd introduced them. Eventually, she contacted him, not because she necessarily wanted another date, but because she needed his opinion on a car she wanted to buy, and she knew that he shared her love of cars. He'd loved the shiny, red, low-mileage Ford Puma almost as much as she did, and even though it was a bit small, she couldn't resist buying it, and was still the proud owner of it now, although with only two doors, and a one-year-old daughter, it was impractical. After Phoebe was born, Grant nagged her to find something more suitable, but she was adamant she could manage, and besides, it gave her the perfect excuse not to travel in the same vehicle as that child of his. She had known about his daughter from their first date, because Grant, who was besotted with the child, hadn't stopped talking about her. She wasn't surprised to learn he had a child, after all, he was in his late forties, but she had expected her to be a bit older, and self-sufficient, like her children were. As it turned out, Grant had been something of a late starter, but she was thankful he only had one child, and at the time, she hadn't anticipated there being any major problems, after all, the kid already had a mother.

At the age of forty-eight, she hadn't expected to become a mother again herself, but Grant was thrilled at the news and was keen to seal their family unit with a gold band, and a mutual exchange of wedding vows. Her dreams of a romantic wedding on the Italian coast were replaced by a quickie at the local registry office, kitted out like an overdressed Heffalump, a mere four weeks before giving birth to their precious baby daughter. Initially, she thought her lethargy, weight gain and scanty periods were part of the menopause, after all, she was knocking on the door of fifty, but when her modest breasts grew to an enormous double H, and her bra started to resemble a hammock, she knew she must either be pregnant or have a grossly underactive thyroid gland, the latter being quickly ruled out by a blood test.

When Phoebe was born, she was perfect in every way, with a mop of fair curly hair, and a delicate slightly turned-up nose. People automatically assumed she was her grandma, but she ignored their remarks, because she was proud to be a member of the more experienced geriatric mum brigade, and she was determined that she and Grant would be good parents, and always put her first, regardless of any unresolved differences they may have had.

As she put her key in the door, Grant opened it forcefully, and for a moment she was taken aback. She was nearly always late on a Friday night, and he knew the score by now, but the sight of Phoebe sobbing uncontrollably holding out her arms for a 'huggle' as she liked to call it was enough to tear at her heartstrings. As she took the sobbing child from her husband's arms, she almost tripped over a pile of carelessly placed bags at the bottom of the stairs, and assuming they belonged to Crystal, she shot Grant a critical look. Phoebe was fretful and overtired, and Chloe knew she hated going to bed if her mummy wasn't home, and although Grant had tried his best to pacify her, she was inconsolable. For a moment, she felt guilty, after all this was preventable, but the sudden appearance of Crystal standing at the doorway grinning like a possessed cat changed her mood in an instant. Grant saw the hatred in his wife's eyes and told Crystal to go upstairs and get ready for bed, and for once she did as she was told without kicking up too much of a fuss. As she climbed the stairs, she didn't bother looking back, after all, Chloe rarely spoke to her anymore, not even on good days, and by the looks of it, today hadn't been a good day for her. She was disappointed, but that was nothing new, because weekends with her dad were not the same now that he was with Chloe, but she remained hopeful, because tomorrow was another day, and she was excited because her daddy told her they were going on an adventure together.

Printed in Great Britain
by Amazon

38601717R00169